Also by JOHN HERSEY

These are Borzoi Books, published in New York by ALFRED A. KNOPF

Under the Eye of the Storm

UNDER THE EYE OF THE STORM

BY *John Hersey*

ALFRED · A · KNOPF ~~~ *New York*

1 9 6 7

THIS IS A BORZOI BOOK

PUBLISHED BY ALFRED A. KNOPF, INC.

Published March 20, 1967
Second Printing, April 1967

© Copyright 1967 by John Hersey

Library of Congress Catalog Card Number: 67–14363

Manufactured in the United States of America

28,055

Contents

Under the Eye of the Storm

1

"See How the Current Takes Us"

A high lozenge of light told Medlar's one cracked and sleep-blurred eye that dawn had come. That dim gray oval was the porthole in the cabin trunk, opposite. He lay listening. There were not many sounds: the rudder post uttering soft bovine grunts at intervals, the tidal currents from the Katama cut purling along the flanks of the yawl, his wife's even breathing in the berth across the way, and the ticking of the round brass ship's clock on the bulkhead over his bunk. Those were all. *Harmony*, he knew, was secure on her mooring; the morning was calm. He sat up . . .

Look at him! The right side of his face is creased with the impress of the cloth folds of the pillow case against which it has lain in a hard morning sleep following two waking hours in the middle of the night. The expression is pinched, chary, and cautious—of a man trying to keep track of small points at a time when the large drift of events is unthinkable. The source of his income and dismay: the slippery mass of the human liver. Though but thirty-four, Dr. Thomas Medlar knows as much about the ravages of contemporary life on that organ as any man on the eastern seaboard of North America. This already famous hepatologist is here on his boat precisely to put distance between himself and diseased livers. The best way to escape thoughts of livers is to pay undeviating attention to the myriad details of his awkward vessel, *Harmony*. His wife Audrey calls him, sometimes, Dr. Meticulous. What an impeccable tool chest he keeps aboard his yawl! How tidy his log book is! . . .

He glanced at the clock and then at the file card he had taped to the edge of the shelf where the radio stood, a schedule of maritime weather reports in his own hand's ordered italic script. Six twenty-nine. He felt the fitness of his having started up like a timed contrivance on the very minute for a forecast from Boston. The elements of existence afloat were measurable and manageable—even by an unconscious mind, schooled by outward habits of exactitude, which could set a head-alarm to wake one just in time for a dimly remembered morning weather broadcast.

He turned the radio on. The weatherman, who called himself Sunny McCloud, was complacent; his voice, though tuned low, had a resonance that must have been fueled by Bourbon and blood-rare steak—an impertinent heartiness so early in the morning. He spoke of continuing flows of warm air and gentle days as if he were their commercial proprietor.

Then, boozily off-hand, this Sunny McCloud told of the making up of a tropical storm, by name Esmé, which might have the mainland in mind though just now she was, he said, a remote sort of shrew—five hundred miles from nowhere off the Georgia coast and meandering.

4

Dr. Medlar did not want to think about faraway gales. He snapped off the radio, lay down on his back, and closed his eyes.

∽∽∽

The rest of this cruise was going to be fun, and that was that. It was all set. Nothing could be changed. During his sleeplessness he had made a list of things to do on this day. A fixed list; an iron list. Morning wipedown, dispose of garbage, inventory check, meet Hamden; other such matters. Thomas Medlar was, in his own view, a fair-minded, warm-hearted man who had dedicated his life to saving lives by saving livers. Alas, he was already, before his thirty-fifth birthday, earnestly sick of the organ of his choice. At that moment in medical school when a specialty had had to be entered on a printed form, he had opted the liver for unashamedly careerist reasons: Among his contemporaries the liver was unpopular, for the heavy rushes in that year were to lungs (carcinoma) and hearts (plastic valves), and the liver was at the bottom of the visceral heap; he had seen his chance. The liver would have its day, and he would be its lonely champion. And indeed his was already a respectfully whispered name in liver circles, yet he had a conviction of failure—not as to professional accomplishment but rather on a score of character. On this point, however, he was rather calm, for he had concluded that all men are in due time failures. They gain power or fame, he had perceived, and it sickens them for want of more; they earn money and it makes them cheaters, pseudo-experts, impostors; they garner praise for a while and it makes them love mirrors; then they eat shit and pretend they are gourmets. If they have done

5

nothing they assassinate the characters of others who have done something. So Tom Medlar had observed. At last they all know that they have betrayed in folly and greed their best possibilities; they are moral failures. In most cases it takes them many years to find this out. Having detected his own inner bankruptcy while still young and vigorous, Tom Medlar had now worked out a way to get through the rest of his days busily, painlessly, and even, much of the time, in high good cheer. His way was to be exact in little things. There was a dynamic force in the word "exact" that had great appeal for him. Exactism came to this: marking off the hours this side of death by being precise about humdrum details of existence which in themselves had no meaning whatsoever. No meaning, that is, beyond their capacity to wipe out the human liver from all consideration—blessed utility!

∽∽∽

He stirred, opened his eyes, raised his arms, and stretched to the full length of his delight at being aboard *Harmony*.

The day was coming on, but the cabin was still dark: the door-boards were in at the companionway, and the hatch cover was closed, and the blue-bellied dinghy loomed upside down on its chocks over the cabin skylight, hooding it like a miniature night. Only the two oval portholes admitted a bit of light.

He looked once more at the porthole across the way. Fog. He could tell it from the sweating on the glass.

A Vineyard fog. He wondered whether the plane bringing Flicker Hamden would be able to land before noon on the island. His friend the computer nut. He always looked forward

6

to seeing Hamden, yet he knew that he was always eventually depressed by exposure to Hamden's obsessions. He and Hamden could never agree. Tom Medlar regarded himself as a humanist, a vitalist; he believed in an inner flame, a secret of life, intuition, love, whispers in the night, and crushing fallibility. Flicker Hamden, to the contrary, characterized anything Medlar said as "rickety antiquated Bergsonian idiocy" and extolled electrical intellectuality and wanted every mortal to be plugged in to a vast cybernetic system of data-sifting, problem-solving, and decision-making. Hamden had an optimism which kept him so far off the ground that the conception of moral failure had never even entered the printed circuit of his mind. All this notwithstanding, it would, as always, at least at first, be good to see him—when the fog broke.

Thinking of Flick he remembered that Flick's wife Dottie was sleeping now up forward in the broad-breasted bows of *Harmony.* He listened for Dot's breathing and could not hear it: she was beyond the thin forward-cabin door, and the clacking of the brass clock overhead chopped into bits such soft sounds as her lungs must have made up there. He thought of the dark life-bruises under her eyes.

Dot had been visiting alone on Chappaquiddick and had come aboard the night before, in a fuzzy cardigan and a very short denim skirt, and pearls, chattering about weathered wood and fantastic real estate prices and Bill Furness, who, when he got drunk at big parties, she said, "had a thing" of guarding doorways and only allowing those to go through who "deserved to pass."

Over scotches at the cabin table in the dim light of a gimbaled kerosene chimney lamp, the two women, his wife Audrey and Flick's wife Dot, had all at once torn into a shrill

7

hen fight about the man Furness, whom Audrey, in any case, scarcely knew; it was the inappropriateness of the girls' fury rather than the wildness of their eyes and the trembling of their voices that had hit Tom hard. He had felt the approach of something dangerous.

Recalling now the heat of their faces, and aware again of a vague feeling of peril, Tom suddenly hardened and day-dreamed with his eyes closed; a crevasse had opened before him, and he took a wild bottomless plunge into desire for anarchic pleasures connected with the memory of both those girls possessed by fury. This chaotic sensuality was upsetting. He—with whom every move called for a plan, a little list, the reassurance of forethought—had an urgent need to check this swiftly rising inner weather. He opened his eyes.

Yes, he said to himself, his heart's pace stirred by those fantasies of astonishing irregularities; yes, fog outside. They'd be late getting away.

In his agitation he arose and dressed and silently made up his bunk. Every move was spruce and controlled; "shipshape" was a high-value word at this point in his racing mind. He raised the bunk on its hinges and looped the retaining strap over its peg, so the starboard cabin settee was ready for what-ever the day might bring—shipshape indeed.

Slowly, slowly, watching Audrey's form for signs of wak-ing, he pulled back the sliding cover of the companionway, and he stealthily climbed the ladder and lifted one leg and then the other over the door-boards, and he stepped down into the ample cockpit and stood to one side to avoid the dripping from the boom.

∾∾∾

Tom sighed. How ghostly and soothing it was up here! The mist-softened boats in ranks, tugging at their mooring lines in the fast-ebbing current, seemed to be moving through the water on lonely tethered voyages. Big yachts, among them a breathtaking black-hulled old ten-meter, lay between *Harmony* and the channel, and a flock of day sailers and cocky open racing craft anchor-sailed every which way in the eddies by the curve of the Chappy shore. Edgartown at the far end was blotted out; the private piers and boathouse docks beyond the channel reached back, like memories of childhood, into a silvery emptiness. Directly across the way stood a topheavy dockhouse, a weatherbeaten cube of pure nineteenth century raised up on out-curving supports for the purpose of enabling elderly ladies to sit out on good afternoons to watch the sailboats leaning at their work—a setting rendered completely other-day and unreal by this thick, moist air.

In the veiled distance Tom heard a deep motor thumping, a one-lunger; some kind of work boat making short trips.

There were calming things to do. He lifted the teak seat-board over the lazaret locker and took from a canvas bucket hanging there among spare lines a round head of true sponge (for he despised, at least on boats, the multicolored, square-edged, synthetic saucepan cleaners to which the big chemical companies gave that name), and he held the lovely once-living form, still nearly alive to the touch, in his two hands, kneading it, and he thought of the slowness with which it had shaped its myriad cavities and vacuoles just for him, of

9

its years of growth in a warm sea so that now, on this foggy morning in Edgartown harbor, he, Tom Medlar, could perform a ritual, could sweep it over the glistening brightwork and brass in and around the cockpit of his beloved boat, squeezing the moisture overboard now and then, performing the sacred morning wipedown of the semi-circular expanse of the old Friendship cockpit that was his special pride—his outdoor throne room, he called it, though Audrey had another name for it: his playpen. The hooded binnacle, the deeply varnished wheel with a white cord Turk's-head on the midships spoke, the wide teak seats and narrow teak deckboards, especially the high coaming, as upright as a church pew, reaching aft in a noble and generous curve from side to side of the cabin trunk—every detail contributed to a sense of an old-fashioned quality, a homely elegance. *Harmony* had a broad-beamed grace; a crew of eight could daysail and picnic in comfort in her cockpit. It was fashionable—"sea-going"—in the big boats these days to let brass and bronze darken with verdigris, and to paint out coamings and handrails, but Tom called that sort of fashion mere laziness; he still polished and varnished all summer—and the cockpit sparkled under the sponge even in fog.

He heard the throbbing coming nearer, and now he saw a dark form gliding between two big sloops at the edge of the murk. It was the garbage boat. Tom remembered the sturdy, stone-faced Portuguese woman pulling alongside early in the morning of a previous stop here; she took garbage ashore. He was intensely happy at her approach. He wondered why. Had it to do with the two who were sleeping below—with the threat he had felt in their sharp, crazy clash the night before? With the unsettling daydreams, of play with them, that had driven him from bed? Was there something about the broad-shouldered garbage woman, as he remembered her, so stoical and taciturn, nodding as she took the garbage bags and sadly accepting a quarter with no acknowledgment at all, that could bring him heavily back to earth?

With a housebreaker's furtive movements Tom descended into the cabin and carried up a carton and two green plastic bags of refuse. Audrey was still solidly out. Above again, he pulled shut the companion hatch cover, so Audrey and Dottie would not be wakened—he wanted to speak with the woman—and then stood waiting at the port quarter. The thudding of the motor was deep and eerily near at hand in the close air, and Tom could hear the rippling at the lap-straked cutwater as the heavy black boat pushed its way to a schooner astern of *Harmony* down the line of moorings.

The imminent coming of this hard-faced woman, a reminder in her hopeless, dark-skinned, poverty-ravaged person of all those aspects of shore life that made escape onto the sea seem desirable, brought Tom hard up against a matter that had often set him wondering: the real meaning of *Harmony* in his life. For one thing, as a young teaching doctor he had not really been able to afford her, homely and cheap as she had been. He owed the bank eight thousand at six per cent; a mortgage on this fat female chattel. As the skipper of an inexpensive craft with distinctly unyachty lines—a big old Maine sloop, or a Boston copy of one, anyway, converted for easier handling to a yawl—he thought of himself as a nonconformist, an oddball doctor, an escapist, one whose protest against ordinariness took the form of being, or playing at being, a now-and-then sea bum who might take off any day for distant islands, hospital appointments two-months-deep be

11

damned. Nevertheless, he had to recognize this other strain in himself: a deep pride in brush-and-polish ownership. He secretly thought of himself, particularly when Audrey came into focus in his mind, as a yacht owner, a person who was getting ahead in the most vulgar terms of ordinariness. This did not fit with his comprehension of failure. What did fit was the burden of meaningless small tasks *Harmony* imposed on him. The ambiguity of his boat life may, he guessed, have had something to do with the intensity of his expectation of the garbage woman's call, for he had two thoughts about her. He wanted to make friends with her; he wanted to tip her, too.

As her chunky boat now came sipping at its bow waves, the garbage woman stood at the crude wooden steering lever on the starboard side, in a massive black rubber raincoat, heavy boots, and an ancient yellow oilskin rain hat under the rim of which stray wisps of her curly black hair were silvered like cobwebs with moisture. Though she must have been surprised to find a yachtsman eagerly waiting for her, with his bundles of garbage already at hand, her face showed nothing but its habitual dark lines of gloom and defiance. Her squat boat had an incongruous row of treadless tires from Vespas and Lambrettas hung alongside for fenders. To Tom, she and her rig stood for the world ashore—social injustice, trash in streets, teenage hoodlum unruliness, stupid violence on television; but she also gave a romantic image of stolid self-sufficiency, of honest labor out of doors. Gripping the gunwale of *Harmony* with her right hand, she took the bundles from Tom at the rail in her left as if they were valuable goods and put them with mother-hen fussing and patting into her filthy wooden bin.

"Think this'll burn off?" Tom asked in haste, for she was almost ready to shove away so soon.

Up from under the stiff brim of yellow oilcloth she gave the sky—which had come down to rest, it seemed from the tilt of her face, on the spreaders of the masts in the harbor—a long, intimate stare. Then she looked down not at Tom but at her cargo of garbage and said in a tiny, evasive, piping treble, "Might be a little some'at out the sou'west when the sun gets up."

Her voice was a shock. Had it been throaty and brutal, he would have been wildly exhilarated by the flavor of New England chowder on her Portaguee tongue, but it was a feeble voice, timid, squeaky, with no trace of resentment of an unfair world, no warmth that should have come from living close to the edge of hell. Tom was horrified by the inaccuracy of the expectations he had had. Nevertheless, he pressed her further. "When do you think it might clear?"

"Can't hardly say 't will."

Tom had wanted this big coastal woman to see and praise his old-fashioned, sea-kindly fisherman's craft (or copy of one), but she kept her stare for the most part on the precious bin. She did not seem to want contact; garbage alone could purify, humanity was tainted. Tom felt a push of anger; he wanted to scare the little mouse that apparently lived in her big, worn body. "Hear about the storm?"

Now her eyes—set too close together in that broad, dark face, seeming slightly crossed in the effort of focusing beyond the creased nose—did flicker briefly toward the topsides of the yawl as she asked in barely audible tones, "What storm was 'at again?"

13

"The one they call Esmé. Off the Carolinas, way out. On the radio."

The garbage woman lifted what seemed an acre of rubber raincoat in a powerful shrug, but her real answer came in a thin, indifferent peep. "Di'n' hear 'bout that'n."

She dropped her rugged hand from the varnished gunwale and placed it on her steering lever.

"Wait a second . . . I wondered . . ." But Tom, disconcerted by her spiritless voice, had no idea what further he wanted to ask her, and he paused.

She gave him a little time and then she said, "I got all them boats." She peered into the fog higher up the harbor. She looked furtively and wistfully for a moment at Tom's eyes, as if wishing her tongue were equal to the task of rebuking him for something—for delaying her those few seconds? Already she had engaged the forward gear and now she touched the throttle with her huge booted foot.

She was gone. Tom saw the half dollar still in his hand; he had meant to give her twice the "usual." She would think that the cheap skate in that old beamy tub had fast-talked her to avoid giving her money. That feebly reproachful glance she had thrown him!

He thought of shouting after her, but it was too late, for the black hull was already melting into the gray vapors and soon there was nothing left of the visitor but the popping of her motor out in nowhere up the harbor.

〰〰

His shoulders shook with a sudden chill, and he turned around and for a few moments moodily stared at the compass,

14

as if he had to know where he was bound in all this fog. He put a hand on the shapely wheel. Underfoot he felt the delicate trembling of his yawl in the current, like that of a high-strung horse; she was alive and impatient with land-locked life, it seemed. Before long Tom had shaken the feeling of disorientation his encounter with the garbage woman had given him, and he had yielded once again to the strong joy of being on his boat. This was a kind of intoxication by quiet. The solitude in the fog-curtained cockpit, with the door shut on the two sleepers below, narcotized all his unrests, and even fleeting twinges of pain in his back from a muscle there that had a way of tuning up like a harp string when he slept on the canvas berth on *Harmony*—even those telegraphic thrusts soon eased, and stopped. He stood in something like peace.

಄಄಄

As of its own will the cover of the companionway slid back, and Audrey's hands, squarish to see but soft to the touch as Tom knew well, appeared over the lip of the door-boards, and then her face above them—and Tom's tranquillity was disturbed only to be deepened. Even with a sleep-swollen face and hair undone, she had a definiteness, a personality which overmatched easily that of the odd boat. She had a beautiful homely countenance—a face which was a playground of unsymmetrical bumps, puffy places, pads, planes, widenings, sharp curves over errant bones, all of which fused together into a vision of a cheerful, courageous, and loving nature. So it seemed at this moment.

"Ugh," she said. A comment on the fog. Then she ducked down and slammed the cover shut.

15

Tom pushed the hatch lid back a few inches and said softly into the crack, "Some greeting!" He closed it quickly again.

Audrey usually woke up in a good humor, and he could count on her energetic grin a great deal of the time. Occasionally, when Tom was most unsure of himself, he wondered whether her dependability was grounded on some kind of thickness, insensitivity. She had been, they said, a fat child, and some of her old friends still called her Pudge; her figure was tolerable now, feminine, slightly coarse, giving an impression, yes, of insulated nerves. Yet she was not callous; she was quick in understanding. There was a periodicity, itself dependable, in her crying out against unchangeable things: that life with a doctor was gruesome, his hours were godawful, he was called out of bed in the middle of the night, he came home bushed, he didn't talk to her enough, he was secretive about women patients, he forgot news, they had no real friends, she was getting wrinkles in her neck, between them they were barren. There it was, they were childless. She had miscarried twice; then no luck at all. Whose fault was anything? Her most telling reproach was withholding reproach, giving gracious space and light and air in which his unspecific guilt could flower of itself. Her anguish came at intervals, riding the cycles of disappointment. Between times she was a good wife. There was a kind of fright in that thought. She might be the breath of his life.

Soon the cover slid all the way back again, and Tom, looking down into the cabin, saw that Aud was dressed in jeans and her turtle-neck Irish sweater with the fancy stitchwork, and she had made her bunk and sponged down the cabin deck and now was pumping the alcohol stove.

16

Without looking up at him she asked, "What did your friend from Boston have to say?"

So she had not been all that asleep. "Mr. McCloud sounded squiffed," he said. "At six-thirty a.m."

"Isn't there an earlier forecast you could pick up? I mean, don't you think it would be a good idea to get all the poop on the isobars and occlusions and whatever-they-are at about let's say four o'clock in the morning?"

"Hooo. It's sarcastic out today."

"What did the man say?"

"Fine. Fine for the next two days."

"Looks just fine up there."

"This'll burn off. Sorry I waked you. If I waked you."

"If. What about the storm? What's her name again?"

"Esmé the pretty one? Hovering. They think she'll go out to sea like a good girl."

"Oh, Lord, what do those people ever know? I don't wonder they drink."

ᔕᔕᔕ

Audrey slammed the pots and wrenched the sink pump and dropped the ice chest lid with a bang—her firm way, Tom surmised, of announcing to Dot Hamden that a day starts early on a boat.

Thinking of those electric clashes between the two women the night before, Tom wanted to float some vague sniffing questions, some oblique trial inquiries, to try to discover, if nothing more, the source of his own outsized reactions to their outsized anger, the source perhaps of those gamey fantasies that had bolted him out of bed; but of course he could not, because the cabin was a kind of echo chamber and whatever he and Aud said at one end would surely be heard up forward by Dot, who must have been wakened by Audrey's clatter.

So Tom stood back and resumed his reading of the fog, which seemed to be floating past now in the same direction as the current, intensifying a sense of a self-willed motion of the yawl through both space and time. This feeling became too strong, and Tom found himself walking forward to check, as if for confirmation of his belief in reality, the pennant of the mooring lashed by its pick-up line to the mooring bitts; then he leaned out over the bowsprit and watched the water flowing past the mooring line, which trembled at its own eddies like a string of some great bass instrument. Only when, seeing a floating fan of seaweed catch itself on the hemp just under the surface, he was again really satisfied that water and weather were on the move, rather than his craft or his illusions, did he realize that the squeaky footsteps of his skidproof sneakers on the foredeck were right over, and close over, Dot's prostrate form down in the forecastle. He wondered if he, too, had been trying to stir her. Did she sleep in the buff? Self-consciously avoiding the clear plexiglas cover of the forward hatch, he went aft.

He stepped down again into the cockpit, and there he found draped around his head, like festoons of glorious pale-colored gauzes hung out for his pleasure by his wife, the fragrances of bacon cooking and coffee brewing—so superior, he thought, taking a deep draught of them into his lungs, to their tastes, in the end, on the tongue. He heard, quite loud, the splattering of fat under the slabs of meat and the repeated *chuck* of the percolator and the push of the burners beneath.

He was aware that his senses were extra alert, out hunting this morning like huge-eyed ospreys on silent wings.

"What do we do about this fog?" Audrey's voice came up through the opening to announce that she was aware of his movements on the boat, and Tom thought for a moment, and then in a blur of laziness dropped the thought, that her question carried a burden. Guardedness?

"Wait it out, what else? Why? You worrying about Flick?"

Audrey's back was turned to him. She was struggling with something—to open a new can of coffee, presumably for another day, with a key, as he understood when he heard the inrush of air at the breaking of the vacuum. Finally she said, "Flick can take care of himself."

Flick could. Independence of action was his shibboleth. Independence and exuberance—which together conspired in a habit of using people, because he could not have both without exploiting anyone who wanted to be close to him. Tom suddenly wondered why he and Audrey had asked the Hamdens to come aboard into the skintight intimacy of life on a boat. They had been seeing this "fun couple," as everyone called them, quite often this last year. Dot, with her sweater-and-pearls mentality; and Flicker—people always spoke of his zest for life. How unspoiled he was. Inner fire. Spontaneity. He was some kind of whiz in a sky-rocketing firm of men who called themselves "social-engineering consultants," and though he himself had never touched a finger to a computer knob, his company prepared the way for its every move by "running a program," as Flick put it. "We ran a program the other day," he had said recently, "on the retroactive contraceptive pill. Fascinating! We may be able to edit remorse right out of the range of social feelings." His exuberance stemmed from, and also fed, his optimism about the future. "Tomorrow" would be a time, according to him, when the analysis of electro-cardiograms and yes, by God, the diagnosis of cirrhosis and hepatitis and Weil's disease and haemochromatosis—all the ills in Tom's field—would be done much better by computers than by mere doctors. Decision-making everywhere, even in the home, would be taped, push-buttoned, and housed in "damned good-looking" imitation-walnut consoles. The earth would be a single farm, the moon would be colonized, the sea would be potable, the sun would be our power plant, intelligent life in the galaxies would be reachable by radio phone, and man in this world would be totally free, provided merely that he would check in from time to time with his infinitude of servant-boxes. Flick's sincere joy in these prospects made a kind of poetry of them. There was nothing science-fictional about them, to him; they were imminent, emergent. His conviction was charming. He was almost, but not quite, irresistible. The not-quite was the letdown part. The not-quite made his handsomeness, his health, his big deep laugh, his hairy hands, the sapphires in his eyes, his hoarse undauntability—it made all his tireless exuberance hard to take for a long stretch, at least for Tom, who was just a plain old liver doc. But on the short haul Flick certainly gave one a lift—and short or long he could, as Aud had said, take good care of the self.

Audrey turned her face up toward Tom and asked, "How will we get word about his plane?"

"We'll just have to wait. Go ashore. Take a cab to the airport. Wait some more. These fogs usually burn off about noon."

She moved to the stove. " 'There's never any hurry when you're living on a boat.' " She was quoting him; now the tone seemed casual, her usual self's steady voice. "Come and get it," she said. She cracked an egg on the side of the pan and parted the shell with care to drop the yolk at the center of the white.

∽∾∽

He climbed down the ladder, hearing and smelling the new frying, and seated himself at the cabin table. Audrey had raised the wings of the table and had set out plastic coastal charts as place mats, and paper plates and cups; nothing to wash later but silver.

No sooner had Tom settled than Dottie came breathlessly out from the forward cabin, all dressed, powdered, brushed-out, red-lipped; it seemed as if she had been ready for a long time and had been waiting for him to come back down into the cabin. The girls' good-mornings were quiet and maybe a trifle too easy. Dot asked if she could help and sat down across from Tom without regard for an answer—which never came.

The impression was of passivity charged with unrest. A narrow face in parenthetic waves of hair, delicate gold earrings in pierced lobes; a warm face with two little chills under the eyes, dark places where all that might be subtended under the vague name of unhappiness—doubts, hurts, unrealized hopes for delightful gifts from loved ones, angers, wrong-reasoned urges to good causes, letters dictated to the self in the night—where everything harrowing had been driven for refuge from the downright healthfulness and cheerfulness of the

21

rest of her glowing face. Whenever Dottie met new people, Tom had noticed, she greeted their opening statements with bursts of too-loud laughter and then, having emitted a few of these claps of agreeableness and of wanting to be noticed and of needing to be liked, she subsided into a melancholy and toneless quiet, speaking when she spoke on a pitch that was two or three notes lower than natural for her, as if forcing her voice down her throat into her soft bosom where she may have thought her real mother-wit lived. She had brought a big canvas bag of knitting aboard. She scratched her scalp from time to time. When she said something she really meant, she gave an emphatic toss of her head, so that her sincere eyes were veiled momentarily by clouds of flying hair.

"What's this about meeting Flick?"

Flicker's plane was due, according to the schedule, Tom said, at ten; he said it would be silly to leave until, at the very least, floes of glare had begun to drift on top of the fog. He paused, and then said drily that he had work to do on the boat while they waited. They ate, after that, in silence.

And after breakfast he busied himself, ostentatiously, in the face of the speechless restlessness of the girls, with an inventory check. Was everything in its place? Forepeak: reefing lines; ditty box; six bagged sails; spare sail stops; heavy anchor, chain, and rode . . . He moved about mumbling. Dot did try to help Audrey, and when she was brusquely sent forward to clean her own cabin, Tom, moving aft with his clipboard of lists, saw the fanned-up embers in Dot's eyes. But he refused to focus on the girls' tightness with each other; he was taken up with busy work, the purpose of which, he realized once with a sinking throb, was to keep himself from thoughts of the flaw in his boat. His beautiful boat—there was

22

her picture, in a frame of rope above the Shipmate stove, taken long ago when she was still a gaff-rigged sloop and had a main boom as long as her overall length, carrying a simply incredible press of canvas, main and topsail and two headsails and bonnets and spinnaker and cheater, huge thunderheads of gray duck cloth above the small white hull. What men they must have been in the old days to use and subdue such power aloft! Ticking off now the checklist of things—portable lights, flares, sail-mending kit, anchor light (oil)—kept him from wondering why he had not hauled her out for the midsummer taking up on her bolts. He surely was, as Audrey called him, Dr. Meticulous, infallible as to niceties—brass fittings threw bright darts of their shininess in one's eyeballs; the batteries in the flashlights were always fresh and would not fail when needed—but he had not done the one fundamental semi-annual job that *Harmony*'s flaw required. He was drawn to lift up the floorboards along the bilges and peek; he suppressed the temptation. Why punish himself? He went above and pulled at the pump. Thirty strokes and she was sucking air; not bad after all. He felt relieved and went below again. Then he wondered whether all his uneasiness hadn't to do, not with *Harmony* at all, but rather with the seething impatience that swirled around him.

"O.K.," he said, as if capitulating at the end of a long argument, "just let me shave and then we'll go."

Audrey already had the kettle boiling for his shave; he took it into the head. When the mirror fogged over with steam, he splashed water on the glass to open up a jagged reflection, and he looked himself in the eye and tried to face the eagerness of both these women to go and fetch Flicker Hamden.

〜〜〜

As soon as he called out that he was ready, Audrey blasted off three times with the pressure fog horn, and Tom repeated the call when he climbed above, and in a while the launch came alongside. They jumped down into it. The launchman looked up at *Harmony*'s stately coaming and sucked at his cheek and then asked for two dollars for the mooring, and Tom paid, and the man took them ashore. There were brighter spots in the fog, now, and they rode a cab to the airport, and there, as Tom had predicted, they waited. And waited. The plane was said to be on its way. A man sent up a balloon and timed its vanishing and doubtfully shook his head. The girls both seemed pale. Some Edgartown types stood around in crazy straw hats frim Eleuthera. No one said much. It got to be noon. The expectation of Flicker Hamden grew out of proportion to his person; he would have to justify himself, on stepping down, by turning out to be some sort of magician, or singer, or gambler with handlebar mustaches. The three sat on a baggage cart.

A drone of engines came overhead, at last, giving an eerie effect of being outside an enclosure, of being heard through windows; Tom and the girls stood in a house of vapor, and the plane flew back and forth over its roof. In the radio shack voices sounded like crockery being shattered. The three sidled over to a screened window and heard, through static, the acknowledgments of the pilot, who sounded dangerously grouchy about being hauled down to earth on a kite string of radio waves. Guided to an approach, he tried once to land, but the plane, never visible from the ground, pulled away with a

24

snarl of power. The controller sent the pilot off on a time-killing pattern. Before long the mist did seem to thin. Another balloon went up, and voices on the air sounded more warm-blooded.

The thrumming of motors returned—and bang, there it was: silver, pregnant, an awkward hybrid built for backwater carriers. The girls let out their breaths in a unison sigh. The airship waddled in from the runways. A door popped easily free like an oval of tangerine skin, and an inner ladder let itself down.

Just then a new bank of fog rolled across the field, and Tom could barely see the file of passengers coming from the plane. For a moment he caught at a surprisingly happy thought: There's been a mistake; Flick isn't among them. The girls were tensely receptive; Tom had the feeling that they both wanted to run forward, find some man, and throw themselves on him, one on each shoulder, sharing him. But the certain one wasn't there! Tom, astonished at himself, was on the edge of a raucous, perverse laugh—when a close couple floating through the mist suddenly divided, and the man veered, and it turned out to be Flick striding toward the three of them with an easy, arrogant bearing, in a gray business suit, with a plaid cloth bag in one hand and flapping the other perhaps to signal what fun the blind landing had been. The grin on Flick's face seemed to come forward in the fog ahead of the rest of him. He threw his soft bag to the ground and, placing kisses on the extended fingers of his right hand, he patted the kisses at arm's length onto the cheeks, first of his wife, then of Audrey. And he pounded Tom on the back, a bit too hard, as if Tom had a fish bone caught in his throat. And all the time he was talking away:

25

". . . It could be really terrific coming down through that crap. It's shallow—we were in blue sky at a thousand feet—this soft big old mattress of fog down under you—didn't begin till this side of Block Island. But Jesus, Tom, it's incredible they don't have guided landing in a place like this. On a foggy island? I mean with some of the equipment they've developed by now it would be just like coming down on iron rails. To depend on tower voice guidance on altitude—that's medieval! That joker chickened out on the first approach—you realize that? He wanted to bugger off to Hyannis, I guess, but it was worse over there, so they finally talked him down back here. You know about the system they're experimenting with at Kennedy? Really terrific—it'll sneak you down through haggis pudding. But boy, expensive! I heard the cost of the gear on a single plane is equal to the entire value of the rest of the plane. Beautiful, sophisticated stuff: servo on top of servo on top of servo that actually take over from the pilot and fly the plane down . . ."

Flick had apparently seen the girls' shining eyes, taking him in but not his words, and he lifted his hatless head and stuck out his lower lip. There had been no expression at all as the recurrent explosive word—"terrific"—had come popping out. The ridge of Flick's big straight nose ran right down in line with the plane of his forehead, which was slanting and unusually shallow, for his flaxen hair hooded part of it; in the gray atmosphere and above his gray suit his skin was pinkly tanned and freckled. He was wholly in tune with the times—that was the maddening thing about him. His first word beyond praise of the danger he had just come through was a sarcastic complaint. "This is that terrific August weather you kept giving us a hard sell on," he said to Tom, thumping him

26

again. Flick's eyes in this atmosphere were piscine and chilly, of a pale transparency of lake ice under gray skies, yet their hardness seemed to suggest, if only by a protective glaze on the surface, much feeling somewhere deep down.

At last the girls began to get their voices going, and the four drifted toward the taxis. As they walked Tom had a feeling of seeing Flicker for the first time: an air of superiority, relaxation, a staggering capacity for imposition. It was as if Hamden had chartered *Harmony*; Tom had a moment of feeling like a hired crewman. The morning up to now had been quiet; the girls had been strung up tight. Now a squall of friendliness and outgoing warmth broke out, and everyone was talking at once, even Tom, to his own surprise, and Flicker's laughter rattled like a punching bag. They drew the same taxi man as before. Somehow Flick made it in back between the two girls, and he began to elbow them like mad, while Tom huddled sidewise in the jump seat.

Flick said, "I hear there's a hell of a storm coming."

"Sunny McCloud says she's hung up."

"*Who* says?"

"Weatherman from Boston. You know she's called Esmé? Those government meteorologists really must be getting hard up. He—this McCloud—says she's probably losing her oomph."

Between the two girls Flicker shot his jacket cuffs. His shirt sleeves were rolled up under his suit coat, and his thick, blond-hairy wrists sliding briefly forward from the cloth gave hints of covered physical power. "God, aren't these tracking systems beautiful? You think of all the thousands of variables in a storm like this—they have the whole picture at their fingertips . . . I say let her come!"

27

In flinging out this dare Flick seemed to be inviting not a rage of winds and seas but rather a great cyclonic turbulence of data, of verifiable and classifiable and trackable phenomena. Let Esmé come in all her shimmering raiment of symbols and numbers!

But then, ebullient and down-to-earth, Flick began to tell the latest jokes from the city. The girls, over-responding, rocked off to the verge of hysteria, weeping through extremities of laughing.

It was not until they were well down Center Street in Edgartown that Flick asked Dottie how the children were.

"Didn't you even call?" Dottie asked.

"I assumed you would."

"I did yesterday. They're fine," Dottie blithely said, quickly drawing back from challenge. "I guess I ought to phone again before we go out to the boat."

Audrey was looking out the taxi window with an expression that appeared to be vacant—at what cost, Tom wondered, of control. The casualness of the Hamdens about their three small girls with pouty mouths and halos of golden ringlets, presently parked on grandma in Rumson, must have struck a kind of terror into Audrey, Tom thought; but her eyes were hooded, secret.

At the harbor a light southwest breeze was blowing and fog patches were still rolling through. Dot put through her call from a glass booth; the kids were, again, no more or less than "fine."

In the launch Flick asked, "Where are we off to?"

"I was figuring on going round to Menemsha," Tom said, "but we only have about an hour more of fair currents. I don't know. It's sort of borderline."

28

Flick snorted. "The current doesn't make *that* much difference, does it?"

"It makes plenty. When it's running strongest you have more than three knots going out there. Nearly four off the Chops. I'm not about to beat up the Sound against that sort of stuff."

"My God, we have an engine, don't we?"

Tom did not answer that question. There had been all that talk about how much Flicker doted on pure sailing, all those tales of cruising—the famous casual boast of diving over the side in Cuttyhunk to look for a bracelet that had fallen overboard, and miraculously finding it on the muddy bottom; and many other suggestions, oblique to be sure, of "experience." Tom looked at the ripples on the steely water; he could not face down Flicker's scorn, for which scorn in return was no answer, though he felt it.

There lay *Harmony*, as they swung in from the channel line, ahead, in profile, a white statement of sturdiness and endurance. Her wound was invisible. Her mild sheer rose toward the dark bowsprit thrust out over an old-fashioned clipper bow, with trailboards above the cutwater in lieu of a figurehead, light blue panels with carved gilt scribing and letters. In pride Audrey pointed her out to Flick. Tom looked at his face and saw the immediate disappointment. This martini-time swab didn't want to be on a powerful, waisty, hard-bilged, wide-quartered old girl that would stand up like a church in a blow; he wanted to lollop on some sweet-lined yacht, a money boat. Yet Flick raised himself in the bows of the launch and lied with fabulous bravery, "Oh, she's a honey, Tom! She's really a sexpot. I *like* her." Then he began to grind his teeth. They rounded the stern, with its lovely oval transom, of the same pale blue, with a carved gilded low relief of a skein of grapevine heavy with fruit and the name standing out in stark black.

∽∽∽

Flick went forward to unpack and change, frequently bumping his head and cursing and laughing at himself and calling out his enthusiasm for this and that. Tom fiddled around inconclusively with the current tables. The girls fixed drinks and sandwiches; suddenly their co-operation had turned out to be the most natural thing in the world. Flick came aft soon in tan shorts and a long-sleeved Basque shirt. How young he looked—how blank! Life hadn't printed a single word on his face.

"This is terrific down here, all this space. I guess it's her beam." Not the nicest thing he could say about *Harmony*— like remarking that a woman had a fat behind. His eyes were scouring the main cabin. "What communications have you got?"

"Communications?"

"Well, Jesus, Tom, stuff like ADF."

"What the hell is that?"

"You're kidding. ADF? Doohickus that beams you in on any city radio station? You never heard of ADF? It's *ancient*. Don't you even have a maritime direction-finder?"

"I have a pretty good transistor radio." Tom felt a tiny push of malevolence, and he added, "I forget what make it is."

"My God, no ship-to-shore?"

"Telephone? A telephone here? Why do you think I own a boat?"

30

Flicker couldn't seem to field that question; he rolled his eyes upward and then looked at the two girls as if for agreement that the skipper was missing some central buttons.

Tom decided to deflect Flicker with hospitality. "Find room for everything?"

"I guess so. I just flung stuff around."

"The waterproofs," Tom said, "go in the locker opposite the door to the head."

"No problem. Didn't bring."

The cordiality was promptly skinned from Tom's voice. "But you said you have some."

"I do."

"Well, for Pete's sake, I assumed you'd bring them. I would have had a set aboard for you."

"I like to be rained on."

"Don't be asinine."

"Honest. I like the rain on my head and shoulders. I go out walking in the rain all the time in town. Right, Dot?"

"Not on a boat you don't. Not on my boat. Not if you have to sit at the wheel for hours on end. It gets chilly here—when it's ninety degrees in New York you shiver here till your teeth fall out. I thought you said you'd done all this . . ."

Audrey was slicing a tomato, and in the hanging silence after Tom stopped one could almost hear the knife going through the deep-red vegetable flesh.

Tom announced that they would have to go ashore to buy a set of waterproofs.

Audrey groaned, "Oh, *no.*"

Pliant and passive even as she protested, Dottie said, "He doesn't deserve them, if he's so stubborn—"

31

"It's my ass to get wet, not yours," Flick broke in.

Audrey said, "Come on, drink your drink, Tomaso. Relax."

Tom said with hurt eyes to Audrey, "He told me he'd bring them, so I left the extra set on the beach. Of course I'd have brought ours if—"

Dottie said, "What difference does it make?"

"It makes a great deal of difference. If we had really bad weather it might make all the difference."

〰〰〰

Tom made them go. After they had eaten, he tooted for the launch again, and all four trooped ashore cross and bewildered. The afternoon breeze had come in off the sea to the south, and the last of the fog was scudding in tatters of low cloud toward the Cape; burgees on masts and flags ashore showed their rippling colors straight out. White sails were flying out the harbor mouth. Tom let it be known, however, as they ambled up the brick sidewalk in front of the Harbor View, that for cruising the day was shot. As he spoke his slim figure, passing through fluttering shadows of the leaves of an overhanging tree, seemed to be alive with lights and darks of exasperation. It would be far too late after this errand to try to get around to Menemsha; the currents were already turning in the Sound. If they hurried they could go out for a sail toward Cape Pogue and back. But on a day like this a solid bank of fog was liable to roll back in about five o'clock—might as well just make the best of the remainder of the afternoon in Edgartown, and lay over. He promised, pulling back suddenly from

32

his accusatory sharpness, that they'd have a really terrific sail the next day. Flick's word.

So they went to Hall's, and Flick, making it clear that he was only doing this to humor Tom, tried on heavy-weather gear, and they settled for a big orange suit of it, and Tom paid with good grace, and they strolled idly along the sunny streets and wandered into Stinchfield and the Country Store and the Orient Trader just to look at things. Flicker threw himself into the mock shopping as if it were the most vital of work, holding up silk prints and sailing shirts and Italian blouses against the fronts of both Dot and Audrey, and he cocked his head, and he snatched the cloth away from them with ogling face-bursts of lifted eyebrows and open mouth as if stripping them time and again right down to the skin. The girls responded with rising excitement, running over to triple mirrors to see themselves, front, side, and back, and fingering the most expensive items, and whispering to each other, now, in an almost conspiratorial intimacy. Tom tried hard not to sulk. Those three made a solid mass of joyful indifference to sailing.

By the time they had returned to *Harmony*, the fog had indeed come back, and it was a legitimate cocktail hour. They sat below in the cozy confinement of the main cabin, and Audrey put out some Crema Danica and crackers, and Tom, chipping with a pick at a chunk of ice in a small wooden bucket, was the host again, on his boat again, and he felt that Aud and Dot had begun to play up to him for a change. Now it was Flick who seemed subdued. Games had teams of threes. They sat a long time over drinks in the darkling cabin.

By the time dinner was over, Flick was bellicose and thick-tongued. His two eyelids seemed to be on independently

33

operated hinges. At one point he challenged Tom: "Why a *sail*boat?"

Tom spoke then of the sense a man got on a sailboat of dealing with forces. Perhaps that sense was "worked up"; but there weren't many ways left, he said, for a civilized man to fight for survival—against anything other than himself. "Ever been out in a sailboat when a line squall hit? You go from dead calm to a fifty-knot wind in one solid knockdown, you know. And that black edge of cloud that comes rolling out off the beach? With those boiling inverted mushrooms at the front of it? If you've ever seen that, you can't forget it. Then when it hits you have maybe ten minutes, or up to half an hour, of wind and rain you just can't face—water's green, with this scum running on it, and a real stiff chop gets up, and the lightning all around you . . . You damn well have to know what you're doing—douse your sails at exactly the right time and run off ahead of it; or if you're on a lee shore keep your jib and jigger and claw off. Yet it's really not that dangerous, really it's not that bad; you just have the *illusion* of a triumph over nature, over the evil side of nature. When it's finished the wind drops out to nothing and the sun comes back, in cleared air, and you think, 'I made it, that was something I did, I got us out of that.' "

Flick said, "Our hero. Shee-it. If you had even minimal communications you'd know about the squall hours ahead of time and get into harbor and be in some bar when the thing hit."

"But the whole point is being out *in* it. Coming through it."

"That's real prime stupid. Human beings ought to be in better control of their environment. You have the means. Or

34

if you had the sense you would have. This boat's a death trap."

"It's not just that, anyway," Tom hurriedly added, a sharp pique darting through his drink-loosened impulse to sentimentality. "There's something aesthetic: the business of heeling slightly in a gentle breeze—two insubstantial things, air and canvas, working with all those marvelous curves and lights and shadows to move tons of wood through solid walls of water. It's . . . it's majestic."

"No, no, come on, Tom, you're ducking the issue. If I were going into boating, I'd want to be in my own century, I'd buy me one of those fiberglas jet jobs—have you seen them going along with those marvelous white rooster tails of water trailing behind? The jet's the most exquisitely simple engine there will ever be on this earth. You talk about canvas! Jesus, Tom, it's all Dacron. Chemical synthesis. Lab stuff. You can't turn the clock back just by pretending it's cotton cloth."

All four fell in their bunks early, not exactly tight but discordant and heavy-headed, and Tom slept fitfully, often turning on the creaking frame of his berth, until, in the middle of the night, he woke to thunder and a few minutes of hard rain splashing on the deck. After that, knowing that a loop of new weather had come through and that the morning sky would be high and glass-clear, he slipped into a deep, safe, harbor-like darkness.

෴

Tom was up early with his *Eldridge's*, figuring the currents, and at six o'clock he began roaring the others out of their bunks. It was a sparkling morning with a dry, gentle breeze out of the north; the front had been weak, and these light airs would not hold all day. Time to get going!

Groans and blasphemy forward. Audrey got up in an uncharacteristically sulky mood, clumsy-fingered and speechless. Flicker came blustering out as Tom was laying out the course lines to East Chop on the Edgartown chart, and the guest began to ride his host for all his finicky pencil work. "Christ, man, can't we just heave up the hook and plunge out into the dawn?" Flick began to chant like an idiot traveloguist: "And so, dear voyagers, we leave fair Pago Pago hull down on the palm-fringed horizon. From here we sail to bournes of purple sunsets . . ."

Dot feelingly said she needed coffee.

Audrey snapped at her: coffee was coming.

Tom said, "Only trouble with the Pago Pago approach, around these waters, is that you'd spend your vacation hung up on Middle Ground or L'Hommedieu Shoal or Squash Meadow. Look here at the chart. Look at these shallows—here, here, here, here."

Flick said, "You were giving us all that savage-forces-of-nature talk last night—but isn't what you really love all this farting around with protractors and tide tables? These figures you squiggle in your log book? Creaky, it's creaky. Give us five years, five-six years, we'll design you a computer no bigger than a portable typewriter that'll do all this bloody navigating for you. And better than you can. No human error. We'll program the damn thing with every buoy from Maine to Florida. Figure in current and drift and leeway and whatever else you want, you name it—and give us five more years and we'll give you a box that you'll just press a button and it'll steer right to your destination for you." Flick stuck out his chin as if delivering an ultimatum.

But there was a strange moment when the time came to leave the mooring. The mizzen was up. Tom, in the cockpit coiling the main sheet and freeing cleated lines while the others forward prepared to hoist the mainsail and genny, was aware that something odd was happening among those three. Flicker, reaching up along the main halyard, was suddenly white as the sailcloth beside his face. Tom's spirits were soaring, as they always did just before he felt the first surge of sailpower on the motionless boat, and, for a flashing moment, seeing the thinly clad figures of Dot and Audrey in sharp relief against the pure sky, he experienced a flashing recall of those searing, chaotic desires that had shot him out of bed the previous morning. At that very instant he saw Flick hesitate. The man was faltering. Good God, Tom thought, he can't pull the sail up, the big shouter wants order, he wants things tied down, he wants the mooring, he doesn't want to leave the mooring! The clarity of the air brought this conviction into dazzlingly sharp focus. Tom saw Flick's clenched jaw.

Then it passed. With a rattle of slides on the track the mainsail rose. The breeze and the current worked at cross purposes, and as the main took hold the boat began to inch up on its mooring.

"Cast off," Tom called forward, "and then get the genny up right away." His first overt commands to Flick.

They were free and moving! Tom spun the wheel and wore off toward the channel, and the current took *Harmony's* keel broadside and swept her swiftly down for Edgartown, till she gibed and came round with a swish; Audrey, who understood everything, was already back in the cockpit trimming up the sheets, and the glistening tower of Dacron began to lean and pull as lines went taut and blocks creaked erect and the whole yawl sighed at the feel of her power. Tom's heart was pounding. What a glorious swift glide down the rows of boats!

Tom tacked close aboard the pilings of the yacht club landing stage, and as *Harmony* heeled to her renewed grip on the wind he looked up and saw Flicker gesticulating and cavorting on the port side of the foredeck like a mad ape, greeting all Edgartown with bombastic political fervor, shouting his exuberance at a grossly unsuitable hour—a calisthenic display after that moment of shocked paralysis at the halyard. Yes, this was Flick's famous zest for life—but Tom had glimpsed a strange prelude to it in that pallor at the hoist, that frozen bite of the big jaws as the man had tried to overcome something in himself.

Bearing off at the curve of the harbor mouth, Tom thought: To hell with him. All the same, it was not so easy to dismiss him as that, for Flick's noisy exultation had dampened Tom's own deep joy at this nearly silent motion through the low-slanting clear rays of the sun. The metabolism of that buffoon was enough to kill anything quiet and heartfelt.

The lighthouse tower out on the sand in this whiteness should have, usually would have, given Tom the peak of his almost dreamlike pleasure, not only in its molded simplicity of form but also because of its symbolic force, standing for the concern of those on shore for those who have gone to sea; whalers' wives waiting for ocean-worn ships to come home; vigilance at night; fellow feeling; a small flame in front of a concave mirror that would send out such a piercing shaft of worry toward the edge of the known world. But all Tom could think at this moment was that the lighthouse was automated now. Electronic controls. Flick's world, a-human and ineluctable.

ᘛᘚ

Tom sailed out toward Cape Pogue until he could come about and fetch the Chops. Now that the trip was under way Flicker simply would not calm down. The air was bracing; he talked like a terror. He was good company. There was no denying that he kept the ball bouncing. "There's this character at the computer center . . . Did you catch the Buchwald piece on . . . So we wandered up to the bar car, since it looked like the train would never . . . They have these real high-smelling cheeses, in the downstairs part . . ." Tom wanted the others to see how perfect the day was—the geometries, complex and dark, of the ferry dock at Oak Bluffs, bits of the faraway Cape seeming to be raised on space-colored floats, the shore-to-shore fabric of royal blue laid out ahead; but Flicker pulled the whole earth into the cockpit and held it there by the throat. Dot's earrings twinkled under softly blowing waves of her hair. Audrey was listening, listening, one hand limp on the fall of the genny sheet. Tom saw that the teaming had gone against him again.

Harmony flew across the gap between the Chops, and Tom tried to shut his ears to the energetic fanatic he'd invited aboard. He scanned the summerhouses on the bluffs of the Chops, with salt-silvered shingles and white trim, and towers and dormers and wide porches, nostalgic images of an old world of which Flicker Hamden would be contemptuous not because it represented privilege, gentility, and bigotry but because it was—to use his word—creaky: few of the houses even had television masts. Tom felt argumentative. He was a mender of suffering human beings, an old-fashioned gut man; this ever-talking futurist made him feel a little dizzy on the brink of obsolescence. He wanted to get something back. "See how the current takes us," he said at the West Chop bell, where the weird sliding of the sea was most visible. "It would be murder against it"—justifying yesterday's painful layover if not the trip for the rain gear.

Flicker went right on, however, his bland, expressionless face opening at the mouth to let out a ceaseless flow of buoyant, null, enthusiastic, insensitive explosions.

But near the northern end of Middle Ground, where the black can buoy was almost pulled right under by the rushing current, *Harmony* hit a tide rip—nothing much in this moderate northerly that came in diminishing puffs, but enough to make the yawl jump and shudder. At the first lurch Tom saw a moment's shadow, no more than a tern's wing's worth, cross Flick's open face, and Flick blurted out—the thought given tongue before his slow inner censor could do anything more than dampen the tone and erase the question mark at the end, "I suppose this fat thing is pretty good in a seaway."

That she was. Tom did nothing with the opening Flick had given him to say what he felt, and what he knew, about the qualities of "this fat thing," *Harmony*; about how the shrewd Maine fishermen had designed their boats to be sailed out to make a hard living in all four seasons, under huge sails in light airs in summer yet also able in winter—what men!— to come thrashing back in from offshore banks in the teeth of whistling sub-zero nor'westers. So they had thought of stability, of making their craft capable of standing up to all sorts of malice of the elements, yet they had thought of footing along, too, to get to market ahead of the others, for dollars' sakes. Hard bilges, flaring sides, great flanks and hips—power, probity, and that strength of character in boats known as weatherliness. What a mockery yacht-racing rules had made of sound design! Men's lives, not their vanities, were designed into the Maine boats. But all Tom said was, "You'll see, she's solid as a stone house."

Later, beyond the rip, out in the Sound abreast of oak-tufted islands, Nonamesset and Vekatimmest and long Naushon, as it became evident even to Flick that the land breeze was dropping out, the puffs having less body and the intervals growing warm and breathless, an inevitable question came about the engine down below. Tom was not surprised; he had guessed that this hard-talking bundle of wires would not be able to stand slatting sails in a dead calm, for he would want to "get some place."

This time Tom rather relished being free with his answer. Oh, yes, he cared about having a power plant you could depend on. *Harmony* secreted a two-year-old four-cylinder Gray which took her along at six knots in flat water. Which would start at the touch of a button, guaranteed. Had just changed the coil, the plugs, the points, the condenser. Said he did this three times a summer, needed or no—corrosion by salt moisture in one of those spots was the cause of nine-tenths of the heart failure on yachts. Talking this way, Dr. Meticulous felt the edge of his own smugness. "I hate to use the kicker," he said, "except when it's really needed." He saw Flick chew that; you could easily read the code of this guy in the involuntary labors of his jaw muscles, for he seemed to eat tough thoughts and bad feelings raw.

"There's no hurry today," Tom said. "Look how we're moving on the land, just riding the current." He sensed that he had worked the issue of the current for all it would give; so he shot one right past Flick to Audrey. "What would you think of ducking into Tarpaulin Cove—or Quicks's Hole would be even better—and anchoring for a swim and lunch? It'll be nice and hot in an hour from now; this is pooping out. Then when the afternoon sou'wester comes in, we can scoot across to Menemsha."

It was Dottie who reacted first to this idea. "Yes, *let's*," she said, leaning forward as if dizzy with fervency and putting out one hand to steady herself on the binnacle hood. There would be a hand stain on the brass: salt and oil from the flesh. Tom would have to wipe it away that evening, with a rag and some Noxon; a prick of annoyance spurred his surprise at the eagerness of Dot's response. Audrey came in fast with a seconding; she urged Quicks Hole. Tom, looking aloft to keep the mainsail full as he headed up toward the islands, was suddenly thoughtful about the sun glints he had seen in both girls' eyes just now. Some sort of kindling had been laid out unbeknownst to him; he didn't want to be a dumb bunny; he must keep sharp.

The last of the breeze, wavering in direction so that Tom could take good advantage of the shifts as he short-tacked on the favorable current into the gut between Pasque and Nashawena, barely had the weight to cut *Harmony* out of the swift tidal stream running through the Hole and to take her up to the empty curve of dunes and bright shallow-shelving beach on the southwest side. They were lucky; there were only a couple of power boats anchored in the bight. Tom slipped *Harmony* closer toward the beach than the power cruisers and swung north away from them and casting off sheets luffed up until she was dead in the glassy water; he called forward to Flick to heave the anchor. Splash! Sails down. There they were. A deserted place under a still, hot sky. After a flurry of furling and tying stops and coiling lines, all four on the yawl stood wherever they were and stared in silence at the empty place: sand, rocks, grass, water, and a huge blue sky for white gulls to write on. But for the horrible stinkpots (those two cruisers simply had to be put out of mind) this was away, away; four human souls in a wild place.

And a wildness seemed to be rooted in three of them. Flicker suggested daiquiris, wanted to know where the rum lived—did they have any limes? Tom said he never drank on *Harmony* until the evening anchor was down; but go ahead. All three of those others skinned down the companionway to squeeze lemons (no limes) and crack ice and change into swim suits. And soon they were in the cockpit—both girls in bikinis. Audrey had had a Cote d'Azur bikini for two years, which she had never had the nerve to put on, but all things were easy in this liberating sunshine. Flick had slipped three old-fashioned glasses in the ice chest; they were fogged now briefly with cold as the pale drinks gurgled from a silver spout. Audrey produced picnic eggs. White grains flew from a tiny cardboard saltcellar; teeth glistened biting into the yolks. The sunbaked boat lay on a plastic bay. There seemed to be much traffic into the cabin and back out to the sun—more rum, something cheesy to munch on; limbs grazing, bare flanks brushing against each other in passage up and down the companionway, breathless laughter, casual hand play (wiping away a splash of daiquiri, patting on sun oil, caressing home a talking point)—Flick's palms in joke and the girls' own fingers in self-loving pleasure flowing over the long stretches of warm skin between the kerchiefs at the loins and the kerchiefs at the breasts. All was indiscriminate. They dived, dried off, drank, ate, licked lips, touched each other as if by accident. Tom was set off to one side by his own prudence, yet he grew slightly drunk on the animal exultation of the others: heat, the salt on the skin, the rum in the veins, the stretch of golden days leading across blue water toward nowhere, nowhere. Dot's bikini was so trivial that the rippling reflection of lights on the water gave a tremulous glow to the undercurve of her abdomen as she stood outside the lifelines, one hand reaching down to steady herself while she waited to dive, her knees bent and spread apart as if she were overcome with lust, and when a few moments later she climbed up the swimming ladder the skimpy dark blue cloth below had been pulled down by her plunge so that circlets of hair showed and pearls of seawater glistened in the creases between her thighs and the now wetted roundness of her belly. Tom saw a bald man on the nearer power boat shamelessly looking across through a pair of binoculars. Sun oil was getting on the teak of *Harmony*, but for once Tom did not care. Flick bellowed like a moose; Dot raised her arms, a post-impressionist's odalisque, and squeezed the water out of her hair. Audrey's eyes were vague, and Tom thought of a Yeats phrase: "dream-dimmed." They unshipped the dinghy and they rowed, several hands on each oar, hilariously catching crabs with the blades, to the curve of sand, and they baked themselves till they had to wash off and hurry back, those three, for thirds and fourths from the silver shaker. Tom drifted with their sensuality. Every moment was

44

sun-warmed, invitations and temptations flew out in ease and heat, glands must have been giving freely of their lubricants. What loose laughter!

In the midst of this Tom realized that he had not listened to a single weather report all day.

He scrambled down into the cabin as if shot out of a gun and turned on the radio and got the Ronettes singing "Walking in the Rain." At once there was motion against the sky in the companionway: Flicker luring Audrey into doing some kind of rock-and-roll chugging thing. The big man pretended he had to duck to avoid the boom, though it was a foot above his head. All three laughed loud, himself the loudest, at his jack-in-the-box motions. Tom turned the button in search of another station, and at the cutting off of the music boos and groans came down the steps from the others. It was the wrong phase of the hour; no news was on. Tom snapped off the set.

Audrey leaned her flushed face into the opening and called down, "Ah, come on, Tommy, that was pretty music."

"Have a heart," Tom said. "It's on dry cells—it's for weather reports."

Audrey looked at Tom for a moment as if he were a total stranger and said, "Good God, Dr. Medlar, you have a whole *inventory* of spare batteries down there under the seat. Haven't you?"

How could he say that it was the principle of the thing? That that device was what Flicker wanted more of on this "fat thing"—a predictor. She was tight and Tom was cold; he was bound to seem to be in the wrong. Perhaps, besides, he *was* in the wrong, and he was choked by that thought and climbed above.

The mood of those three shaded off after that, and fifteen

45

minutes later Audrey and Flicker were below, stretched out on the padded settees on opposite sides of the cabin, sound asleep, and Dot, her body all pink in her two bits of cloth, had sprawled into a limb-flung sleep on the canvas cushions on the cockpit seat.

Tom sat near the other man's nearly nude wife waiting for the wind. The bald gent on the power boat, with his binoculars slung on his neck at the ready, was smoking a huge cigar. Gulls were crying in circles above the lily pond beyond the dunes. Tom felt rueful. He knew that it would have been the very top of folly to drink in mid-passage, especially now that it was clear he would have to sail single-handed over to Menemsha. Drunk skippers wreck boats. But he thought of the skins grazing against one another; he thought of Flicker Hamden's handsome abandon, and of the undecipherable dreams clinging like pale-colored lenses to Aud's eyes, and of Dot's pathetic yet touching eagerness to give, to do, to be whatever was wanted. Tom keenly felt his separateness from the others. Dot stirred and sighed; he stood up. He saw a piece of bread left on top of the cabin trunk, and he began to break it up and to toss bits into the clear water. The gulls, alert at a great distance to this opportunity and suddenly muted by greed, banked and glided down to swoop and snatch at the floating food. One was a bully. Tom, furious at its cutting-out tactics, threw his coke bottle at it, but it flew safely away with leisurely strokes of its rain-cleaned wings.

Then out across the open Sound Tom saw what seemed to be magic shadows on the water fallen down from a cloudless sky—the first streaks of the sea breeze, breaking the quicksilver glaze of the dead calm that had come with the turn of the tides. These streaks widened into pools of dark on the wide, steaming mirror. Tom went to work, to be ready when the afternoon breeze had gathered enough body to reach along the island surfaces and come down into the bay of the Hole. First the little spanker went up; then the main. He waited a bit. The metal wind vane at the main truck wavered, then turned with some purpose toward the southwest; the sail trembled up at the head. Yes, air was moving in—air that had come like instinct-driven migrating wildlife from far shores, from Hatteras, Dry Tortugas, Yucatan. Tom thought in a flash of Esmé, out there somewhere to the southwest, and for a moment he was furious with himself for his laxity in not having listened to a forecast all day. But then he busied himself—got the anchor up and shipped it and coiled the line and lashed the Danforth's triangular blades and long cross bar into its cradle abaft the mast, and quickly hauled up the jib and ran aft to the wheel. An eddy was throwing the bow of *Harmony* the wrong way. No matter; a puff came and filled the sails and Tom gibed her comfortably around to glide out toward the Sound. The crew slept.

How serene to be alone on a well-loved boat on an easy beam reach in smooth water! Tom felt alone, and now, busy at the helm, he accepted solitude and began to think it a blessing. He headed for the lowest point in the great dip of the skyline of Martha's Vineyard between Chilmark and Gay Head, holding half a point to windward of what he took to be Menemsha itself, to allow for the current which was now just beginning to run up the Sound. This was the perfect angle of sailing for *Harmony*, a hair higher than wind abeam, heeling at a lazy slant, rushing along with a swishing sound through the ripples as myriad maps of foam floated past a daydreaming geographer at the wheel, islets and reefs and atolls and shoals of spindrift thrown out by the creative bow waves. With her sails trimmed right, she was in balance; she would hold her course without his hands on the spokes of the wheel.

By the time *Harmony* was half way across the Sound—the wind holding so light as scarcely to ruffle the water, which was now moving more surely in the same direction as the air—Tom had thoroughly lost himself in the wide afternoon.

His gaze was making a casual sweep of all those things that bear watching—the luff of the tall sail, the telltales, the cleating of lines, the carelessly dropped fall of the main sheet, a winch handle not stowed—when he became distantly aware of a glittering pair of eyes aimed at him. He came back with an inner crash to his company: Dot, across from him, sleep-puffed, lazy, stretching her drowsy nakedness, and looking at him. Tom met her eyes, and he saw the most blatant and pathetic invitation deep, deep in the blue irises. It was so urgent as to be a cry for help. It said: Now, don't wait, now's the time, we're alone, they're asleep down there. Help me! Change me!

Tom's heart began to run. How easy it would be to untie the little bow at the hip! The oiled legs were already spread. *Harmony* would sail herself. Enter, possess, serve, and never regret. Either to break the spell of those pleading eyes, or simply to figure the risks, Tom stood up and stepped to the companionway and looked down into the cabin. Two enchanted sleepers lay on the berths, in thrall to the narcotic gurgling of the boat's motion, dead to the betrayals of this world.

48

Harmony held her course like a good friend.

Tom stood over Dot, looking down at her. Her gaze, still pouring into his face, seemed to Tom to say so very much about Flicker Hamden. Tom's own warmth, withdrawn in the role of mere witness in the hour at anchor, now began to bank up fiercely, yet at least part of what he felt was pity, cold against his pulsing.

He was on the verge of bending down and reaching out a hand to Dot's cheek when she began to shiver. His eye slid to her skin, so desirable and so available a few moments ago, and he saw there countless tiny gathers. Goose pimples. She was chilled by the ocean breeze. That begging look! Her eyes must have been pleading for cover not by a man, not by him of all men, but simply by cloth, warm cloth. He was horrified by his misreading of her messages. His face began to burn. He turned rapidly and descended the companionway ladder and went forward between the sleepers—Hamden was snoring in a sleep of filthy righteousness—to the forward cabin, where he tore a blanket off one of the bunks, and he carried it back up on deck and spread it over Dottie.

She turned her eyes up to his with a look of luxuriating gratitude, as if he had indeed served her and unknotted her, and the lids of her eyes drooped as the pupils seemed to roll up into her head—and she was fast asleep again, eased away by his gift of warmth.

෨෨෨

Tom sat down at the wheel, all alone again. He felt a slow anger rising, but it was not strong. The genny needed trimming; he slipped the handle into the leeward jib sheet winch,

49

not far from Dot's form, and casting off the cleated fall took a few fast cranks. The rachets clicked their peremptory sounds into the hull.

"What's happening?" It was Audrey, from below. Tom was surprised by his sharp elation, relief, at hearing that steady, good-natured voice.

"You're missing a hell of a sail. That's what," he called.

Dot did not move.

Tom went forward to the companionway once more and looked below and saw his wife lying on her back, a sweater spread on her, staring straight upward, her eyes unusually wide and dark. "Come on up and join me," he said softly. "I'm lonely up here."

"All right, darling," Aud said. She made mouth motions, indicating a drink-dry tongue. "Twenty more winks, O.K.?"

But she did not come. She may have fallen asleep again, Tom supposed, and he sailed on in a breeze that was now folding little tucks in the water. He had to point higher, as the current was running more swiftly, and he hardened up all three sails, coiling the main sheet when he had trimmed it down. The sun was on the shoulder of the afternoon, and a haze hung on the air like a vague report; a mildewy dampness that rumored of immense depths of the sea far away off soundings. He realized that he himself felt chilled, but for some reason he did not want to go below to fetch himself a windbreaker.

Half a mile from the Menemsha bell Tom began to rouse the crew. "You've got to see this entrance," he shouted down into the cabin.

"Be right up. Be right up," came quickly and briskly from Flicker.

Audrey was awake, too, uncovered in her bikini. Tom had the impression he had interrupted a lazy conversation, perhaps about himself, between those two; they were lying on their sides facing each other across the cabin.

He turned and shook Dot's blanket-covered shoulder until she awoke in the act of stretching, mouth pulled, one bare arm reaching out. He pointed to the bluffs of Chilmark, where the scrub oaks were lighted yellow-green by the lowering sun, and she sat up making sleepy sounds of delight; she pulled the blanket he had brought her close around herself and hugged herself in it.

Flicker climbed up with a rowing shirt over his trunks, and in a few minutes Aud appeared in blue cotton slacks and a pale yellow sweater.

Near the bell, which clanged seldom in the calm sea, they handed the sails; Flick helped Audrey furl the main. Dot sat huddled and passive in the blanket. All three were amazingly fresh-eyed and observant, pointing out sights for others to enjoy.

Tom turned the ignition key and said to Flick, "Now hear this."

He pressed a button, the starter gave out a gong-like cry, and the engine did indeed respond at once.

"Music," Flicker said, but with less admiration in his voice than Tom would have liked to hear.

Tom headed for the mouth of the jetties. The tidal current was running out so fast from the broad reserves of Menemsha Pond that between the jetties waves of the water's swiftness were veed together as if this were a river descending from hills, and *Harmony*, swaying and straining, barely moved against all that force alongside the great angular chunks of stone. Bathers from the beach to the left, two women in floppy hats, and some boys with a barking golden Labrador stood on the breakwater watching their entrance. At the end of the left-hand jetty Tom swung his boat sharply to port into the basin, where, in still water, *Harmony* seemed to shoot forward. Quickly picking an anchorage between two fiberglas cutters, Tom swung in a big half circle, killed his speed, drifted ahead, and finally called to Flick to heave the anchor.

A man on one of the glass boats made a circle of a thumb and forefinger and called across, "Very pretty!"

Did he mean anchoring on a single pass like that, with plenty of room all around, or did he mean *Harmony* herself?

Tom, walking forward on the deck, glowed with sunburn and windburn and pleasure. Flick and Audrey were on the foredeck, looking at a whirlwind of gulls over the dunes beyond the Creek. Tom spent some time checking the hold of the hook because he had dragged once here on thick kelp on the bottom; the other two moved aft.

Straightening up, looking around at the whited Coast Guard boathouse with its launching rails slanting down into the smooth basin, at Dutcher's Dock with two raunchy commercial swordfishermen tied up alongside, at the sportsmen's playland of flying bridges two and three deep at the outer end of the town quay—at this quaint place so sophisticated that the tourist touches had themselves been absorbed into the general air of silver-shingled authenticity—Tom felt a current of release; he was pleasantly tired, full to the brim with a day of sailing delights, ready now to unbend with the others.

He wanted a drink with the others, wanted to redress his stiffness of the noon hour and to commune with them in that spirit of mindlessness they had achieved, that indiscriminately shared reveling in the dumb works of fingertips, tongues, lips, eyes, limbs, hot skins—but it seemed that during his securing of *Harmony* a vote had been taken by those three beyond his earshot to go ashore first, before cocktails, to take possession of the place by planting feet on it; they were not really sailors, any of them, not even Aud. He felt he owed Dot a debt—not an explanation, because she surely had no inkling of what had gone through his mind, and she may not even have been fully awake. He wanted to be agreeable; he wanted to laugh with Dot's husband Flick. So now he took the lead, jumping down first into the dinghy, holding it steady while the girls and Flick got in, and he rowed them ashore.

∽∽∽

The lights of evening bathed Menemsha, and Tom took them into the simple shack of the fishmarket on the dock, where in a glass-sided tank great lobsters, like knights in the jousting ready-tent, faced death with stupid calm, and bluefish and mackerel and striped bass, already staring with the knowledge of what death brings, lay on cracked ice—still lifes with glints of iridescent silver, blue, aqua, and pale, pale gray of shadows under rocks in shallows. Tom ordered up some clams, and a college boy, working there to get away from his family's middle-class ethos, in boots and dirty sweatshirt and jeans, hair too long, upper lip surly and spoiled, pried open a dozen and a half, wincing each time he squeezed the steel wedge, and having cut the white muscles laid the clams in their dripping halfshells on a round metal tray. They ate them right there by the market scales, sucking the sea fruit off the rims of the shells; Flicker made slurping noises. The damp cement

53

floor, the deep *bump-clack* of the ice room door thrown shut, the sunset light, the edged saline taste of the clams—Tom savored, if more inwardly than those three at noon, a rush of unthinking sensations.

But now it seemed the others did not want to let themselves go. Tom was out of phase again. Audrey spilled a dribble of clam juice down her chin and onto her yellow sweater, and her embarrassment and annoyance were too large for the case; fire spread on her cheeks. Dot ate one clam and made a face. Flick began talking about the city in homesick gloom: how he had walked across Fifty-seventh Street at eight o'clock one Sunday morning, with not a living soul in sight—a science-fiction feeling of being the only survivor. He was, Tom suddenly thought, trying to think them away from this room with a redolence of the substitute for the odor of sex—the smell, among others, of mackerel, the cuckold-fish.

It was Audrey who asked with burning eyes, "And what were you doing walking the streets at that hour on a Sunday?"

Flick patted her on the shoulder and said as if to a small child, "Hrrumph. Your Uncle Fillmore don't let no grass grow under his footsies."

Tom couldn't believe the charge for the clams. He had had them in other summers from that same battered circular tray for what?—three cents a clam? He thought the college boy, a product of the new math, had perhaps never learned simple addition; he pressed his questions; the boy barked the name of his boss, who came from the chilly caverns beyond the thick door in a fishing cap with a long black plastic visor and confirmed the robbery, to the penny, in very sour New England tones that seemed to say, "Dear Lord, spare us from these summer people." Tom wound up bilked and humiliated. There was too much money around . . .

But then rescue came—the arrival at the dock of one of the crusty swordfishermen, a high-pulpited vessel painted a strange brown of deserts, of dust, of utter dryness, named *Thalia IV*, with the pennant of a catch on the ratlines of her crow's nest. All hurried out on the dock. A huge, muscular, steel-blue torso was heaved out on a crane and was weighed and was dumped on the dock, and the man in the black-visored cap settled a price with the fishermen. A seagull with an eye brimming with defiance perched on the torso by the rip where the sword-nosed head had been severed and began pecking at the pinkness. No one drove it away. Tom took his lackluster crew, their three set against his one, back out to *Harmony* for drinks.

They were soon settled, glasses in hand, in the cockpit in a quiet frame of mind as the circle of the sun seemed drawn down by an attraction of brilliance to brightness toward the piercing flashes of the Buzzards Bay light, already lit, on the Texas tower over the open sea out to the left of Cuttyhunk. Tom, puzzled by his isolation, was slipping farther into it.

∾∾∾

Flick said, "Hey, case the haunted pirate ship."

There had appeared between the jetties a big lumbering trimaran being pushed slowly by an inadequate, whining outboard. It blundered into the basin, its high freeboard and three massive floats clearly making it difficult to maneuver in a crowded, windy anchorage. A corpulent young man with a

55

purple face under a Bahama straw was at the tiller, and he
looked furious that his craft, with which he had evidently
determined to impress yachtsmen from Maine to Florida, had
proved so awkward, and in its clumsiness so very unnautical. A
pretty, soft woman—Flicker let out a low wolf whistle at the
sight of her—wearing pajama-like slacks and dark glasses with
mirroring lenses, was drooped over the anchor line forward in
what appeared to be the last stages of exhaustion and vexa-
tion; she looked around with eyes that seemed, in their reflect-
ing, to be ovals of just what she saw.

"All right! Let go!" the man called to her, though his
ugly, gigantic duck was still moving.

She slipped the anchor line, holding her hands up in a
feminine gesture of distaste away from the snaking coils of
Nylon. When the line went limp she made it fast.

Flick said, "Listen to the way that snotty son of a bitch
talks to her."

"That marriage won't last long," Dottie said in a dry
voice.

Flick's face snapped around toward his wife's; he gulped
at his drink as if to wash down the reaction that had started
up his gorge.

The wind carried the trimaran, settling on its anchor line,
hard down on one of the glass boats, and it was clear that the
fellow was going to have to try again. He had overconfidently
cut his engine; he scrambled out on the after-frame to start it
up once more. Flick snorted. The trimaran man's purple face
lifted up and he roared to his wife to get the God-damn hook
up; he made the error seem hers. The little mirrors looked at
heaven and became heavens. The soft arms tugged.

"The bastard," Flick said.

The outboard was racing in neutral, throwing out smelly fumes.

"Is it up? Is it up?" The anchor was obviously off the bottom, for the bulky triple pontoons had begun to drift. "God damn it! Get it up!"

The woman nodded. Was she weeping behind her mirrors? The man took the nod for a signal that all was clear, though the anchor line still hung down straight. He threw the motor into forward gear. The big craft began to creep into the wind.

"Incompetent meathead," Flick said, and then he emptied his drink, holding the glass back with the ice against his teeth while the last drops trickled down his throat.

Tom looked at Audrey; he felt he had to see her face. Was she disturbed by the display of trouble, over there, between a man and his woman? Where had Audrey drifted off to during the day? Why did he feel so alone? Her eyes were on Flicker—and no wonder, Tom thought. Flick's response to the red-faced skipper of the trimaran was absurdly exaggerated; the brilliant social engineer seemed looped on a single drink. But Audrey had a cat-like look, watching him— inscrutable, alert, waiting in too-perfect poise. Then Tom saw the moment arrive when, with an acuity of peripheral vision that she had, she became aware of his own eyes on her face. The cat stare was instantly wiped away; she arose, moved to Flick, took the empty glass from his hand where he still held it high as if thinking of hurling it across the water at the head of the red-faced man. She went below to refill it.

The hulls were turning, and the wind caught them. The big craft, while still headed mostly upwind, was sailing on its pontoon sides and was drifting across-wind. The skipper accelerated his motor—too late. What was bound to happen, happened. The trimaran gathered speed. Its anchor, only a few feet off the bottom, picked up the anchor lines of three peacefully anchored yachts, aboard which, as it chanced, there were no crews just then. Flicker whooped, half joyous, half furious. Audrey's head came up to see what had occasioned that bellow. The tangle was beyond belief. The trimeran, buzzing like a hornet, was tugging at the entire raft of vessels.

Tom thought of those crews, having gone ashore from their shipshape boats, decently anchored, probably to enjoy a lobster in peace at the Home Port, coming back later to this mess.

"Cut your motor, you bat brain!" Flicker roared.

But the skipper of the trimaran was too busy shouting garbled phrases at his wife to hear instructions from any quarter. The blue smoke of the laboring motor's exhaust blew off in sun-touched puffs. The skipper looked around, head held high, as if out on a perfectly normal run in his elegant craft and waiting to drink in the pretty sights; he had become aware that many eyes all around the basin were on him, and he would look nonchalant at any cost. The four vessels nestled together in a hopeless snarl. Tom felt helpless himself, a mere onlooker just as during the noonday picnic. Audrey was reaching out Flick's new drink. Flick seized it, gulped it half down, jumped to the quarterdeck, pulled in the dinghy painter, crashed down into the cockleshell, and was pulling away with the short oars hell-bent for rescue before Tom could even catch his breath to decide what to call to him.

Something made Tom look at his watch: it was just before six-twenty-five. "Jiminy," he said, and he rushed below, as though nothing were happening out on the surface of the

58

basin, and he snapped on the radio and tuned it for Providence. A newscaster came on strong, with a horrifying bulletin about a babysitter whose dogs, a Doberman Pinscher and a Weimeraner, had attacked and killed the baby she was taking care of, and at the same time Tom heard Flicker and the skipper of the trimaran shouting rancorously at each other. Flick's advice sounded poor; the skipper had found a meddlesome target for his rage. The newsman said the crazed dogs had turned in due course on their own mistress. Tom kept listening with two distressed minds, and when a weatherman, replacing the gruesome newscaster, finally spoke about the wavering of Esmé—she was now lazing back toward the Carolinas—the report was all mixed in with cries of "Get the hook down" and "Christ, man, what do you think I'm trying to do?" So that in the end Tom had no more than a layered, ambiguous impression—the storm veering indecisively toward the mainland again, the two fools up there crying their manhood into the wind. Tom turned the set off, but he had no desire to go above. It was going to be a good cruise; that had been decided, that was all set. He sat thinking about Audrey—that look of a cat, poised, waiting.

Then he heard a powerful motor, and several new voices all shouting, and he did climb up the ladder. The Coast Guard was having difficulties over there with Flicker, who was waving his arms like a symphony conductor and sounded very drunk. It took an hour to straighten everything out. By the time the Coast Guard came across the water towing a subdued Flick in the dink, it was nearly dark and the wind had died and tiny gnats were flying.

2

The Swimmers Beneath the Bow

They were barreling into the blue west with a good capful of breeze. What a morning! The dome of winds sparkled like a child's eye. Gay Head was already far astern, pale against paleness, and *Harmony* was coming up now on the Texas tower, Buzzards Bay light, which stood up stark and angular out of the swells on its tall, hollow, red steel shanks, a mechanical monster, alien to the sea. Flick thought it beautiful.

From here, from this known point, Tom would set his bearings for the long run in the open ocean.

They passed close to the tower's hissing feet, where barnacles clung to the steel, and they all looked up at the underside of the dizzying platform, so high, to where a derrick peeped over one edge dangling a swaying cable with an ominous bare steel hook on the end of it. Just then a Coast Guard sailor condemned to duty up there slammed a metal door in its metal frame in the metal housing, and the crash rushed down the metal legs, and it seemed as though the very waters of eternity clanged.

The course Tom set, with that everywhere-sound still

ringing in his mind, was two hundred sixty-six degrees, for Block Island, twenty-six miles away across the open sea.

There had been a change in plans. As they had sat at the cabin table, at anchor in Menemsha, looking at, but not eating, the canned peaches and glazed coffee cake that Audrey had set out for the early breakfast Tom had insisted upon, they had all heard together the morning weather report from Providence. For once the forecast had been precise, because the Weather Bureau was now issuing detailed advisories:

At six a.m., Eastern Daylight Saving Time—in the hesitant, semi-literate voice of a meteorological technician, a man used to reading drift meters and pressure gauges but not pages with words on them—*the tropical disturbance designated Esmé was centered two hundred and eighty miles south-southwest of Cape Fear, North Carolina. It is presently moving northwest-by-west at approximately five miles per hour. Wind speed now seventy miles per hour, an increase from last evening. This intensification may continue. The erratic path of the storm makes it impossible to predict its future course. Seaside property owners from Cape Hatteras, Virginia, to Cumberland Island, Georgia, are advised to prepare for exceptionally high tides, heavy seas, and damaging winds.*

Tom, ballpoint pen poised over his open log book, had talked about this bulletin in the reassuring tones of a calculating fellow. These cyclonic storms, he said, had a tendency to loop around in a clockwise curve and go out to sea, as this one had seemed to be planning to do the day before but seemed not to be doing at this moment. Esmé was a good four hundred and fifty miles away from Martha's Vineyard, as of that broadcast, he said, and if she did decide to swing up and out, and supposing that she might graze these offshore islands, as

62

these babies had often done in the past, and guessing that her forward motion might be a bit faster than at present, then you could expect that conditions in these parts would become a mite unpleasant after two or three days. . . .

There was silence from the others. Flick's cheeks were flushed. The girls both seemed to be staring at the red patches on Flick's face and not listening to Tom at all.

As though sitting in chilly cross drafts, Tom felt two sorts of danger, and neither was the danger of the storm. That absent-minded fixedness of both Audrey's and Dottie's eyes! And Flick: Tom imagined that Flick wanted to talk again about storm-tracking; that it was not reality, but rather the beautiful linking up of circuits that might whisper to each other about fragments of reality, a process rather than an essence, something very far from this real boat and that real storm, that interested the man. Doubly frightened, Tom sat and listened to his own tongue running away.

There would eventually be heavy rains around here for a day or two, the tongue was saying, even if Esmé carried straight along her present path and pasted the Carolinas. The tongue therefore suggested that instead of puttering around the Elizabeth Islands and Buzzards Bay for half a week, as they had thought they might do, and then gradually piling up the westing toward home, they should rather take advantage of the fine weather that was likely for the present and hit right out for Long Island Sound. If there had to be a storm, the chances were good that doing this would put them out on its harmless fringes. If there had to be a real snootful, it would be best if *Harmony* could be snug on her own three-hundred-pound mushroom anchor at home. The tongue suggested either Block Island or Newport for the first night—

either one a superb sail on a day like this—then Hamburg Cove the second; then home. They could sit out the rains ashore, if rains came, and then sail around the Sound for the rest of the time. How did that strike them?

How could it strike them? They had accepted it; Tom himself in his cold sweat had accepted it. And ever since then the girls had been in skittish moods—Dottie talking a lot, laughing often, on the razor's edge of being wild, and Audrey irritable yet inexplicably glowing.

Flick's response had been to turn on the full flood of his charm. As they heeled along he kept exclaiming and flinging his arms in praise of the adventure they were having, and somehow these acrobatics seemed to result in his constantly being waited on by both women. Subtly he required their services but not what they served. They brought him sun cream, coffee, Kleenex, binoculars, a pillow, a hat, dark glasses, sourball candies, his camera, a chart, a book of crossword puzzles. He spread all these commodities in a casual display around him, using and consuming nothing, keeping the things, in some mysterious expectation, for "later." The coffee grew cold, and Audrey threw it overboard, prudently to leeward, and replaced it with hot, which in turn grew cold. The collection of the loot of the girls' pampering constantly increased.

For the third successive morning Flick had not shaved, and a seedy crop of blond bristles covered his chin and cheeks; he apparently felt that he was roughing it in the hardy way of a seaman, but Tom could not help thinking him lazy and vain in the worst sense—convinced, that is, that women would think sloppiness an irresistible corrective on a man who would otherwise perhaps have been too handsome.

64

Now Flick stepped below, alone—going to the head, Tom assumed. Apparently it crossed Audrey's mind that Flick might have repented his stubble and might be intending to shave after all, and she called down after him, "Let me know if you want some hot water—won't take a minute."

"No, thanks, doll," he called up from the cabin. "Don't anybody come down here for a while."

Perhaps, Tom thought, Flick was changing into bathing trunks—but why in the main cabin, why not forward?

In Flicker's absence the cockpit grew silent. Audrey gazed off to the southward, scanning the horizon, it seemed, for a black cloud the size of a man's hand, a harbinger of Esmé. Dottie took the binoculars out of the case, and without looking through them she began to flex them at the central joint that controlled the distance between the eye pieces, open, closed, open, closed, over and over, until Tom felt like yapping at her for God's sake to knock it off.

Then noises of a catastrophe suddenly began to come up from below—a garbled roar, falsetto shrieks, a clatter of pots and pans. The girls both sat up straight, and they looked at each other in a reflexive and intimate sharing of a preparation to laugh. And now indeed the racket below was capped by a long run of bass laughter of operatic villainy. One last pathetic falsetto outcry. The bass *ho-ho-ha* of a desperado once again.

One hairy hand, then another, gripped the sill of the companionway, and slowly up over the edge came Flick's head wrapped in a bandanna he had made from a Hermes scarf of Dottie's; there was a black cardboard patch over one eye, tied on with marlin cord. The big nose, reddened with lipstick, perched on the sill in a stealthy pause. The uncovered eye darted here and there.

65

Rills of pretended fright and laughter poured from the girls. Tom felt a warmth at the center of the puzzling glumness that had settled in him even during this glorious sail, and he smiled.

Up came the rest of the face. Between the teeth, its line transecting the unshaven jowls, was Audrey's breadknife dripping ketchup.

Both girls shrieked, and Dottie flew across the cockpit, and the two wives hugged each other, giggling and squealing.

Very funny and attractive, Tom thought, already analyzing, tidying; what made it so attractive was Flick's having gone to such trouble for one moment's naive gag. But the prank was spoiled for Tom by the globes of tomato sauce falling on the pallid, scrubbed teak, marking circlets of crimson, and he tried without success to be casual as he dived into the lazaret for his sponge to wipe the spillage away.

As he sat back down at the wheel he looked at the girls, both still gasping at the end of the flurries of their laughter, and he thought of their coolness with each other when they had been aboard with him before Flick's arrival. Then he began to wonder where that black patch had come from.

At that moment it occurred to him, as for some reason it never had before, that *Harmony* had a bad liver. Her flaw was a rotten liver down there in her belly next to her spine. She was a sick boat. Then Tom saw that that small cold core of glumness he had been feeling all morning had to do with his sincere hatred of livers, the hatred that was forever invading his mind, his hatred of every element of the huge, viscous, muddy, reddish-brown gland that took up so much housing in the human gut, hatred of any and all Spigelian lobes, Glisson's capsules, omental tuberosities, fissures of *ducti venosi*—

66

detailed and closely focused hatreds which he had begun to suspect were simply encodings for other kinds of deep, deep hatreds lying there against his wishes in the right side of his own abdomen, manufacturing gallons of spiritual gall. To his mind the liver was surely where the worst sins had their bed: anger, pride, envy, and laziness. In this century the other sins, having other seats, had become almost virtues: lust was a sign of vigor and civil liberty; covetousness was the hot key to success; gluttony was excusable because merely compensatory. But those other four, the ones he now thought of as the liverish sins, they were the miseries that caused most misery. He didn't want them in himself; he wanted to be a decent man. He had used to believe in surgery, but you could not isolate anger and carve it out from all that slippery tissue, pride was not divisible, and envy grew on being cut. Laziness—the biggest trouble-maker of all, the enemy of the word "exact"—was wildly self-regenerative.

He suddenly wanted to go below and be by himself. The girls were still intermittently chuckling. Flick in his pirate get-up seated himself again in his nest of spoilage, and he began giving the girls foxy looks with his uncovered eye. That patch?

"Listen, big bad boy," Tom said. "Will you take the helm a few minutes?"

Tom stood up, realizing that this was the first time since the Hamdens had come aboard that he had yielded the wheel to anyone else. "The course is two six six. Try to keep right on the button, O.K.?"

Flick stepped to the wheel and, with one hand on a spoke, remaining standing, he bent his knees and shaded his eyes, buccaneer-style, and scanned the horizon and sniffed at the air

67

for a scent of hostility. He started to growl and then as Tom plunged down the companionway he gave out several deep barks and finally began to bay like a moon-broken bloodhound. The girls flew into new giggles.

Tom wanted to confide in his logbook. He had checked the very minute of *Harmony*'s passing the Texas tower but had not written it down; and he had other messages of precision to enter: course, wind direction, wind velocity, barometric pressure, tide and current data. And inner measurements? Vectors of mental drift? He dropped onto the settee on the port side and slid in under the cabin table, and for a moment he covered his face with his hands. And he saw vividly against the darkened screen of his eyelids: Audrey. She seemed to be waving him back, pushing air with her hands, warning him against something unseen; there was an urgency about her gestures, yet it seemed to him, without his seeing it at all clearly, that her face was serene, radiant, and sensuous. Tom tore his hands away and opened his eyes, and he turned on the seat, reached up to the bookshelf, lifted out the little maplewood lee-bar, and took down his precious log book.

The book fell open at the front cover, and Tom knew at once why he had wanted to come below.

Into the black, cardboardish end paper of the book ran a ragged gash which, deep into the page, began to circle and scoop, and it ended in a hole about the size of a hen's egg. Tom searched then for other clues and soon found on the settee beside him, crudely and tactlessly left in the open, a pair of nail scissors, his ball of marlin twine, and numerous scraps and trimmings of the black stuff. He picked up the ball of twine and put it to his nose and drew in the smell of boats, caulking smell, rope-locker smell—the smell which, savored in

68

deepest gloom of wintertime, had the power of evoking far-away sunlit wavetops, a canted mast, splashing bow waves, a warm summer breeze on a helmsman's cheek. But the smell did not help him this time; the breeze was right there, above, and he was on the heeling boat right then.

He flipped the pages of the log book and carefully entered the figures that were in his mind.

Then he went above again and walked the length of the cockpit and said, "Thanks, Flick, I'll take it."

"Kee-rist!" Hamden said, harking back to the old joke about the parrot whose cage was covered in daytime by its female owner just long enough for her to couple with a lover. "*That* was a short night!" Didn't Tom trust him? He shrugged, winked his one eye at the girls, and gave way to the skipper.

Tom sat down astraddle the wheel box and looked at the compass. Flick, having kept the girls in stitches, had obviously not been paying the slightest attention to the course and had worn off by nearly twenty degrees.

Tom said nothing. Bringing *Harmony* up to her course he hated himself for saying nothing.

ରରର

"Oooh, Tommy! Look! Over there!"

Audrey, on the high side of the slanting cockpit, was leaning forward and pointing to leeward with a bare arm flung straight out to its fingertip, and her face was wearing a mask of pure childishness—eyes huge, mouth hanging open, cheeks reddened with circus delight.

Tom, turning his eyes to see whatever she had seen, warmed to her reflex of calling out to him. Had she realized how angry he was? She had called him Tommy, and he knew that she used the diminutive only at the extreme ends of the range of her feelings: when she was full of love and when she was furious. This time the sound had been good, and he was taken aback by the strength of his gratitude.

"Whee! There!"

He saw three porpoises leaping. In the sunlight the wet gray backs gleamed like stainless steel. There came two more! A calf! All on *Harmony* cried out with envious pleasure at the sight of such carefree play; each strong jump built a shining arch of exuberance. Silver games on a clean blue day! There must have been a school of a dozen, and all of them, with bursts of aspiring to a higher element and splashless falls to the home one, were driving in at a shallow angle toward *Harmony*'s fish-like hull.

"They're coming in. They'll be at the bow," Tom said. "You'd better get up there to see them."

The other three ran forward, and soon they were perched at the windward side of the bow, Audrey gripping the jibstay, the pirate next, and Dottie outside with a hand on the lifeline, all three bent at the waists, Flick with his arms around the two girls; and Tom was alone—at his own suggestion, alas. Often he had seen these friendly creatures playing at the forefoot of *Harmony*, shimmering blue-gray under the surface, seeming to speed through the water with no effort at all, nuzzling at the breast of the boat, rolling, listening perhaps to the bow waves' rush or to the wind's singing poured down to them through the thrumming stays and chain plates and hull, looking upward with little pig eyes, their undershot mouths seeming to smile and smile; and now, as the school came close aboard, some leaping alongside with wet blowing sounds and others taking turns at the bow under the eyes of those three, and as Tom could see the human backs jerking in response to exhilarating glimpses of the sheer fun of those swimmers, and as the three heads turned to shout and share and almost rub cheeks and kiss, Tom felt a flood of melancholy self-pity. He had told his crew to go forward; he wished he had not; he wished he could see the bow-play himself. Was the little calf there, learning a new sport? Could the porpoises, rolling to turn up their eyes, see the human faces looking down? Did they with their good minds think the people were having a gloriously happy time up there on the boat?

Audrey, leaning forward with that florid arm across her back, drew his attention and held it. What was the hint of grief in her straining now at such pleasure? He remembered; seeing her bending over in this way reminded him. One morning at breakfast time, about a month before, he had gone into the kitchen of the apartment and had come on Audrey, bent forward over the counter with almost this very curve of the back, with her forehead down on a wooden cutting board, her hands flat on the Formica on either side of her head, in an attitude of sudden illness or profound worship—an attitude, at a level of myth that seeped into his shocked mind, of preparation for human sacrifice; light blue smoke poured out of the toaster, whose timing mechanism was flawed and which she had apparently been watching. He put a hand gently on her back, feeling the two rounds of the pushed-together shoulderblades. Her face came up, streaked with runnels of tears, and she looked at him as if from beyond an unbridgeable gulf. She turned away and would not speak. He tried to connect her pain with a minor quarrel they had had a couple of nights before, when each had downed an extra martini before dinner and both had, as the evening unfolded, made less and less sense about their lives.

But only now, at *Harmony*'s wheel, seeing her back bent again, being hugged, did he make the true connection. He saw that small bedroom in their first apartment, with the faded cornflower-patterned wallpaper and the brass bedstead Audrey had found, which he loved to polish, and the fragrant Bouvardia, for which she had such a specific green thumb, in the small sunny window; a Sunday afternoon, a series of unsatisfactory games of backgammon, restlessness, a dark turn away from the benign mood of the second third of her term, off to the flicks to try *The Hustler*, a worried murmur, taxi home, lying on her back with legs up, brow wet and sheet-white, the gynecologist away for the weekend, the g.p. off for the day and the answering service for his cover vaguer with each call, the unmistakable pulsing of the pain, its rhythm speeding up with the inexorability of a *bolero*, the look dawning on Audrey's face that all the euphoric plans, the dollhouse anticipations, the beforehanded purchases—the bassinette, the tiny nightgowns soft as chick down, the insanely premature *Winnie the Pooh*, bought to appease recollections—all those things were looming as folly, as embarrassment. Then from this tone of genteel loss the occasion suddenly went to the outer limits of grimness: the mythic flood loosed on the bedspread, a writhing struggle on the bathroom floor to hold, to keep, or else to bear, and at last the empty, cauterized, never-to-be-the-same look . . . Tom could not remember much about the second time, which had been much less violent, perhaps because far less a surprise, but all the myriad pictures of the first were arranged and stored in his mind like the frames of a stop-action film . . .

72

The show was over. The three up forward straightened up, and looking off to starboard Tom saw the porpoises wheeling away toward shallows again.

As the crew came aft Tom half expected to see tears streaming down Audrey's face again; not at all, she was in a rapture.

Flick began shouting to Tom. "They want to talk with us! They're trying to get in touch!"

Dottie's face was oddly twisted, and as she jumped over the high coaming down onto the cockpit seat and then to the deck, she said with an edge of impatience, "Oh, Flick, let it rest."

But Flick couldn't, and he began to rattle on about the Lilly experiments with dolphins in the Virgin Islands, and about the patterns of dolphin speech, which, squeaking, he began to try to sound out, and about their responses to synthetic stimuli, and about the possibility that they might be trained one day to help with fishery as sheep dogs help with flocks—and then he was saying that some day computers might help us find the keys to open talk with all the creatures around us. There was a rapidity and a flatness to Flicker's utterances now that seemed tuned by some rheostat of obsession—his talent, his joy, his limitation.

Dottie, hearing that mechanical rigidity in his voice, began to kick up her heels—talked loudly about the porpoises' dear little eyes, cutting into, and breaking off, Flick's steady hum.

Tom searched Audrey's face. He could not find the portentous shadows, bending-over shadows, he had fully expected to see. He only saw that she was welded by some kind of solid-state connection to that monotone of inner passion in

73

Flick's voice. Communication, indeed! Who could ever begin to know what another being was really trying to say?

∽∽∽

In the next hour the breeze slowly dropped away. Long before the chop began to flatten out Tom felt the softening of the air on his cheek, and he saw the needle of the Kenyon slip from six through five and four until *Harmony* was easing through the sea at just better than three knots, and he felt her big genny go weak each time the mast fell away from the wind on the rise of a swell; he knew he would have to start the engine sooner or later.

A subtle change was coming over the sky. The air was still clear; they were out of sight of land, and the horizon was sharp as the edge of a table all the way around. It was far ahead, to the west and south, and very high above the earth, that a huge transparency of vaporous change was becoming visible. A thin gray hood was being pulled up the sky.

Tom doubted whether the others had noticed any of this. He had heard the brass clock strike eight times—the strokes of noon according to ship's-clock code; and he suggested beer and sandwiches, and the girls went below.

Flick was still going on about understanding wild animals. "Like the mix of voices on the overseas phone—you know how the bits of sound are all scrambled up on the transmitting end and then reconstituted into words by the receiving end? Some day we'll be able to do that—more than that—with say a cat's *meow*: unscramble the tonality and inflection of the *meow* and reconstitute it into human words that the cat meant. We already have translating devices for human languages."

74

"Cats might be a good place to start," Tom said. "They see right through people."

Tom observed for a moment the literalness of Flick's mind causing him trouble with this line. He would have to reject the idea of cats' having X-ray eyes before he could understand that Tom had meant that it might not be altogether comfortable to get into conversation with them.

"No," Flick said, "I was thinking of the vibrations of their voices—so easy to chop up and analyze."

By the time lunch was over the sails were slatting. Tom knew he should turn on power, but he wanted Flick to demand it. He went below and dead-reckoned *Harmony's* noon position and noted the tenuous weather change in his log book, which first fell open again, as if of its own sense of outrage, to its violated endpaper. As he was sitting at the cabin table, hearing the boom sway and the loose cable of the topping lift drum along the big sail, the expected call came from the cockpit.

"Hey, Medlar, fella, whatever you do, don't shoot that albatross."

That was all Tom wanted. He went above at once, his expectancy eased, and started the engine. Audrey moved forward to lower the sails, and Flick, suddenly happy, followed her.

Within an hour the sea was flat and shiny and immense, and the afternoon lights were eerie, for *Harmony* seemed to be moving into a huge open mother-of-pearl-lined shell of weather, one wing sky, one wing sea. A tip of a bluff of Block Island was visible now at the inner hinge of the shell, twenty-five miles away, and so pellucid was the air that Tom thought that with a powerful glass he would have been able to see men on that cliff-tip, perhaps bending and rising in a steady persistence of some kind of stone-lifting work; in his imagination the sight of them was sharp. The afternoon *looked* silent, but all the evident stillness was held at a distance by the sounds of *Harmony*'s exhaust, now popping in the open, now steamily muffled, as the gentle glazed swells rhythmically lifted the boat's little metal anus out of the water awhile, then put it under awhile. The dinghy, under tow from the stern on its taut painter, whispered on its path of foam.

Audrey, peering into the vast distances of the afternoon, saw a mast ahead, a bit to the right, so far away that the hull under the swaying spar was not yet to be seen. She pointed it out to Tom, and he, thinking to please her, and with the landfall already made, changed his course slightly to pass close to the oncoming stranger.

This vessel, approaching near at hand many minutes later, turned out to be a jewel of a cutter with a brightwork hull, its mahogany planks deep red under the glistening varnish. Everyone on both boats waved, and Tom, looking at Audrey as he spoke and holding her eyes, told a story of a hailing at sea—how old Joshua Slocum, at the turn of the century, having taken three years to sail around the world single-handed on his sloop *Spray* and having floated through raptures and nightmares of seamanship, standing one day under full sail homeward along the north coast of Brazil, met a steam vessel which proved to be the battleship *Oregon*. She came alongside him, flying signal flags that meant, "Are there any men-of-war about?" Slocum in his tiny craft, not knowing that the Spanish-American war had recently started, knowing little more than that he had done a great thing in sailing

76

around the world alone, hoisted an answering signal: "Let us keep together for mutual protection."

Let us keep together. Audrey's eyes turned casually enough to the passing yacht. She asked for the binoculars, and Dottie handed them to her.

"It's called *Vesta*," Audrey said behind the glasses.

Tom went below and took *Lloyd's Register of Yachts* from the bookshelf and carried the fat book above and laid it like an offering in Audrey's lap. She loved to look up passing boats, and she read aloud the description of *Vesta*, and while Flick sat silent she and Tom and Dottie made up scandalous stories about the owner, who was from Houston, Texas, and had shamelessly rendered his sea-going adventures tax-deductible by registering the boat in the name of his firm.

ᏬᏬᏬ

But: "You didn't tell me . . ." It was true that he never uttered a word to her about certain things—some that seemed not worth telling, some that would have burned his tongue to tell, some that he thought, rightly or wrongly, she should be spared out of kindness. Not a word had he ever said about that afternoon in the boatyard.

He had decided to do *Harmony*'s fitting-out himself that spring—the second year the fat boat was his. Boatyards dislike having owners playing at working on their own boats: dilettantes of labor having "fun" sandpapering, arrogantly mislaying tools, leaving scars of incompletion, making idiotic mistakes that fall back on the yard crews to rectify in a hurry just when the worst rush is on; but Tom, willing to pay for hours safe from a phone that might be connected to a liver, had

77

bribed old Burkett to break his rules. Tom sat in the cockpit awhile, that afternoon, getting in a boat mood. It was a day at the end of April when the soft air bore sun-drenched promises. *Harmony* was cradled near the top of the launching track not far from a great-headed weeping willow down whose undulating tresses the gold of a new season's life seemed to trickle and drip as if the sun's rays were condensing and accumulating on the sap-sticky tendrils. The whole tree was a celebration. Tom, putting off going down into the winter-musty cabin, dreamily watched the tree's big slow hula dance. But then he thought of the puzzle down in *Harmony's* guts, and he made himself go below.

He had seen the strange clue the previous weekend, on his first day of work that spring. He had been cleaning out the bilges and, lifting the forward floorboards out, had come on it: the huge bronze ring-nut at the head of the forward of two great bolts that ran all the way down to the lead keel. The nut stood free of the wood of the keelson by a full eighth of an inch. In winter storage the boat sat on her keel instead of dangling it, and the weight of the hull had driven the flaw up into full view.

Thinking about it during the week he had remembered two happenings from the previous season that he had not previously connected in his mind: in midsummer the jib had sagged and he had taken up firmly on the forestay turnbuckle, and in late summer there had been a pesky seepage into the bilges. Had he pulled her up too hard and somehow hogged her bow?

Now, armed with an enormous wrench and a tiny can of penetrating oil, he went below to tighten the nut. He lifted up the floorboard. He could not see too well, and he climbed

78

above-decks to take the canvas hood off the cabin skylight. Below again, drenched with a shimmering light reflected from the willow, he took a close look. What he saw sent him hurrying to the ice chest to fetch his ice pick.

There was a washer-shaped depression in the wood of the keelson around the throat of the bolt. Tom probed with the ice pick at the edges of this circle, and then his heart really sank. The wood was spongy.

He drenched the little wound with red lead and fitted a steel plate under the nut to distribute the pressure, and he took up hard on the bolt.

Boats, like men, all have flaws. Perhaps it was knowing this that had led Tom to be charitable and to forgive *Harmony* hers. Since the earliest pushing off from a sea beach of a dugout log, sailors have searched for the perfect craft and never found her. Every vessel seems to have her weak point—an overhang aft that will take a spanking from steep following seas; a prow giving way too generously to cheeks which pound a heading chop; an obscure leak, elusive, dormant in fair weather, always there again whenever the boat begins to work her seams in a seaway. The sea's seeming denial of the very possibility of perfection is one of its lures. It took Tom a year, until after he saw how the plate he had installed had bitten into the diseased wood, and after he had begun a thorough study of dry rot, to realize that his red-leading and the plate itself had not halted the infection but had in fact sealed it in and undoubtedly made things worse. There was only one thing to do: remove the sick wood from the boat. Take it out and burn it. But how? Every frame and floor beam was tied to the keelson. It was a surgeon's nightmare—not liver at all, come to think of it, but a nonregenerative vital organ that simply could not be excised either in part or as a whole, a very spine. Nothing to do but trust the thickness of the timber and tighten the nut again and again, a thread at a time, winter and summer, year after year. Only this summer he had not done it.

Last winter with the help of old Burkett's disenchanted eye Tom had found out the cause of the rot: In a moment of laziness, or carelessness, or making-do in the old Yankee way to save a few pennies, the boatbuilder had made an unforgivable choice of wood for the keelson. *Harmony* and her gear were exquisitely assembled, like a masterwork of parquets and inlays, from great woods from the corners of the earth: Honduran mahogany for wheel and coaming trim, seats and decks of teak from Burma, Norway-pine planking, a dinghy of Port Orford cedar, spars of spruce from Nova Scotia, hackmatack knees, white-ash battens, honey-locust cabin bulkhead, cherry-faced drawers against butternut cabinetwork—and timbers and frames of white oak, as hard as the screws that bound them. But when it came to the biggest piece of wood of all, the keelson, running like an inoperable backbone all along the hull, the builder had settled for a timber of cheap wood from roundabout his shipyard—a piece of local red oak. Burkett, on his hands and knees, reaching with the oilstone-narrowed blade of his clasp knife down into the bilges to chip at the big timber, had shaken his grizzled head and said, "Knew bettuh. He knew bettuh." There just wasn't any doubt. It was a lousy piece of red oak, *Quercus borealis*—notorious for checking and cracking and harboring insidious spores.

You could be sure the builder had not told the man for whom he had built the boat. It was a secret place in *Harmony.* Tom, sitting now at the wheel, staring off into calm air that was pure and limpid as elemental truth, reflected that he had not told his crew, his companions in pleasure and danger, about that secret place. He had never told his wife Audrey about that secret place. Her accusations were absolutely justified. There were things which—assuring himself that "honesty" was too often used in human intercourse as an outlet for vicious cruelty—he was satisfied to keep to himself. But Flicker, damn him, harping on transmission of data, with even his porpoises who wanted to tell us something. What was it they had wanted to say just now at *Harmony*'s forefoot? What was it? What was it?

∽∽∽

"Would you take a crack at the pump, Flick?" And then, in response to the blank look that came from the one visible eye: "It's right under you. Take off the seat cushion and lift up the seat flap."

"Here, I'll show you," Audrey said.

Soon Audrey and Flick were shoulder-to-shoulder, leaning over, their backs to the cockpit, and they were evidently lifting all the items of Flick's treasure off the seat cushions in order to get at the pump.

Tom dropped his eyes away from the hips and buttocks of those two, which, angled out toward him into the open area of the cockpit, were expressively responding to activities that their bodies screened from view, and to give his eyes something to do, he checked the compass; for some time he fastened his gaze on the little black lubber line and on the degree mark of his bearing on the floating card, and he tried to rivet the two together, steering *Harmony* down a railroad-track course.

81

He began thinking of Hamden's reflex whenever he, Tom, gave a command; no matter how courteously he framed the order, Flick seemed at once to dissolve into a bearing of vagueness, evasiveness. He seemed not to be able to comprehend what Tom was saying. Even making allowances for Flick's not being the experienced sailor he had made himself out to be at wintertime cocktail parties, this response of fogginess was obviously not based on his failure to understand words Tom spoke. Rather he seemed not to be able to believe that Tom, "idle" at the helm, could possibly mean to command him to jump about doing physical labor, and in a big hurry, too. Communication was not just a matter of what Flick kept calling "input," it was not just a question of clear and faultless utterance—especially when it came to command; giving commands and acceding to commands required a thorough-going interdependence. Tom thought about skippers of boats who scream at their crews, men who suffer a metamorphosis on sitting down at their tillers or wheels—mild and courteous ashore; imperious, tyrannical, unreasonable, hysterical in command on the water. Tom flattered himself that he was not like that, for he saw himself as more gentle and patient, if anything, at *Harmony*'s wheel than anywhere else, but now he realized that one specific goad—this response of indefiniteness of Flick's—might make an unpleasant commanding officer of him. Flick's elusiveness was surely a veiled form of insolence. The pirate get-up, which he apparently had no intention of shedding, intensified the effect.

Now Tom, with eyes still glued to the compass, heard the gagging sounds of the pump's beginning to draw, and after a half dozen strokes the first splashes of salty foam, then hard water, into the forward part of the cockpit, from where the bilgewater would drain away through the self-bailing cockpit's scuppers. He was both soothed by the sound—for the command was after all being obeyed—and disturbed by it: There was a solid flow from the pump, in due course, which spoke of the extent of the seepage around the keel bolt.

Tom looked up and saw to his astonishment that Audrey, not Flick, was at the pump.

Flick was sitting across the cockpit, leaning back in grand piratical style, arranging his loot all around him.

Tom had not heard any words spoken while he had been gazing at the compass, but now he had the feeling that Flick had somehow conned Audrey into doing the work for him. Command, indeed!

"Hey," Tom said in a sharp tone, "I asked *you* to bail."

Flick's uncovered eye turned slowly toward Tom. The pupil appeared to be in the process of melting; its look was going vague again. "She wanted to," he said, and he pointed a long forefinger at Audrey as if she were an object.

Without breaking her rhythm, pulling up and pushing down, Audrey said, "I enjoy it."

"That's very damn funny," Tom said. "You've never once told me in all the time we've had this boat that you got a charge out of pumping."

"Well, I just started enjoying it."

Was she making fun of him?

Dottie, sitting on the port side of the cockpit half way between Flick and Tom, suddenly broke in like a tattle-tale at a playground quarrel. "She wouldn't let him."

Tom began to tremble. "Listen, you lazy prick," he said, "when you're on a boat you have to do your share of the work."

83

Flick, in his woman's scarf and eye patch from Tom's log book, bathed Tom with a one-eyed look that seemed to come from a thousand miles away, and he said, "Why?"

"It's true," Audrey said, still rocking up and down. "I wouldn't let him."

"The reason why," Tom said to Flick, "is that sometimes things have to be done in a hurry, or the whole crew gets in danger. Much as we might all enjoy it, you can't have anarchy on a boat. There isn't even time for democracy." Tom realized that his anger was making him pompous.

"Surely no one's in danger now," Flick said from his great distance, waving a hand out over the level silver sea.

Tom felt very much in danger; his anger flamed into rage. "God damn it, Audrey," he said. "I don't like this. I ask this guy to do his first lick of work and—pumping's man's work!"

"A woman can do it. As I am demonstrating. Forty-eight. Forty-nine. *Fifty*." She broke off to rest awhile.

Flick began shouting. "What do you mean, 'first lick'? I've been hoisting and dousing and furling and pitching the frigging anchor overboard and hauling it up again. I've been extremely co-operative. In my opinion. Anyway, the girls are right, as usual: Audrey wouldn't let me bail."

They were having fun with him. Tom could see that they were enjoying themselves no end. He wanted to cry out to Audrey that they weren't being fair.

But it was Dottie who spoke next, and she was in a state. "He's a parasite! Watch out, Audrey. He'll suck your blood. He'll drain you till there's nothing left of you but dust, dust, dust." Dottie leaned over toward Flick's circle of pirate treasure and snatched a Kleenex from his box, and Tom saw that she was weeping.

84

At that moment Tom intercepted a look between Audrey and Flick that carried him over the brink into knowledge he would have given anything not to have had. He took in both faces, her two eyes and his one locked in an unguarded moment of conspiracy, false security and—what Flick preached for machines and humans alike—totally open communication. They gave themselves away. Was it a surging feeling of triumph over Dottie that had led them to be so incredibly reckless?

Tom had a momentary impulse to throw *Harmony*'s big bronze gear-shift lever (it sparkled! he polished it every evening!) into reverse. Couldn't he move the boat, its now lost crew, his understanding, the terrible incaution of those two, backwards in space and time into the scene they had just been through, then push the lever forward again, so they could take a slightly different course out of it?

But he did nothing. He sat limp at the wheel. *Harmony* moved forward through the flat sea. It was all being printed in his mind with a dry-aired clarity: the huge sky with its reptilian eye-scale of gray mist winking up from below, the loom of Block Island now a dark heap along the horizon ahead, the molten-metal sea sliding past at an irretrievable rate—a scene, in all its parts, of immutability, the sharpness of sight itself seeming to say to the inner eye, "*This* is the way things are, there are no other possibilities"; Dottie snuffling into fluttering paper tissues, having lost far more by giving herself away than those two, being two, could ever lose; Flick projecting his enormous feelings right through that childish birthday-party disguise, immensely sincere in his absurdity, the one eye throwing an open shaft to Audrey, the other covered by the cutting from Tom's beloved book, the lipstick-rouged nose a drunkard's nose, the bristling skin about the mouth touched with the most enviable pain; and Audrey, leaning slightly forward, everything about her so utterly familiar, and most familiar of all the softened cheeklines, the eyes expressive of an almost pitying sympathy, the lips on the edge of a pout, and colors here and there of lightness, of humor, of whole-heartedness, and of that same unbelievable pain of desire—the expression Tom had so long ago come to think he owned as his.

Something had to be done; the moment had to be ruptured. "Darling,"—the word leaped to his tongue—"would you take the wheel a minute?"

Audrey was on her feet, her face arranged almost too quickly; there was a crudeness not properly hers in her alacrity. "Sure, darling," she said. That word flew again—to his ear, this time. It was firmly spoken, without a trace of awareness of irony, it seemed.

"Keep her as she goes."

"How far do we have yet?" Was she holding him? Did she mean that she was . . . she was at least sorry?

"That's what I want to check, among other things."

He went below. He stayed a long time. He was sitting staring at the raped endpaper of his log book when Dottie came stumbling down the companionway. She stood for a moment at the end of the cabin table with a look on her face much like the one she had given him on waking up in her bikini the afternoon before: Help me! Change me! He wondered now exactly what she *had* meant then. Her warning to Audrey a few minutes ago had told Tom that she had intuited the whole truth long before he had understood a particle of it. How long had she known? And what did it matter how long she had known? And what if he had used her body under the sun in the cockpit while those two slept below? Would that have changed anything? Almost as if she understood his unspoken questions, Dottie vaguely shook her head and went forward; soon he heard her sobbing.

He turned on the radio to drown her out.

~~~

He was thinking—scarcely hearing whatever was being transacted on the radio; one endless marathon of commercials—thinking of his old theme, so often carelessly uttered over cocktails on *Harmony*, of escape and confrontation. That, he had said again and again, was the point of sailing. You got away from the world and faced the universe—your naked self in its relation to chaos. A cruising boat was where, disconnected from society, you could get down to rock bottom about your place in it, and in nature. Big chatter over drinks. Had he ever imagined that the talk would come home? Those two were alone up there now, free to exchange their telltale looks. What bothered Tom most of all was that he had been so opaque—so unwilling, or so unable, to perceive the loss he had obviously suffered some time since. How long had this been going on? Now confrontation had been rammed down his throat by a remark of Dottie's and a vibrant glance traded by those two, and the paradox was that there was no escape. He was on a boat and could not run.

Slowly there began to trickle through to his mind something compelling about a sound on the radio. He focused his attention. A man was slowly reading. It was the hesitant meteorologist with the dry voice of the morning advisory. He was saying that just after dawn Esmé had suddenly begun gathering speed, and that she was veering again. She was rushing up the sea at nearly thirty miles an hour, northward. Tom turned off the radio without even hearing the man out, and he went above. Audrey's face was pink and oblivious. Tom sat to one side, letting her go on steering. There was no escape.

~~~

It seemed to take forever to skirt the northern point and get around to the entrance to the Great Salt Pond. The sky and the sea and the bluffs were gray. Tom was back at the wheel again, and the concerns of the approach—watching the bearings on the creeping islandscape, light thoughts of navigation, checking the chart, ticking off the buoys, keeping the log—all those familiar mechanical rituals of boat life began to absorb him and save him. Flick had at last taken off the scarf and the eye patch, but the lipstick was still on his nose. He and Audrey appeared not even to have noticed that every aspect of existence was now changed; they were on guard, they were being discreet—and they seemed to have no idea that they had given themselves totally away and that their prudence now had an almost comical transparency. Dottie had made a disconcerting recovery; she was right back where she had been beforehand, cheerful, agreeable, trying to please everyone. Flick had casually dropped the oval of black cardboard with its laces of marlin on the seat cushion, not two feet from Tom, and Dottie had picked it up and kept twirling it around her index finger, as if in this way she could assert Flick's being entwined, still, with her.

They bore down on the heavy jetty jutting out to the northwestward and swung in through the throat of the Pond;

88

with a vague thought of Esmé, Tom noted the Coast Guard station to the right of the entrance. It was a fairly long pull across the wide sheet of Great Salt Pond. The place was crowded with sportsmen's boats. Tom took *Harmony* to the end of Champlin's pier to fill up with gas; standing on the dock after they had tied up, he quietly asked the attendant, a leather-faced man in khakis, whether any moorings were available.

"Are you serious?" the man said; he was loud and cheerful. "With this harrycane supposed to be coming, we was all filled up ten minutes after they switched the weather report around on us—what was that, the two o'clock?"

"What's he saying?" Audrey, apparently having heard some interesting word, stirred in the cockpit. Dottie, sitting beside her, looked pale.

"About a mooring," Tom called back over the ticking of the gas pump.

"Are you going to take a mooring?"

"They have none."

"Oh."

Had he and Audrey come to this kind of inconsequence? He was not interested any more in forecasts, portents; nor did he wish to discuss them. He and Audrey talked about a mooring without a word about the meaning of taking a mooring. The concept of precaution was no longer a serious one for them to discuss; he had a moment of wondering, for he could not clearly remember, what his insurance policies on *Harmony* actually covered. He took on water and a thirty-pound chunk of ice, and he tipped the man with a weathered face a dollar on a total charge of less than four dollars. Was he, he wondered, paying off a kind of debt to the Edgartown garbage woman? The indifference of the marina attendant as he stuffed the bill into his trouser pocket was sufficient rebuke to his folly. There was no one for Tom to impress—least of all himself.

He cut up the ice into chunks, which Flick handed down to him as he fitted them into the ice chest. After handling each piece, Flick loosely tossed his fingers this way and that to shake off the chill. Flick was acting somewhat put-upon; perhaps, Tom bitterly thought, he felt that Audrey should do this ice work.

They cast off. For an anchorage Tom eased over toward the old steamer pier. There seemed to be hundreds of power boats of all sizes moored and anchored in the Pond. Tom looked for an open place, for he remembered that the water was deep here and he wanted plenty of scope on which to swing in backing winds. But everywhere he went there were stinkpots, and as the other three, a team again, picked out names on transoms—*Ma's Mink*, *Edannboblu*, *Magic Carpet* with dinghy *Throw-Rug*—he went in widening circles, as if searching for something dropped overboard. There was no good place. Finally he anchored, shaking his head, in twenty-odd feet of water not far from the nun buoy nearest the steamer pier. He noticed that a light breeze had come in from the southeast.

They went ashore to Deadeye Dick's for dinner; it seemed to be understood that the cabin of *Harmony* was too cramped to contain them that evening. They rowed to the New Harbor pier and climbed ashore and soon entered a room steamy with seafood smells.

After three drinks and a half-eaten swordfish steak with beer Flick got the idea that he wanted to rewrite his will. He borrowed a stub of a pencil from the waitress and he began to scribble on a grease-spotted doily with lobsters and jellyfish printed in red on it.

"Don't worry, Dottie," he said. "I'm going to take care of you. I just want to give old Skipper here my inventions, you know, my thought on fixing up sailboats, all the rights and royalties and perquisites attaining thereto." He wrote in a scrawl, apparently setting down "perquisites attaining thereto." "My idees. I don't know how much they're going to bring in if anything. Might be nothing, might be a potful. Can't tell yet. How many witnesses you need?"

Tom said, "Never mind all that. We can do without your boat gimmicks."

"How many witnesses for a last will and testamen'? Audrey? Dear Audrey, how many?"

Tom said, "I don't want any part of your thinking-and-talking God-damn machines. Leave me out."

Audrey said, "I think it's three."

"Got just the right number."

"Christ," Tom said, shifting ground, "you can't use the people you're giving it to for witnesses."

"Miss. Miss!" Flick snapped his fingers at the waitress.

The girl, a frowsy-haired fat fisherman's daughter in a dress of synthetic fabric through which the pattern of the lace of her slip showed, and through that the white outlines of her bra, came to the table giggling at the sight of Flick, as she had giggled earlier: the streaks of lipstick still ran down his big nose.

"Sign on the dotted line. It's jus' a legal statement, do us a favor, honey."

The girl shook her head and backed away. "Uh-uh. None of that," she said, turning as if to run.

"What's the matter, baby, don't you want to get in-

volved?" Then Flick turned limpid eyes on Audrey.
" 'Mericans don't care any more. They'll hear a woman
scream on a street, she's right under the street lamp; they can
see these guys frisking her—nobody liffs a finger." Flick stood
up and, bumping one table, went into the kitchen. There were
shrieks of laughter from two women out of sight. Soon he
came out again, waving the doily. "O.K., honey," he said to
the waitress, "your Momma signed, and the other lady. Come
on, just your John Q. Hancock. You can read it. Here. Look.
It's harmless."

But in the dark in the dinghy on the way out to the
boat—the wind had almost died—he said, "Audrey? You got
that paper of mine—did'n' you put it in your bag? Gimme
back. I'm gonna cancel. Stuffy ungrateful bastard."

"Tear it up. Tear it up," Tom said.

Audrey wouldn't give Flick the doily. Flick said, "I know
you, Audrey Medlar. You want your cut. Right? Fiffy per cent.
Right?"

"Isn't that a drop of rain?" Dottie asked. "Didn't I feel a
drop of rain?"

It was in fact beginning to rain.

"That's good, then, isn't it, Tom? If the rain comes
without any wind, doesn't that mean the storm isn't going to
be too bad?"

She must have taken everything in—the broadcast below
decks, the exchange on the pier about the mooring. Poor,
silent Dottie! She had it backwards. He did not tell her that
but, rather, to encourage her, he said without lying, "The
wind certainly has dropped out." But to himself, slowly, rowing to the scanning of the lines, he recited the adage:

Wind before rain, soon to your ale;
Rain before wind, 'ware a fierce gale.

92

∽∽∽

Tom stood on the foredeck in a furious wind which drove raindrops hard against his waterproofs, making a sound of dried peas in a gourd. It was seabottom dark. He did not know what time it was; a halyard rapping against a spreader had wakened him. The tiny battery-powered anchor light hanging from the forestay, swaying in the wind, cast a dim glow about it, making a shimmering globe of luminescence out of the raindrops flying past. Water ran in sheets down across his bare feet. His waterproof hood was drawn tight around his cheeks and chin; wet pellets struck his face. As wind-puffs rose in intensity they set up haunted-house whistlings at the tops of the tubular wooden chafing guards on the shrouds. The halyard was still slapping at the spreader with an importunate doggedness, like someone steadily knocking at an unanswered door, desperate to come in from the discomfort and fear of the vast, windy darkness. He listened to the whistling and beating and thought of the various things he should do. He had been roused from his berth and impelled to go above by a habit of thinking: Details matter. They really do matter. Put them together and they do matter.

He had been stupid not to bring any light above. He went aft and stood for some moments at the companionway hatch, wondering how he could get below to switch on the spreader lights without dripping all over everything; he knew he could not, it was hopeless, he would just have to grope and drip. He pushed back the hatch and went below as quickly as he could, and he fumbled over his bunk for a flashlight, found it, blipped it at the clock—three forty-seven—went aft to the power panel box behind the companionway ladder, poured brilliance into the box, found the switches he wanted, and flipped them: spreader lights and binnacle light. He tossed the flashlight on his berth and climbed above.

Now the whole boat was bathed by the floodlights that shone down from the spreaders: big raindrops driving slant-wise the length of the boat, everything white and everything varnished and everything brass glistening with varied tonalities; and, all around, the black water pocked with a hissing goose-flesh. Tom lifted the binnacle hood and looked at the compass, its whited points and degrees pinkly glowing under the tiny infra-red bulb. The wind had indeed backed. It was north of east now. To be exact: East northeast a quarter east, seventy degrees. He supposed it would settle in at northeast for a few hours, perhaps many. He wished now he had listened with a less muddled ear to the afternoon forecast, and that he had picked up a late evening one. Details accumulate; they count. He would have to remember to check and log the barometer reading and time when he went below later.

He started swiftly to work. He set up canvas chafing gear on the anchor line at the bow chock. He took up hard with a winch crank on the halyards and reset the halyard stops to hold them away from the spars; the rapping ceased . . .

He paused then, as if trying to decipher the real message of this wind. A ferocious puff came running, and hard bits of water pelted his cheeks, and he became convinced—almost said out loud to the wind, "I believe you. I do." And he set about two heavy and fateful chores to manifest his conviction that Esmé, deceitful and unpredictable, had simply outrun all her beautiful data that Flicker loved so much.

First he undressed the yawl—for he had heard of vessels ripped from their anchorages in gales by flapping sails that had come unfurled from their booms; he mistrusted the

94

shock-cord he had installed to hold the sails in place. He took the mizzen off and stowed it for the time being in the cockpit. Then—far more trying task—he opened the gate-latch of the track on the mainmast and pulled down the slides of the luff of the mainsail, and wormed its foot forward along the boom track and got the whole heavy sail off at last. He damped the bulk of it down temporarily atop the cabin trunk by criss-crossing over it the free end of the working jib sheet.

He went below to the forward cabin and turned a light on there. Dottie and Flick both stirred, both turned their faces to the opposite outer skins of the yawl, and both lay oblivious. Dottie wore pajamas; Tom could spare a corner of his mind to notice that.

He burrowed for the two empty sail bags and put them out in the main cabin. Then, with grunts and thumps and clankings, none of which seemed to penetrate to the aware-ness of either Hamden, he lifted the heavy fluke anchor out of its seating in the forepeak, and he laid it on the deck directly under the hatch. Next he opened the hatch part way on its forward hinge, so that not much rain could drive in, and he fed out the inboard end of his heavy anchor line—beautiful creamy new nylon stuff.

Within a difficult hour he readied his ship. First he crammed the sails into their bags, dropped the mizzen into the main cabin, and lashed the mainsail, inside its bag, into the dinghy cradle on top of the cabin trunk, using two strong spinnaker guys and webbing them tightly back and forth many times. Then he lifted the fluke anchor and its chain and nylon line up on deck through the forward hatch; and he weighted the line, sixty feet from the chain, with a heavy spare flywheel that had been stored for this very purpose

95

in a cockpit seat locker. He started the engine and swung out to the right on the light-anchor line and got the fluke anchor down and the flywheel overboard; then swung left with the motor's help and managed to raise the Danforth anchor—for he did not believe in having two anchors down in winds that were sure to shift.

He was committed at last to the storm, whatever it might bring, with his vessel stripped and his heavy fluke anchor down on a weighted line.

He was burning inside his waterproofs, but a push of elation worked at his throat. He had known what the significant details were, had known their relative importance; and now he wanted to let loose into the baby-teeth of the storm a shout of invitation and defiance. But he stifled the cry before it had built to actual sound, because he saw a ghost beside him.

It was Audrey. Her hair and nightgown were sopping. How long had she been there watching him? Her face turned toward him as he looked at her; it glistened in the rain as though smeared with cold cream; her hair was plastered on her forehead; her lips were pulled back—a smile?—a chill?— and her teeth flashed in light reflected from the deck. Did she want to speak? Did she want to say, "Can I help you, darling?"

Could she help? Could she make amends? Could she do anything now?

What could he answer? Go below. Leave me alone. You're getting soaked!

Not getting. Already. Everything was already as it was. He stood on the foredeck beside his unfaithful wife in the wind and rain, looking out, as she looked, too, into the darkness upwind.

3

The Cone of Uncertainty

Tom started up from a short sharp sleep into a universe of wind. A howl combed through the rigging of *Harmony*; every spar and cable, every hard edge set up a note of its own. Rain clattered on the skylight and washed with a deeper tone on the decks. From time to time the whole boat gave a rapid series of shudders, as if chilled by thoughts rather than by the wind. The yawl seemed to be sailing widely back and forth on its anchor line, as the gale caught first one cheek of the bows and then the other, and on each tack of this veering the wind canted the mast and the boat heeled over as if reaching under full sail on a day of moderate airs. A constant rattling and slamming of lines and blocks underscored the whine of the whole instrument of the yawl. The hull rocked and slapped on a smart chop that had worked itself up in the confines of the Great Salt Pond.

All this Tom took in from his bunk, with his eyes closed and his mind resistant. He had not slept enough. He did not want to enter the new day yet, if at all. He was against the blow; he took it personally.

He opened his eyes and looked across at Audrey. She was hard asleep. He wondered if a bad conscience could have a narcotic effect; then he realized that the sort of obsession she was inhabiting carried no sense of guilt with it. Her sleep was fresh and innocent, her body pure, for what was happening to Flick and to her (she must have imagined) had never happened to mortals before. But her hair was haggard; it seemed to have been blown straight out into strings by this wind. Even her cheeks appeared to be drawn down sadly by the ferocity of the gale, which seemed to Tom's mind to be raking through the cabin, though his senses told him that the air within was weirdly still. Here in the inner box of the boat the wind was a force of nerves.

But in the very midst of bracing himself he began to think of details, the bane and boon of his life, and at once he was standing, peering out through the oval porthole above his berth. He saw chaos filtered through chaos, a lowering, soaked day looming beyond a glass streaked with drops and lines and sometimes sheets of rain; yet he made out soon that *Harmony* had held and was holding. He had marked bearings abeam at the anchorage in the evening light the night before; he lined up again the end of a wooden pier with a gable of a house up the moor far beyond. He was glad he had set the fluke anchor. *Harmony* was holding fast.

Knowing that, he could look for signs of the day through the bleary glass: greenish scudding water, power boats straining and careening, the immovable land mass crosshatched by slanting curtains of rain, the nap of the foliage cowering as close to earth as could be, as if with a vegetable patience waiting it out and saying, This will pass, this will pass.

He had waxed the porthole glass, in and out, and the

downpour danced across it in agile globules. Sometimes, when a sudden spillage of solid water curtained the opening, the wind, getting at everything, made tiny waves across the vertical surface which looked like the ripples of sand in a tidal pool, and through that brief filter Tom saw a horrifying corrugated white power boat beyond.

As the yawl sheered out on a starboard tack and the glass was drained of all but a few scurrying drops, Tom saw the marina dock: a mess of trouble. The glimpse was not long enough to make out more than that things were distinctly not right along the pier.

He looked at the clock: nine minutes past six in the morning.

Once more he checked the bearings ashore, the pier and the gable. This time *Harmony* must have been on a different phase of her constant oscillation; the pilings of the old dock stood forward out of line. Had *Harmony* after all dragged a bit? Tom began at once to think, sorting out his mind under the gruesome symphony of *Harmony*'s standing up to the cruel wind, what he would do if she dragged. Step one, step two . . . Ending, no matter what course of steps he took, in the unthinkable. But then he realized, with a surge of relief, that the wind must have shifted during the night, probably going round now slowly clockwise in the cyclonic pattern; and *that* would account for the pier's being out of line on one side of her swinging. Thank God, she was well rooted in the mud.

Here came Flicker Hamden bustling out of the forward cabin, slamming the door back against the bulkhead with his elbow, his unshaven chin belligerently jutting forward, his eyes yellowy and rheumy. No struggle to rouse him this morning!

99

"Christ, man," he said, his jocular tone thinly covering a real resentment, "you told me cruising was the most relaxing pastime this side of—what did you say?—the Turkish baths?"

Tom, shocked by Flick's inconsiderateness, put a forefinger to his lips and then pointed it across at Audrey.

Flick ducked and made a face, as if to dodge a blow of surprise, and he disappeared into the head, banging the door shut and knocking the close bulkheads with knees and elbows and overriding the storm with athletic pumpings and noises of splashing and of blowing through water. This was a morning to show his vigor.

Tom looked out the porthole again, with its fugitive drops running almost horizontally, and reasoned out the wind direction: a point or two south of east. Good in one way, for part of the bulk of the island, rather than a mere sandspit, stood between *Harmony* and the pile-driving air; but bad in another way, for by the mariners' rule that put the eye of a storm like this two points abaft the beam of a vessel nosing the wind, Block Island—and *Harmony*—must be more or less northeast of the center and therefore almost dead in its path, where the longest and worst would come.

The barometer? Tom tapped its face with a forefinger. Twenty-nine point seven, and falling. But that told little; the speed of the fall was what mattered. It was six-fourteen. Logging the figures in his memory, he aligned the needles as on any morning.

He turned on the radio; it was almost time for Sunny McCloud. But Boston could not be heard in this noise, not if he kept the radio low so as not to waken Audrey; nor could Providence. New London was selling bread. He held New

London, and a song came on: "Liar, Liar." And then another, the Righteous Brothers with "You've Lost that Lovin' Feelin'." Then praise of a caked bleach. New London was not interested in this storm. "Nobody knows," the Chiffons lamented, "what's going on in my mind but me." Six-thirty passed. Tom turned the radio off.

Flick came slamming out of the head, and Audrey, all too fittingly aroused by Hamden's racket rather than by the storm's or the radio's, turned her head and sleepily said, "What are we going to do?"

Flick stood in the door to the forward cabin, seedy in his rumpled pajamas and slovenly bristles, waiting for Tom's answer.

"Sit tight. Right here."

Flick asked, "This a good place to be?"

"Can't say it's an ideal anchorage, but we're stuck with what we have. We're holding, anyway. So far."

"Shouldn't we go ashore?" Audrey's voice, in her state of slowly emerging awareness, seemed defenseless and trusting, and it wrenched at Tom and made him angry.

"In what? Scuba suits?" At once he repented this foolish sarcasm, realizing that Audrey had not had a chance to get her bearings. "Couldn't very well make it in the dinghy now." It was the big oaf, the snorter and splasher, standing in the doorway, who made him angry.

Who made him angrier now, by saying (and especially by using a pronoun which, in seeming to distribute the blame, aimed it, to the contrary, through a reverberating irony of tone, all the more tellingly), "We should have followed the forecasts closer. We got kind of sloppy yesterday." It was the nursemaid's "we." Such insolence! Why hadn't *he* glued himself to the radio, if he intended to treat himself to this big "we"?

"Look, chum. There's a difference between tracking and predicting. This one out-foxed the boys. Nobody knows enough about storms yet. It still takes human guesswork—"

Flick whirled away and went forward and slammed the cabin door. *Harmony* timed badly her next shudder, which came at this moment and seemed to express an old boat's disgust at her owner's way of handling things.

Tom lit the stove and set some water to boil. He would shave in the midst of peril and demonstrate to—to Audrey—that—that—

She was standing by her berth in the narrow space by the folded-down table, dressing. She always turned her back to him in modesty when she let down the top of her nightgown and put on her bra; he saw now her soft back . . . A fierce gust spoke in the stays and spars above with the voice of a crying child. Audrey, her sympathies aroused, leaned to the porthole on her side and looked out; there she would see the wide and, on that side, almost boatless expanse of the Pond, greenish and foam-flecked all the way to Indian Head Neck. She held her face so close to the glass that two plumes of fogging fanned out from her nostrils; then she swung around to Tom with a look of total recognition of what they were up against.

"We'd better have eggs," Tom said in an everyday voice, so controlled that not even his control could be heard in it. "This will be a big old working day, just sitting here. Good fat breakfast, O.K.?"

In seeing the surprise and fear ease from Audrey's face,

Tom felt he might presume to ask her a dreadful question, ask for an explanation, an accounting. How come? What was the story? What had gone wrong? She was still his wife; she still trusted him; she looked through the streaming glass, saw wet hell, turned to him, heard his calmness, responded, felt safe—a lot safer than he felt. This sequence gave him rights; he had a right to whisper a question. What went wrong, darling? Those two wouldn't have to hear.

Whoosh. Another gust. How *Harmony* heeled under bare poles!

The moment for the question, if it had ever been there, was gone. Audrey bent to make up her berth; Tom turned to do the same on his side. They were working together, and it was too early in the morning to talk.

The water came to a boil. Tom took a steaming panful into the head and shaved. Interstitched with the wailing of the storm and the creaking of *Harmony*'s timbers, which in the tiny toilet seemed very loud and urgent, he heard through the thin bulkhead to which the mirror was fastened sounds of a quarrel. Tom felt, under his generalized anxiety and pain, a blurt of smugness. Audrey would notice his clean chin; perhaps she, too, could hear now the mean squabbling up forward.

But when he emerged, feeling greatly refreshed, and saw Audrey at the stove, staring at the frying pan as if unable to decide what to do next, he was suddenly let down. He cruelly searched his mind for ways in which he had neglected her. There was that crying child again. Audrey snapped out of her reverie and looked upward. Then she reached in the icebox and took out a package of bacon.

Those two came out from the forward cabin. No sign of a

quarrel. No sign of a hurricane, either. Sunny skies! They were holding hands! Tom thought that this was Flicker Hamden's most appalling effrontery yet. How could he inflict such a mockery on Audrey—to say nothing of Dot? Was he being big-Daddy-when-the-wind-blows?

Dottie looked frightened, but Tom felt that he should bear in mind, no matter what might happen later in the day, that she had been able to work up the spirit for quite an ugly spat with Flick, fear or no fear.

"What's the check-out hour in this motel?" Flick said. "Just got a call from my secretary, says I'm needed back at the firm."

"It'll take a while to pack," Dottie said, bravely going along with Flick's joke, which fell flat with Audrey, who evidently could not take in anything but that teenage hand-holding; and as for Tom, half of him was checking off mental lists and half of him was chilled to the bone with regrets and apprehensions. Both the Hamdens sat down, waiting for service.

Tom watched Audrey getting breakfast, and with all of him he admired her so much, there came a moment of feelings so strong, that he actually had to remind himself of the dangerous storm, and of precautions. And when, as *Harmony* heeled to a whistling blast, he did concentrate on the storm and realized that its power was far from its peak, his feelings about her grew all the more intense; there was only a short time, he told himself, in which to repair, take back, forgive, shape up, make amends, atone—to put back together again the one important relationship of his life. But then two fried eggs were in front of him, and bacon, and hashed brown potatoes, and buttered toast, and steaming coffee—his re-

quested hearty breakfast for which he had no heart. He tried
to eat; Audrey's handiwork was all paste between his tongue
and the roof of his mouth. It occurred to him that Flick,
seeing him push the food around on the paper plate, would
think he was afraid of the storm, and with a Protestant anger
he forced the food down. The mass of it lodged itself, to his
senses, just under his Adam's apple. Of course Flick didn't eat
much; the son of a bitch was in love.

If there could be Protestant anger there could also be
Protestant self-reproach. Tom sucked probingly at his own
smugness, as if at meat lodged between his teeth. He felt
superior to Flicker. Even hating livers he led a more useful life
than this tinker. He was interested in inner man, Flick only in
electronic extensions of man, devices that dangle from him
like prosthetic limbs and mechanical graspers. He, Tom,
wasn't afraid of the storm, not deeply, because he knew as a
man what to do, whereas this big unshaven slob . . .

But then Tom had an insight that made him almost want
to cast off and lose *Harmony* and all aboard: The cuckold
always feels superior to the one who has wronged him. With
this understanding all the succulence went out of his smugness, and he just felt mean. He felt driven to do something.
He stood up and went to the closet opposite the head and
took out his waterproofs and thin non-skid boots.

"Please tell me where you think you are going?" It was
Audrey, speaking out of what?—old habit?

You can worry about me still, can't you? He almost said
it out loud. Instead he said, "I've got to check things."

"Things! You and your things! Why can't you just sit it
out the way you said we were all going to?"

"The chafing gear—," he lamely began.

105

"You'll let the storm into the cabin," Audrey said.

"For God's sake, darling, we can't just pretend it isn't there."

"Oh, go ahead, go ahead. You're going to take us out for a little sail, aren't you? I know you."

Tom dived into his waterproofs to avoid thinking about that thrust. She knew him. Yes, she knew him. He lifted the hood over his head and pulled the drawstrings tight around his cheeks. A little sail?

He threw back the hatch and climbed the ladder and rose outward into a medium of violence for which no phase of his life had prepared him.

A brutal push from behind, foul and delinquent, like that of muggers on a night street, drove him down, and flinging out an arm as he fell he grasped the upright pipe stanchion of the boom gallows, and there he clung, astonished, sobbing for breath with lungs which were not elastic enough, it seemed, to deal with this air that stole air. That's hail coming at me, he thought. The downpour had looked like rain from below but must be hail, for it crashed against the hood of his waterproofs and stung his skin like a solid scattershot. But no; there were no pellets of ice on the deck. It was just driven rain. His wet knuckles were going white gripping the pipe of the whatsit— the gallows! Aware that the main boom rested overhead on that frame called gallows, he conjured up a detail: He must take down harder than ever on the main sheet to hold the boom from jumping the frame and smashing all sorts of gear. But wait, he told himself. Gather strength. Count to twenty. Count your blessings . . . four, five, six . . . Jesus, how quiet it had been in *Harmony*'s cabin, how he yearned to be below! And this was only the start; it would get worse later.

All at once he began to worry in earnest about the chafing gear he had set up on the anchor line during the night, that bandage of canvas strips he had wound around the Nylon rope to protect it from fraying, and he felt sure that this straining and bucking would cause even the rounded edges of the bow chock to saw right through the line in no time, and he commanded himself to go forward and see to it. But wait! That wind would take him right overboard: he couldn't just stand up and walk forward and check the chafing gear . . . A little sail? A little sail? . . . He reasoned that he would have to crawl, he would have to slither over the coaming onto the outer deck and crawl along it, gripping the handrail on the turtleback of the cabin trunk—so *this* was what that prissy, varnished handrail had been for, all this time! Tom started his move over the coaming. With a heart-thump of self-congratulation he thanked God and his own foresight that he had taken the mainsail off and bagged it and strapped it down. He heaved himself along, lying almost flat. That screeching in the rigging—he had never heard anything like that. Heave. His face was close to the lovely tight grain of the wet teak deck. Heave. We're going good now, he told himself. Was everything better, or was he just getting used to this gang-war wind? Had he thought it had sounded like a crying baby?

Gradually, very slowly, he began to make each move in a rational way. Once he had dealt in his mind with the first shock of the greatness of the wind he could begin to act, to make sense of each action. He got to his knees. Scrabbled along. Came to the end of the handrail by the mainmast. Got a good grip on the bulwarks. He was on the port side, and rainwater was coursing down the scuppers as along a city curbstone after a cloudburst. Still hard to breathe; mouth away from the gale, gulp deep, hold it, move forward. The lashed-down club of the jib—he could climb up it, so to speak, toward the bow; the small boom was made fast to the deck by its own jib leads. Shinny up it lying down.

Now he hugged the mooring bitts and could see the anchor line running out through its chock, and he saw that the wide strips of canvas (they really were canvas) that he had wrapped round and round the anchor line were doing their work very well. This gave him an enormous lift. He had set up the chafing gear in the dark, and he had set it up right. He had allowed plenty for the stretch in the Nylon line and plenty for *Harmony*'s surges forward that came between gusts, letting up the strain. He had made a double thickness, two bandages, in effect, and he could see that the outer one was so far scarcely worn at all. His lashings were firm. He knew his business! He could take care of . . . A *little sail?* How bitter she had sounded!

To look at the chafing gear he had to face the wind and beating rain, but he gulped air and looked again; it helped his morale. The anchor line was safe for many hours. He had ensured that. This was something he had done right.

Easing back down along the deck he kept a sharp eye out for "things." Everything except the cotter pins of his own life seemed secure. The main in its bag on the dinghy chocks was perfectly snug; he was exceedingly grateful—that edge of self-satisfaction again, even under the pummeling of *this* wind—that he had stripped the sail in the night; difficult then, impossible now.

Soon he was sitting in *Harmony*'s beautiful cockpit, somewhat sheltered by the cabin trunk, back turned to the gale, used to it now. Absent-mindedly, automatically, he picked up the cockpit sponge and passed it back and forth over the brass of the binnacle hood, counting the strokes. Four, five, six. His blessings.

He looked up for the first time from the immediacy of the boat and surveyed the world blowing around. At once he saw that several power boats, their windage too much for their hooks, had dragged down in the earlier northeast wind and had smashed against the marina pier—a scene of havoc all along—and that the lee shore beyond the pier was also strewn with small craft, and some not so small.

Tom felt a rush of anger at all driving-license skippers, as he called them; men with some money in pocket who, because they have passed road tests in automobiles, think they can steer anything with a wheel, and buy stinkpots and go to sea and hail sailors in open waters, calling through a bullhorn, "Which way is New London? Don't gimme those compass numbers. Just point." Idiots. Wasters. Spoilers. Pier-wreckers. He became quite angry; inappropriately angry.

Then a new gust of the gale came, and the crashing of raindrops against his hood was almost overpowering, and the anger was blown away, leaving a painful vacuum, into which, in a moment, grief poured. How could he ever ask Audrey the questions he wanted to ask her? How could so much of life be a waste?

Somewhere there was a muffled new knocking. Had some rigging parted? It was near at hand. A solid thing, not just a beating rope end. He looked around. *Knock knock knock.*

Then he saw Audrey's face in the round porthole, low in the forward bulkhead of the cockpit, put there to provide ventilation above the engine. It was sheltered from the rain by the overhanging ledge of the stepway across the front of the cockpit, so Tom could see clearly through it. Audrey was rapping on the glass with the knuckle of her middle finger—marvelous that he had heard her in all this shrieking. Would he have heard any noise other than one that Audrey made?

When she saw that she had his attention, she began to signal with her forefinger, first pointing at herself, then pointing out through the glass. Incredible! She wanted to come out and join him.

He felt suddenly playful. The grief was gone on the violent air like the anger before it. He laughed. He fell to his knees and bending far forward put his face close to the glass and made cross eyes. Then, flapping his hands close to his rib cage like a seal waving its flippers, he invited her out.

But she drew back her face at the closeness of his, and he saw then that both Audrey and Dottie were in their waterproofs. Flick was not. The girls wanted to taste the storm together. Let them.

Tom raised up and pushed back the hatch. Dottie started up the ladder first; her eyes were big, excited.

When her head and shoulders were in the wind, she stopped; she cringed down. Audrey was pressing up the ladder beside her, and Tom saw some sort of eagerness in her face, too. What had Flick been saying to work them up this way? Or did their excitement come from his, Tom's, having been outside in the wind? Why wasn't Flick coming up to sample the weather?

Audrey raised her head above the hatchway just as a heavy gust came across the Pond, and it was as if she had been struck a solid blow from behind. She ducked.

Both girls backed down the companionway. They had

already had enough storm. Their faces, tilted up, were pale and appalled.

Tom himself was ready for shelter, and taking help again from the firm boom gallows, he got his legs up over the hatchway doorboards and dropped down the ladder. He slid the hatch shut and felt the stillness of the air as if it were a palpable heaviness all around him; he might have been under water. He took his dripping rain gear off and hung it from one of the catch hooks of the ladder. He felt himself trembling inside.

He turned to face the others. "Pretty good breeze," he said. "We ought to make Hamburg Cove in about four hours in this."

A little sail. He saw from Audrey's eyes that she understood he was joking, answering her jibe with a light heart; but Dottie blurted out, "Tom! You're not going to take us out in *this!*"

"God, Miss Dorothy," Flick said, "he's putting you on." All the same, Tom caught Flick looking into his face for confirmation.

He gave it for Dot's sake. "Sure, Dot, I was kidding. We're going to hunker down right here till it's over."

Suddenly, with that announcement, there seemed to appear a frightful problem. What were they going to do while they waited? How were they going to deal with each other in this confinement? The wind whined in the rigging, and they had nothing to say to each other.

Tom knew he had an advantage over the others: He had "things" to see to. It was almost eight o'clock. He turned on the radio. On the hour came bulletins, and they were all commonplace—an auto wreck on the Connecticut Turnpike,

three teenage girls returning from a state beauty contest, all
killed by a car that had run out of control across the center
strip the wrong way; an eighty-six-year-old woman burned to
death in a tenement fire, origin thought to be a kerosene
cookstove; police in Norwich called by neighbors, having
heard screams, to a home where a milk deliveryman, said to be
intoxicated, had put a woman customer of his dairy, who had
left a note in an empty bottle that she didn't need any milk
that day, across his knees and had spanked her with a ping
pong paddle. But not a word from the broadcasting studio in
its solid building in a solid town about the closest trouble and
fear of all, not a breath—until the weather report; and then it
came in the most matter-of-fact tones. High winds, currently,
in New London, from the east, gusting to sixty miles an hour,
with a forecast of heavy rain and winds verging on hurricane
strength through the day, clearing at night, tomorrow fair and
mild.

"Fair and mild," Dotty wistfully said.

"Be quiet!" Tom wanted to hear each word.

But that was every bit of it. A musical commercial had
come on—a total moral jolt in the context. Tom fought off a
feeling that he was going to get into a labyrinthine argument
with Flick about communications, in which he would have to
say that all the sophisticated electronic equipment in the
world wouldn't cure this kind of inanity; it was beginning to
look as if we needed tracking devices for storms of social
idiocy . . . But he didn't want to quarrel with Flicker today—not on that level, he told himself, and he turned his
back on the man and checked the barometer again. God,
it *was* plunging. It now stood at twenty-nine point five and

had fallen to this immoderate low point in less than two hours.

Tom took the log book from its shelf and squared it before him on the table, and he thought: Now here, just inside the upper cover, *is* the substance of a quarrel!

To still his revived anger, Tom listened to the voice of the storm. He had come to think of the gusts as great words which an ear, a trained ear in a wise head, but never a device, never a machine, might be able to make rhyme and reason of; and now one came, a howling long monosyllable, under which *Harmony* strained as if its every wooden part were being stretched to new lengths, and Tom tried, himself straining, to get the word, and he felt that he almost had it, but the word ended with a crack of something loose above, a hard consonantal ending, and the gist eluded him.

Then with deliberation Tom lifted the cover of the log book and turned it back flat, so the cut endpaper lay exposed to view. Tom looked around at the eyes. Audrey saw the cut page and looked up at once into Flick's face. Dottie saw it and looked up just as promptly into Tom's eyes. Flick saw not only the cut but also that everyone else had seen it.

Flick looked as if he might yawn. Now, when Tom wanted his anger, he lost it in astonishment at Flick's brazening. The man looked bored. It was going to be a long day, this; his telltale jaw muscles were relaxed, his eyelids rather heavy.

In order not to be routed altogether Tom flipped the book open and began briskly to write in it. Every item he logged was factual yet somehow muted, understated; data could not express Tom's views of this ferocity.

He felt drawn to it. Closing the log book and putting it back on the shelf he had an impulse—he began at once to

113

think of it as a duty—to go above again. He told himself he wanted to make extra sure that the mainsail in its bag was secure.

But he paused. Those other three were talking about Joan Plasson, an acquaintance, a fiercely ambitious woman they all knew. Under the moaning of the masts and lines, amid the heeling and shuddering of the hull, they were gossiping. They were not interested in whatever he might have written in the mutilated log book, but only in how—Flick was saying it—Joan periodically got a bad back, and it always seemed to be just after she carried on a public flirtation at some party, right up to the brink of scandal, with some older man who was crucially important to the future of Perry, her husband, and then undoubtedly had to march home that very evening and have intercourse with old Perry—and *zing*, muscle spasm.

Tom stood up and reached for his waterproofs, and nobody asked where he was going.

When he slid back the hatch, Flick said in an outraged tone, "Hey, can that! It's drafty in here. I'll start to sneeze."

The girls both laughed at this threat; Flick's eyes came up to Tom's for a moment, and Tom saw a blur in them, something frozen just behind the twinkling lenses. Let them gossip for their health's sake. He pulled the hood drawstrings tight, and though he saw Audrey saying something good-humored—she could afford it—to Dottie, he could not hear the words. He climbed out.

This time the shock of emerging into the gale, though expected, was almost worse than the first time, perhaps precisely because experience did not seem to ease it. The shock in Tom's mind was at the possibility that a dead and usually bland and even sweet thing, air, might be capable of a schemed, not simply random, malevolence, as it hit, tested, tried to upset, probed for a man's weakness, and hinted with its howling voice at deliberately evil intentions. Tom, gulping for breath and bringing every canny ability he had into play to steady himself, remembered the word "majestic" he had used in speaking to Flick of the concept of smooth sailing; the dark side of majesty would be tyranny. Dictator wind: the only aim of despotic power was to satisfy insatiably sick drives. Kill! Kill! Find scapegoats! Punish the innocent till they seem guilty! These thoughts rushed through Tom's mind as he clung once again, to gather his resources, to the upright pipe of the boom gallows; then his reserves slipped a sickening notch as he thought (with a curse on the common fund of "modern" psychiatric understanding in which he, like everyone else, crudely shared) that he might be projecting something of himself onto the surely inhuman wind.

The sail. He had come up to take care of a detail. Holding on tight with every move, he made it to the lazaret and reached down inside and put his hand on one of the spare lines—a spinnaker guy. Realizing that the wind, whether or not it meant to be evil, would make an irretrievable snarl of the line if he tried to carry it forward coiled, he unstopped the hitch around the loops and grasped the bronze fitting at one end and drew the rope out free. It flew out at once astern like a long gay streamer. He fought his and its way forward to the mainsail in its slings, and literally lying across the bag of synthetic cloth he applied this additional lashing, webbing it back and forth around the handrails on either side of the trunk, and took it all up as tight as he could. This left him hot and weak, and it showed him what it was like to do even a small jag of work out in a whole gale—or perhaps it was a hurricane now.

He lay resting on the trapped sail, and he looked out over the harbor. Worse confusion than ever. The boats that remained were sheering wildly back and forth; two stinkpots were entangled, one of fiberglas beating to splinters the broken beam-ends of an old wooden sister. While Tom watched, the anchor of a small cutter tripped right out and the vessel went down the Pond broadside to the wind, nearly capsizing altogether. No one seemed to be aboard. Tom watched until the boat, almost lost in the rain, seemed to have struck a rock along the shore beyond the marina. All sorts of debris was floating in the water: timbers, floats, flotsam, planks; and there went a motorboat awash! Tom did not want to look to windward to see what might be bearing down on *Harmony*.

Harmony! A thought of her flaw struck Tom like a poke in the ribs. He scrambled with recovered energies back to the cockpit, raised the starboard seat lid, and began to pump. As he rocked up and down, he was taken with a vision of himself in safety—but what a strange picture! He was at the table in the dining alcove in the apartment at home, and papers were spread out across the tabletop, and he was chewing a pencil—making out his income tax return. He was in the act of cheating the United States government of thirty dollars here, eight dollars there, forty-five on another item. Only he didn't think of it as cheating, really, for these were merely those small everyday short cuts and white lies and "clean" peculations that everyone indulged in, consciously or unconsciously, as a matter of course; indeed, began to think of as part of one's natural rights; took advantage of for fear of thinking oneself a damned fool otherwise. They were one's

private levies against government policies with which one dis-
agreed. Tom, swaying over the bilge pump yet holding on to
the coaming for dear life as he watched the sportsmen's toys
on the Great Pond being ripped from their moorings, began to
laugh out loud at his glimpse of safety—the long columns of
figures, the tiny and easy and respectable untruths! The wind
tore the laughter from his lips and flew off with it along with
all its other captive wreckage.

The pump ran dry quite soon; the push of the storm
seemed not to have told on *Harmony*'s sore place. He dropped
the seat cover.

Now he wanted to see whether the engine would start.
Not that they were going anywhere—but just in case the time
might come when he needed to take some strain off the
anchor line. Not wishing to alarm the crew he pushed the
hatch six inches open—good Lord, they were playing cards on
the cabin table—and he shouted, perhaps far too loud, for
what with the rain crashing on the hood over his ears he could
hear only the storm, "Going to crank up the motor. Don't
panic. Just testing." And he pulled the cover shut, not waiting
to read their upturned looks.

Sliding to the rear of the cockpit, he checked to be sure
the gears were in neutral, and he cracked the throttle and
advanced the spark, and he turned the ignition key—and
then, as though not really caring to know the answer, he
paused. An inflated, much-patched inner tube floated past:
some summer-visiting youngster's water plaything, crazily
turned loose now. There was so much storm noise; would he
be able to hear the engine? He pressed the button. He did
hear the clang of the starter. But the rain tattooed his hood
and he heard nothing else. He advanced the throttle and,

bending down, looked at the panel of instruments on the lazaret bulkhead: Good old engine! He could see the tachometer needle, a wavery line of white through a wash of rain, standing at the angle for eleven hundred revolutions per minute. He turned off the key at once and felt pleased.

But the satisfaction was brief; he was restless. He thought perhaps he'd better go below again; he could only take so much of this breath-snatcher of a wind. He climbed over and down.

With his back to the three and the hatch closed he stripped off and hung up again his streaming slickers, and this time he pulled off his boots. He was bent over fussing at his drippings with the deck sponge when Audrey said, "You really are hell bent on going some place, aren't you?"

"Just in case, just in case," he said toward the floorboards.

He stood and faced his boatmates. Flick had the girls playing blackjack. They had emptied a box of wooden matches and were using them for chips; Tom had a quick thought, which he recognized as pretty mad in the context of a hurricane, that you could set fire to a boat playing with kitchen matches that way. Flick was dealing. He faced an ace on his own hole card and bet it up and up. The girls stayed. He turned his hidden card—a lousy three! The girls laughed at his bluffing with rippling delight that overrode the wailing above. Dottie won. Her face was suffused with a pink glow of pleasure.

They had shut him away again, their three. Tom tried to tell himself that they didn't understand as much as he did about the storm, and that therefore they sheered, like these boats at anchor, between unknowing fear at one extremity of the swing and equally blind overconfidence at the other. They

118

thought him finicky. He was the one who hadn't taken a drink at Quicks Hole. For each of his precautions they had to make some gesture—Flick egged on the girls in this—of indifference.

But how, above all, could Dottie sit there blushing with the fun she was having? How could she look so radiant? She must have some need for defeat, Tom thought, remembering the hand-holding of that pair coming out of the forward cabin. All this must have happened to her, to them, before; perhaps often. Watch out, Audrey! They're using you for their game!

But Audrey was saying, "Sit down and take a hand, Tomaso."

"I want to see if I can get some weather," Tom said, and he slid in by the radio.

At this moment the storm furnished its strongest gust of the morning. The boat was on the port tack, so to speak, and the grappling hooks of this sharp flurry pulled at the masts, and *Harmony* heeled farther than ever, and shuddered, too.

"Watch your matches," Flick warned, and he put a hand over the dealer's pile and reached his other hand out, fingers outspread, to cover Audrey's stack, but she had moved quickly with both her hands, and when his came down it folded over both of hers. It stayed there, conveying whatever needed to be conveyed, until the fat boat had righted herself and the shriek of that particular blast had fallen to a moan. Then his hand came away as from a hot stove.

Tom, fiddling with the turning knob of the radio without having turned the set on, in order to pretend he had not seen the handplay, wondered how all of them could sit there in such peril and not come out with some big truths that they would have to face sooner or later; but the thought of truths reminded him of his vision of safety a few minutes earlier, and of his packet of untruths over Form 1040. He barked out a short, involuntary laugh.

Dottie asked, with her head tipped to one side, really wanting to share in any jokes that were going, "What was *that* about?"

"About verities."

"Oh, for Pete's sake, Tom," Audrey said. "Cool it."

"No," Tom said, suddenly wanting to justify himself, and covering up by taking a new direction, "I'd just said I wanted to see if I could get some weather, and then we got *that* sample of it."

"Har-de-har," Flick said, and Tom noticed, perhaps for the first time, that Flick's two front teeth were awfully big, almost as prominent as the Mad Hatter's. Cuckold's contempt, he told himself, the old Calvinist juices flowing strong.

It *was* time to cool it, and he almost pounced on the radio, and this time he kept sweeping the bands until he found a good loud Long Island station which seemed to be interested in little besides the storm—a man kept repeating warnings to shore dwellers to evacuate their homes, and he announced the locations of emergency shelters in various public schools and firehouses, and in due course, on the hour of nine, he paraphrased the latest Weather Bureau advisory. He was no meteorological technician; he sounded as if he had theatrical ambitions. Esmé's skirts now whirled in winds of seventy to eighty miles an hour. It was now expected that the eye would be off Montauk—less than thirty miles away, Tom immediately calculated—at about one o'clock that afternoon, and if the rate of advance remained constant the whole show should be over by six or seven in the evening. The winds could be expected to shift more and more toward the south and then west, and it was expected that skies would be clear before sundown. Then the announcer began to give free play to warnings about what such winds could do, and he recalled many lurid details from the blows of 1924, 1938, 1944, 1954; from storms named Carol, Diane, Hazel. He was beginning to sound a bit like Batman, and Tom was in the act of reaching out to throttle him with a turn of his thumb and forefinger when they were all startled—Tom so much that he stood up, ready to grab his waterproofs—by a loud crashing sound. It took some moments for him to realize that the clatter had been on the radio. Now the announcer's voice came back part way, and it had lost all its lisp and orotundity; it was far away and small-boyish. "My God! The tower. The tower's going. Am I still on? Are we on, Larry? It's buckled, the big tower, the guy wires must be holding it from falling. It's aimed right for . . . Am I on? Larry? Supposed to go ahead? . . . A technical problem has just risen at the studio shack of—" And that, with a little crackle, was the end. Silence.

They had all heard clearly enough. They sat speechless for some time. Then Audrey, perhaps angry that Tom had now indeed let the storm into the cabin, said rather petulantly, "You kept telling us it was stalled. 'Hung up off the Carolinas,' that's what you kept saying."

"Darling," Tom said, "that's what *they* kept saying. Don't hold me responsible"—he couldn't resist the chance—"for the Weather Bureau's think-boxes not knowing what was going to happen next."

In this moment of defending himself, Tom felt his first deep stab of fear. It was connected with his not-quite-rational uneasiness of a few minutes earlier about the possibility of a deliberately malicious intent in the searching wind. What if the whole storm had a mind? What if it was a willful living organism that refused to be predicted, much less controlled, by arrogant puny human beings—Flickers with their mechanical extensions of their tiny arms and brains? Tom felt like an ant hearing thuds, through the ground, of approaching footsteps; the mouth of the anthill was darkened by the shadow of a huge shoe. He'd seen some orchard trees being sprayed once. What about the inchworm, or whatever it was, in the apple tree—what did he think of the wet fog of poison that came from nowhere and enveloped the whole banquet-tree and choked him and his brothers to death? Mindless chance—a kind of storm of death? This fear hadn't to do with any big phony idea of a divine plan. This was the thought—which he knew in the moment of thinking was unscientific and probably worse than that, but the knowledge did not shut off the thought—that Esmé might be alive, intelligent, and bitchmean. And looking for, among many other objects, the yawl *Harmony*, with its cargo of human beings who had made a mess of their lives.

Flick's way of meeting an explosive situation seemed to be to ignore it. He asked Tom, quite pleasantly, "Shall I deal you in?"

"Sure, I'll take a hand."

"Wait a minute, Flick," Dottie said in a most cheerful voice, "we'll have to give him some matches."

Matches were money. They were going to give him some money, with which he, too, could play their game. He wondered why he kept his mouth shut. Audrey! Audrey! Watch out! This involves us both!

As the matches were counted out and the first deal of hole cards came around Tom had another glimpse of a scene of safety. His office. A woman, Josephine Lawlor, a boozer, who had been in two or three times before. She felt twinges. Down there on the right side. He knew she would not believe that she had had her money's worth unless he gave her what she called a "complete physical," so he sent her into the examining room, and there, in time, he came to her; she was in a split starched white examining gown, and Miss Spellacy, also starched and very white, both in cloth and skin, was standing by for propriety's sake. Blood pressure—low enough for a fine longevity of endless hypochondria. A close lamplit look into sticky yellow eyes. A laying on of hands, a kneading of flaccid meat. Rubber gloves; apertures. "We'll shoot a couple of pictures, Mrs. Lawlor. Miss Spellacy will take care of you." And a murmur to Miss Spellacy: Get blood and urine. And when Mrs. Lawlor came back, dressed, she quite obviously felt much better already. He wrote out a prescription, "temporary—till the tests are in," and called her drugstore after she left to tell the pharmacist to give her placebos. And he made a notation for Miss Spellacy's later attention: Mrs. Lawlor, O.V., $25. . . .

A smile—not pleased, not bitter, but tentative, puzzled—on his lips, he bet twenty-five matches on his first hand and lost.

And so they played cards, eroding the cliff-like minutes with little waves of non-committal activity. Few words were needed for their transactions. After a number of hands Dottie won the deal, and her love of the dealer's power, so odd for one so accommodating, made her seem greedy and a tiny bit fierce. But it was all for fun—just matches. The wind pummeled *Harmony* and made the shrouds cry. At last the game grew dull, and Audrey, who by then was dealer, simply stopped passing out the cards, and she picked up the big matchbox and began stuffing the matches into it any old way, but the box soon filled, and she had to take them all out again and align them to fit them in. Flick kept bringing up one topic after another, cheerfully enough, but the conversation, like the storm, was gusty, intermittent. Occasionally Tom stood up and checked the pier and the gable. Often he looked at the clock. For a time the rain seemed to be letting up, but the wind squalls were bad. Audrey served Cokes.

Crump.

Something hard and heavy dealt *Harmony* a blow, with a sound of cracking wood, on her right flank, forward. Tom was on his feet in an instant. His first thought was that a boat had tripped out and run down on her, though he did not remember having seen any craft to windward—and for more than an hour the wind had not shifted. That horrible cracking sound: had a rib gone, or some planking? It was ten twenty-three; he must put that in the log book with its endpaper ruined.

Crump—it hit again. Tom pressed his cheek against the porthole on the starboard side, but all he could see was deck and rain and waves. He plunged into his waterproofs and boots and climbed above.

The shock of the wind was undiminished; perhaps it was worse than ever, this time, because now there was a hazard that had not been there before. He held to the gallows pipe, gulping for breath.

Then he moved to the right and went over the coaming onto the starboard deck, and he saw at once that there was an enormous dark shape—a capsized hull?—lodged against the

124

bows. He hauled himself rapidly forward by the handrail and bulwarks. He looked over the bow and saw a roof.

A cabin—a shed—a small boathouse. It was skewed to the right, three quarters under water. It was snarled on the anchor line, had pulled the Nylon rope straight down from the chock, and was caught somehow.

Crump. Even here in the outer noise he heard that blow, or felt it all through his frame. Those assaults were too serious; they would demolish *Harmony.* He crept aft and undid the light lashings that held the boathook and mop. In this wind every act took far more time than usual; the cords of the lashings were wet and had seized up, and he had to brace one foot against a lifeline stanchion and wrap the crook of one arm around a ventilator funnel to keep himself from being blown away, and he had to tie the mop back down once he had loosed the boathook, meanwhile wedging the boathook under a thigh so *it* would not take off.

At last he was able to creep forward again, this time to the very pulpit of the bow, and he reached down along the anchor line to see if he could free it from this nightmarishly misplaced structure, whatever it might be. Holding the hook straight downwards off the bow took all the strength of both his arms. How swift was the wind that was trying to snatch it away from him—eighty miles an hour?—a hundred miles an hour?

He soon found that there was no hope at all of freeing the anchor line this way. It was held down as tightly as if the house had been built right from its foundations on it. What was brought to bear at the point of snarling? A hook, a hinge, a nail? Would it claw through the rope? He tried to reach a foot down to see if he could push the roof away, but the wind took the big sail of the waterproof legging and slammed his limb back against the bow cheeks. It was no easy matter to get it back aboard.

Crump.

He had to make a decision. To delay might be disastrous, to rush might be worse. He put his hooded head down on the deck to rest his neck—for just to hold one's head up in such a blow took fortitude and muscle—and to think. Did he have all the facts he needed in order to decide?

He knew at once that he had not, and he began to make his way aft. How weak and tired he felt without having made a significant move!

What about the boathook? Might need it later. He dragged it along. He paused on his way back down the deck to lash it down again—and here he won a tiny lift to his courage, for he had had the presence of mind, in refastening the mop, to leave ends of the cording free, so now he could make fast the boathook without having to untie the mop again. That was not a matter of chance; he had thought it through. He could think of things. He and "things."

Crump.

He hastened below. Without pausing at the foot of the ladder to take off his dripping togs, he moved forward through the cabin.

"Darling, you're getting everything sopping."

Through the hood he heard her. Would she call him "darling" forever? He did not answer but went into the forward cabin and clambered over gear and sailbags far up into the forepeak, and he ran his hand along the skin of the hull and up and down the ribs around the area where the blows must have been delivered, and he examined planks and

126

frames, and as far as he could see there was no checking or cracking anywhere. Robust *Harmony!* She was going to knock the house to pieces.

All the same, he wanted to back away from the bows before another of those enormous drumbeats came. One more "thing" to observe. He slithered backwards down from the forepeak and stepped into the after cabin and looked out the starboard porthole. The pier. But where was the gable? Oh, God, there it was. Out of line to the right. They were dragging anchor now. Just no question about it: *Harmony* and her assailant were on the move.

He turned and faced the three.

Flick brought the flat of a hand down hard on the table and said, "For Christ's sake, what is it?"

Tom did not want to answer, he wanted to think. Where could he think? Not forward: one of those awful blows would knock any sense right out of his head. Not above: Esmé would talk him out of a rational decision. Not here in the cabin, where those three pairs of eyes and Flick's question pressed him to hurry too much.

He stumbled into the tiny box of the head and pulled the door shut and sat down on the john in his waterproofs. He would think about what to do, about how to deal with the bitch storm, about fate and whether and how to fight it— sitting on the crapper. He'd better cut. That was his first thought. The house might stove a hole in lovely *Harmony* any moment, and she'd go to the bottom, and they'd all drown in the wind-fanged Pond. Beach her to leeward? The chart showed rocks beyond the marina pier and rocks in the mouth of Cormorant Cove farther on, and even if she found a sand shoal she might trip over and fill in the fierce chop far from land. Or, as the wind was blowing at this moment, from the southeast, she might even drift right out the channel to sea. He would need to be able to control her, have steerageway somehow; the engine would not be enough, not upwind. Better put on the tiny storm trysail that was made of cloth like iron. Without it the engine would never be strong enough to bring *Harmony* head-to-wind, in case he needed to turn, or was driven out to sea and wanted to heave to. He thought then tenderly of *Harmony*, and at once in a reaction against his love for his boat he began to search his mind for the small print in his marine insurance policy, and he could not for his life remember what in the line of storm damage was covered, or whether total-loss-by-Esmé would bring him money . . . That kind of thinking would sink them for sure . . . Once he had the trysail on, wouldn't it be better to keep control of the boat, take her out through the channel and hug the lee shore of Block Island? If he could control her it would be madness to try to sail around in the Pond, with hazards on every side. A little sail. Was Audrey going to be proved right about him, as she usually was? But surely this wasn't his choice; it was being forced on him. Or was it? Shouldn't he just cut and let fate take care of a beaching? Why fight it? To salvage what?

Crump. He stood up at that and looked at his face in the mirror. The orange hood was drawn tight around his forehead and cheeks and chin, and all that showed was an oval of indecision. Mercy and knowingness, though, of a doctor's face were also there; he could see traces of a doctor in the face . . . He wondered what it was like for a dying man to look in that face; he remembered one of his patients, a month back, a remarkable old man named Ellis, a retired judge of the

128

circuit court, rare primary carcinoma of the liver, lying on a hospital bed and saying goodbye to him. Ellis had great shrubs of eyebrows and a record of probity and compassion. He was so weak that he could barely raise his hand but he wanted to shake hands with Dr. Medlar. He knew. His face was sallow and his eyes glittered, but he was a man of powerful character; the look was outward. He clearly did not wish to express thanks or sorrow or fear or regrets; instead, Tom felt that Judge Ellis examined *his* face with interest and concern. It seemed to be a look of encouragement more than anything else. Why should the dying man offer such a message as that to the well man? What did that glimmer of concern mean? Tom shook the man's hand for a long time. Judge Ellis died late that night. Standing before the mirror now, Tom felt a belated blow of grief for old man Ellis. Then *Harmony* shuddered at a gust, and Tom shook his head as if to throw off confusion—to align grief with appropriate objects in the context; to defy the memory of the old man's jaundiced look of concern; to be a doctor; to be husband to Audrey, will she, nill she; to be at least himself. His face was wet from the storm's rain, and it was pale beside the flaming orange of the waterproof. The eyes?

He opened the door to the head and stepped out into the cabin.

"What the hell were you doing?" Flick asked. "Throwing up?"

"Some kind of shed or house has floated down on us," Tom said. "We're dragging, and I've got to cut. I'm going to ask you to help me to bend on the storm trysail, Flick."

"Whatever that means." Flick shrugged; he was trying in extremity to be humorous.

129

Tom saw that Audrey was all right; they were all going to be all right. Audrey was not going to make a bitter crack about the little sail he was going to take them out on. They had all badly needed a decisive word; they looked quite cheered up.

"Darling," he said, "would you and Dottie secure everything down below here? I mean really get things buttoned down. We can't have a lot of groceries and pot lids flying around down here."

"Sure, Tommy," Audrey said. "What are we going to do?"

"Going to get the trysail on and cut and then see what we can make of it." He knew that all decisions after this one were going to have to be reached more swiftly than this had been.

How nice it was to be below! He clung to being in the cabin—found a number of things he needed to do before he could go out in the storm. He took a long look at the Block Island chart to fix every shoal and promontory and bell in his mind. He looked up, in *The Boatsman's Manual*, all the reminders on heavy-weather sailing and on storms and hurricanes—not to learn things he had not known but simply to bring every trick he might need into the forefront of his memory. He took down his log book—thinking, What does it matter at this moment if there is a cut in a black piece of cardboard?—and he entered, with the most careful discrimination, only those observations that might affect choices later; then, having written them down, he knew he would not forget them.

While he did these things the house struck the boat once . . . twice . . . again. He was being too deliberate. But—

From the locker under the port bunk he took out four

safety belts, and he showed the others how to put them on. "Over your waterproofs. You step through here, you see, so these two straps go under your crotch, and then the main belt goes tight around your waist—listen, you'd all better go to the head before you get yourselves locked into these chastity belts. Then wherever you are, whatever you're doing, even if it's only holding on, you attach one of these snaphooks on these free straps to the lifelines. Gives you about three feet of play."

Flick said, "He'd make a good airline stewardess, wouldn't he?"

Dottie was horrified. "You mean we have to go *upstairs?*"

"Above. On a boat we say 'above.'" It was Flick again, with that "we" again. He was really tuning up.

"We'll all be much safer up there," Tom said. "After you get your belts on I want you to put on life jackets. The orange ones up in the forepeak, Audrey. I'd get them but I think I ought to get to work. Oh, one more thing. The Bonamine. Where is it, Aud?"

"In the medicine cabinet in the head."

Tom fetched the little bottle, and he pumped up some drinking water, and he offered the pills around. Dottie and Audrey took theirs, but Flick shook his head. "It would make me go bye-bye. Sleepyhead."

"Don't be a damn fool. This is one day you're not going to fall asleep, I guarantee. It's Dramamine that does that, anyway."

"Never touch the stuff."

"Look, I'm taking one." And Tom did, to show that taking a pill was not unmanly.

"Nighty-night," Flick said.

"Oh, come on, Flick. A sick sailor's a burden."

131

"Unh-unh. I made a New Year's resolution. No more bonzies. I was on 'em for a while there, did you know that? Was hooked on seasick pills. So I said to myself, 'No more. I've taken my last last bonzy.'"

But the house hit *Harmony* then, and Tom shrugged. He turned suddenly to Audrey and said, "You'll have to be his governess. I'm going to be too busy to take care of him today."

Audrey played her part. "I'll put a didie on his darling little mouth," she said.

"I've got to go above now," Tom said, thinking of the uses of the word "darling." "Don't forget to batten down every damned thing down below here, Aud."

"You see?" Flick said to Dottie. "He says 'above' and 'below.' Not 'upstairs' and 'downstairs.'"

"I'll need your help," Tom said to Flick, "as soon as I've checked some things."

"Aye, aye, Commahndah."

Before going up, Tom took one more look at the bearings ashore. Oh, yes. *Harmony*'s anchor had given up thirty or forty feet. There were now only two other craft whose anchors had held. What a pity, Tom thought; the kedge had been beautifully set, and *Harmony* might have been the only vessel in the Great Pond to ride it out from beginning to end. But now—

Now it really was time to climb out.

On this round, the shock of emergence—of being reborn into the outer world—was worst of all, because now the storm was no longer an adversary for mere anchor and line, not an enemy simply to hold bottom ground against; now it was an elemental exposure within which he was going to have to be a sailor. He was going to have to cut and sail his *Harmony*—in *this*.

And *this* had changed, it seemed to him. There was an insistence now, a steadiness, and even though the frightful wind was still coming down off the land, it was no longer coming in gusty williwaws. It had an even force, as if there were no island in its path, as if it had blown the land away. Could one really speak of a lee shore any more?

Tom faced aft, gulping at this flying air. And saw the dinghy. It was half full of water: rain and splashes. They could never tow it; it would swamp and be a dangerous drag. Could he possibly, even with the help of all the other three, haul it aboard and turn it over and lash it down on the cabin trunk? The mainsail was in the dinghy's cradle. He would have to cast the dink adrift—but even to free its rain-tightened painter from the cleat would be ferocious work in this. Cut. He would have to cut it free. There was nothing to do but cut away his last connection with the shore.

Once more Tom had a small reason to congratulate himself, and at this moment even such a smallness loomed into a powerful consolation. In putting on his waterproofs and safety belt, he had gone to the trouble—as a matter of course, he now told himself—to take his big lockspike knife out of his trouser pocket, to slip the loop of its lanyard over the safety belt, and to put the knife in the pocket of the waterproof jacket. A real marlinspike-seaman of a sailor feels about his knife as a violinist does about his fiddle. The knife's fid opens shackles and forces the lay of ropes for splices, and its blade, often honed, makes sausage of hemp and Nylon and goes into wood as into butter. Weapon, rescuer, whittler, friend. Scalpel.

Oh, yes, he was a doc first and last. He was wildly glad that he had made the little move that now rendered the blade accessible at once; otherwise he would have had to go below and tear at his waterproofs and fish it out and be angry with himself. "I am going to drown in smugness," Tom thought, and the thought gave him great pleasure.

With his left arm crooked around the mizzenmast, Tom swung aft and pulled the knife out by its lanyard and opened it and in one slash cut the dinghy painter. He was astonished by the speed with which the cockleshell ran down the pond. It sped as if self-impelled by terror. Tom leaned a long time looking at it, telling himself, as he lingered, that he must hurry. How wide the greenish, spindrift-flecked pond seemed to have grown, and how tiny the dinghy eventually became in the distance! Hurry, Tom . . . There it is, just a speck. Tom saw in his mind that sun-soaked and now incalculably precious moment when the dinghy had touched the sand that afternoon at Quicks Hole, in the sensuous tropical heat, when he had been a watcher of what seemed to be the freedom and joy of those three, back before the end of innocence and trust, and long before the onset of this world's-end wind. He lost sight of the dinghy in the rain.

Now he knew he must turn and face the gale. He must see if all was in order for the hoisting of the little bikini of a sail. He dragged himself forward along the starboard deck, observing as he went. The mainsail was well tucked in. The halyards were all slapping again, but no matter; they were well cleated. It was going to be hell freeing the main halyard so as to hoist the trysail, and getting the sail on the track, and pulling it up.

Crump. Tom put his head down on the deck, for it

seemed that this had not been a blow of house against boat but of thought against mind. The flaw. *Harmony's* sick place. The thought was simply there, a nasty obtrusion. He knew that there was absolutely nothing he could do about the flaw, and that its existence changed nothing—it had been there all along. It was only that it had not entered his mind once during his recent calculations about what he should do. How queer! What a shock to that smugness in which he had been taking such delight! Might he be forgetting other important considerations? As to the flaw, there was nothing to do but ignore it—bank on the thickness of the keelson. One simply could not think about *Harmony's* breaking her back.

Having faced the flaw at last, Tom found himself prepared to act. He must stop this nonsense of checking "things" and go below for the trysail.

He climbed down. It struck him at once that Audrey was making a glorious game of securing everything loose. The cabin was stripped—plastic cups, ashtrays, pillows, condiments from the galley shelf; all had disappeared. She had taken the ice pick out of its sheath by the ice chest and had removed the glass chimney and globe from the gimbaled kerosene lamp and had even unscrewed the electric light bulbs from their sockets. She had evidently stowed these objects, and others, in the lockers under the berths, and she was now lashing down the seat covers over the lockers with some spare lines from the forepeak. All this, with Flick and Dottie helping, was being carried out in a spirit of mockery. Safety had become a big joke. Well, wasn't it, after all?

Tom went forward and saw that the smallest of the sailbags, containing the never-tried trysail, was of course at the bottom of the heap of spare sails. He burrowed and heaved and dragged the little bag out. This sail was the epitome of Tom's precautionary fervor. Every salty character along the line—the sailmaker's front man, the owner of the boatyard, even a snotty young Coast Guard inspector—had praised Tom for ordering and having a trysail, yet all of them had eyed him in a curious way, when discussing it, as though being sensible were a sure sign of being a little screwy. He had ordered the sail to be made of ten-ounce Dacron; synthetic sheet metal. Only twelve feet up the luff and four feet along the foot—an absurd little handkerchief on a mast three times its height and a boom four times its foot-length. He had had it on just once, to fit it. It had looked silly; he had ever since been somewhat ashamed of it. There it had lain in its bag all this time, waiting for this day.

He frugged into a lifejacket.

When he re-entered the cabin, carrying the bag before him and obviously appearing in orange jacket over orange waterproofs to have been inflated like a swimming-pool toy, the other three, so playful in their preparations, all laughed at the sight of him; but in the middle of their laughter arrived the pale skins and suddenly wan mouths of realization: It was all quite a lot more than a cabin game of hide-the-unidentified-flying-object.

"Come on, Flick," Tom impatiently said. "Get on your horse. I said I was going to need your help."

"I'm all set. Rarin', pardner."

But all he had on was the webbed safety belt, which dangled outside his sport clothes like some shameful under-harness; a rupture truss.

"Get your stuff on and let's go."

"You said it: Let's go. I'm a big grown boy, Thomas. Dr.

Medlar wears what he wants to wear, and Dr. Hamdown wears what he wanna wear. I told you I like rain. Right on little me."

Tom felt, as if rubbing it between thumb and forefinger, the hard-set texture of Flick's stubbornness, yet he thought he must try again. "Look," he said, "I'm going to need every bit of your strength—all day. Waterproofs'll help you save it. We bought them for you!" He was sorry at once he had said that last, which put him so in the wrong.

Flicker's face was suddenly washed clean of all its flippancy and contrariness, and was dead in earnest. "What's your intention, Tom? What are you planning to do? I think I'm entitled to know what the plan is . . . We are." Did that afterthought-plural include both the girls, or only Audrey and Flick himself? How proprietary could he get?

"I told you before all I have in mind. I'm going to cut our anchor away and then see what happens. With the trysail on. We'll put that on first."

" 'See what happens' doesn't quite satisfy me."

"You mean the think-machine wants a more rational program?" Tom heard the raw childish bitterness in his own voice.

It did not soften his bitterness to hear Audrey intervene. "We want to know what's going to happen to us, darling."

He would say it to Audrey. "I'm going to have to see what we can do under power and trysail. Maybe we can stay here in the pond, but I doubt it. I don't know if we'll even be able to come about. I think we'll probably have to go outside. There'll be a choice if we do—either stay under the lee of Block Island, where the big seas will be broken but the water will be very confused, I'd guess—backwash from swells looping around the sides of the island—wind chop—and if you can't hold up to it there and the storm's prolonged, you risk the lee shore, Rhode Island, Connecticut; or the other choice is to take a chance on the open ocean and at least hope to keep going as the wind veers. It's not"—here his eyes shifted back to Flick—"an easy pick—not a choice of caution or daring. It's just something you have to wait and see about, see what makes sense."

Tom half expected some abusive line about chicken shit; but the big man looked rather pale.

Dottie's eyes were huge; she kept swallowing, perhaps in an unsuccessful effort to speak.

Audrey spoke for her. "You're bats, darling. You really are. Why not just let her drag slowly down the pond? Might take all day and the storm be over."

"Her side would be bashed in by that damned house. We'd sink in the middle of the pond."

"Then why not cut and just let her go ashore inside here? Why prolong the agony?"

This was the question Tom could not really answer. All he could say was: "I want to have something to do with what happens."

Flick was looking hectic. He was going to press for the open-ocean alternative, Tom felt. He looked hungry and quite dangerous. "Let's go, boss," he said.

"What about the waterproofs?"

"You heard him, darling," Audrey said. "He refuses to wear them."

"Don't *call* me 'darling.'"

"*Really*, darling. You're out of your mind." But there was an unfamiliar unsureness in Audrey's eyes.

138

"Calling me crazy—you've done it twice just now—doesn't solve anything."

"Oh, Tommy"—here suddenly for a moment was Audrey herself, the known Audrey—"I'm sorry. It was just a . . . an expression."

"O.K., mulehead," Tom said to Flick, "*andiam*. Hand me the sail when I get up."

Tom climbed the ladder into the storm, took the sailbag from Flick and wrestled it to the deck. Then, shocked yet again, he watched Flicker clamber out, watched for the shock to hit the other man, the thief.

Tom should have known that Flicker Hamden would have a style all his own. Flick scrambled down into the cockpit, turned, gripped the cabin trunk, stood up facing the storm, and began to shout. He was soaked through in an instant. He looked wildly happy. Soon both of his arms were sawing the air; he looked like an Italian tenor—a little fat, rapturous, self-important, wooden-armed. The wind caught in the cavern of his mouth, blew out his cheeks, and ripped away his shouts, so Tom could only hear thin, fluttering vowels, ostensibly of celebration: "Ah! . . . Ooooh! . . . Ha! . . . Uh-h-h! . . . Hiyah-h-h!"

Tom began flipping his hand at Flick, beckoning him to get to work.

Flick saw him, and opened his mouth wider than ever. "Ha-a-a-ah!"

Tom rolled over and began sliding and crawling along the deck with the sail under his belly. He looked over his shoulder and saw that Flick was following—and saw, too, that Flick, unencumbered by life jacket and waterproofs, moved about much more efficiently and easily than he did.

139

They were at the mast. Now began the experience of work in this mad air. Both together held the sailbag with their knees, both grasped the clew of the sail, pulling it from the bag, and both strove to get the first slide of the foot onto the track on the boom. Flick was strong. He clenched his jaw and made a struggler's face. Together they seemed to be frozen in this first effort. The wind, screeching in the stays, fought to tear the heavy cloth from their hands. For a moment Tom felt caught, as if in a photograph, in an eternity of not being able to move or change expression. At last they heaved together. There! The first slide was on.

The slides, one by one, were like the shocks of emergence into the storm; experience did not seem to help. Each slide asked a peak labor of alertness, timing, and strength, each wanted a long day's work from two laborers. At last the foot was all attached; now the luff had to be fastened to the mast. How could there be strength enough to finish this job and *then* deal with the storm? The little lipped metal grips tore at Tom's fingers as he guided them toward the track, and the more sail they threaded into place, the more the fabric shook back and forth, like a powerful dog trying to break a captive creature's neck.

Flick was strong, and he was responsive to Tom's lead, and he sang out like a sheet man on a full rigger, happy as a puppy. The rain was streaming across his face and his clothes were dark with wetness. For a moment Tom was in awe of the force—was it no more than the wind?—that had brought about his co-operation, so intimate, so interdependent, so willing, with this robber, of all men. What did he and Hamden want in common?

It was all bent on. Tom signalled to Flick by gestures—

for this word-snatching storm was clearly going to train them to be deaf men, speaking through charading hands—to throw his weight over the boom and onto the bunched sail, which Flick obediently did, and Tom turned his attention to the cleat of the halyard, and he began to fight the wet linen rope, to free it. He uncleated the line part way, passed the loose end beside Flick over the sail, and Flick moved, and with several turns of the rope end Tom stopped down the convulsive cloth. Then he pointed below, meaning, "The girls. It's time for them to come up."

They slid aft, the two partners in work, on opposite decks of *Harmony*, and when Tom pushed open the hatch both their faces looked downward. Audrey reached up—toward him, Tom!—a paper cup of steaming coffee. Miraculous Audrey! How had she thought to do that? How long had it taken to put on the sail? Tom saw that Audrey had filled a thermos, too, for later; at this moment Dottie was spooning sugar— they'd need that—into the mouth of the container. Wonderful women! He and Flick could not possibly have drunk from paper cups in the gale, for the coffee would have flown out and down-pond just like the words the wind had pickpocketed from within their mouths, but hot coffee would be so fortifying that it would justify the effort of climbing down and up again, to drink it.

Tom gestured: After you.

Flick was dripping at the foot of the ladder when Tom got down. Tom felt so grateful to Audrey for this sign of confidence, and suddenly so hopeful, that he reached his wet face forward and kissed her dry cheek. Audrey, in the act of putting the coffee pot down, was surprised; annoyed; suddenly wore a worked-up pleased face. "Sorry," she said. "It's instant.

I know how you two loathe instant coffee." Two? *How* know? She ripped several sheets of paper towel from the roller over the sink and dried Tom's face; repeated the consideration, vitiating Tom's gratitude, by drying Flick's face and then his matted hair.

As soon as his face came out from behind the towel, Flick began telling the girls how super it was to be out in the storm. "It's like free-falling through space," he said. "You put out your arms and you just *fly*." And Flick demonstrated in the still cabin, groaning with pleasure.

In spite of Flick's rhapsodic grunts, Audrey remained prosey and skeptical. She asked Tom, "You really think we'd be better off up there, do you?"

"No question about it. Safer—and far more comfortable. You'll get used to it pretty soon. It's a noseful at first, don't be surprised. But you'll get onto it."

Tom saw that she believed him, and that Dottie, who appeared to be speechless with anxiety, hung on his words. The heat of the coffee and their acceptance of what he said worked together as a bracer he needed after the work at the mast. They made him think that he knew what he was doing.

"Mind getting your gear on? We'd really better get started."

Crump.

Tom waited for the girls to be ready; he wanted to be close to them when the gale first took their breaths away. He motioned Flick up first; it would be good to have him sawing away at *La Bohème*, or whatever he'd be putting on, when they arrived in the big windy gray opera house of the outdoors.

Audrey. Then Dottie.

Then he. He found the two girls crouching in the first

142

full shock down on the deck of the cockpit. Sure enough, Flick was standing over them, gesturing grandly and burping out great sea-lion roars. This wind was like a scandal, amazing and ruinous; yet for Tom, for the first time, the surprise and awe were diminished. He made flat-hands motions to the girls, meaning, "Stay right there. That's fine." And moving forward he clapped his hands at Flick, applauding his aria, and then beckoned him toward the mast.

Their next career—the chore might last forever and become a life work—would be raising the sail. Tom crouched by the mast wondering what to do first: unstop the sail from the boom, set the winch handle, uncleat the halyard the rest of the way? He positioned Flick to tail the halyard off the drum of the winch as he cranked.

Then came a new surprise: It was all easy. He unwound the halyard end from the sail, uncleated it all the way, and simply pulled the sail up. It shot up like a self-service elevator, only faster. It exploded as it rose into a shaking that caused a chattering series of reports as of a machinegun. Right through the waterproof hood, right through the acoustical opacity of the storm, *rat-a-tat-a-tat-a-tat-a-tat-a* . . .

He wrapped the halyard end around the drum, and set the handle, and cranked; Flick tugged at the tail. They got it cleated down taut, and that was that. That was all too soon that. He did not want what had to come now.

He motioned Flick aft, made hand signs meaning, "Wheel. Spin it to the right." So that, backing off the cut line, *Harmony* would throw herself onto the starboard tack: more room in the pond that way.

Then Tom crawled to the bow and wrapped his hands around the anchor line, and he clung to it for a moment as to an idea—that he would simply haul it in, pull up the anchor, and sail away on a cruise that couldn't miss being happy. Ha! That word for people with solid marriages, or maybe for people lacking imagination. The thought of cutting was suddenly excrutiatingly painful, as though active and reflexive modes were bound into one. There would be something self-wounding about this cut. The nasty thought of cost came in from an oblique angle here and made Tom furious—not at the notice of loss but at himself for having the thought. Fluke anchor, twenty feet of chain, more or less a hundred and twenty feet of three-quarter-inch nylon anchor line, still as white as cottage cheese in its newness. That rope was murder: forty-seven cents a foot. Times one hundred twenty. Let's see . . . Oh, yes, *and* the flywheel. *And* the dinghy already gone. *Harmony! Harmony!* There were, there had been, money problems in their lives. The basic chafe was the affectation of a scorn for money. The shabby values of materialism, all that. But when it had come right down to it, concerning their own kitchen, the value question had been which had more—Norge or Westinghouse or G.E. or Hotpoint or Whirlpool? He had a throttle-hold on the creamy white and slightly slippery nylon anchor line, as if he wanted to choke out of it the answer to the question: What of value am I about to lose? He had risen to his knees. He would pull the damned thing up. Sail away cruise. Happy.

But his self-directed right hand was reaching into the pocket of his waterproof, and out leaped the knife on its elastic lanyard. Beautiful, glistening stainless-steel object. Spike lying one way, its dirk-point safely couched between two flanges, and the big dorsal sailfin of the blade, with its dark thumbnail slot like a hair of a new moon on a northwind

144

night. It was a sea thing, all right; lying in his hand it looked like a snub-nosed, flattish fish.

He opened the blade—whetted to a wedge of vanished metal. He held it up so it cut the wind. He could have used it at the operating table: it would inquire its way through flesh rather than crudely cut.

He looked around. There was only one other boat left at anchor. Couldn't he just wait here, holding his knife at the ready? How fine to be the very last! The seas were a dirty green; foul sick froth out of some devil's washing machine was flying from wavetop to wavetop. They were now almost half way to the end of the long marina dock, so much had *Harmony* dragged. The rain seemed to be driving horizontally above the water, like the parallel lines that make fantasy out of the grimmest reality on a television tube. The wind pushed at his neck and shoulders. Wait. Couldn't he wait? To be the last and best?

Crump.

He rose to his knees and brought the cutting edge of his knife gently against the taut elastic artificial fibers. The wind made his surgeon's hand grossly waver. Could he wait at least for a lull? How would he move aft fast enough to take command?

How hard it was to cut! Here went umbilicus.

He pressed and drew the knife edge once. Razor edge! One strand of the full-stretched rope was three quarters severed; another short stroke and that strand broke with a loud crack and withdrew forward right through the chafing gear at the chock and down toward the house and the waves like an insidiously spiraling sea snake slithering into its element.

Now that the commitment had been made, Tom was

resolute, and *snick, snick, snick:* with three strokes and two loud reports, the remaining serpents leaped forward and away and down, and *Harmony* was on her own.

Tom saw the house in the water, like a huge, sluggish beast hardly knowing it was free, heave a shingled shoulder and slowly, soggily turn—but it was fifty feet away . . . It was a hundred feet away! Jesus!

Tom scrambled aft on the high side. *Harmony* had gone off surely enough on the starboard tack. The sail had not been trimmed, and it still was giving out its machinegun reports. She was falling broadside to the wind, and she heeled over hard; the tip of the boom was in the water. Would she falter and fill in these first moments? Flick's jaw was slack, and he was blinking at the stinging rain drops; he looked suddenly different. The crux of his opera seemed to have escaped him entirely.

Tom moved as fast as he could, crashed into the cockpit, hurting a hip, seized the main sheet, and with all his strength hauled at it, to trim the chattering sail. By God, it began to draw, and *Harmony* suddenly recovered a certain composure, as, shivering like a wet dog, she rose a bit, took a bite of the wind, and began to go with some purpose toward Indian Head Neck.

Elbowing Flick aside, Tom took the helm, standing, and at once he felt great pride in *Harmony*, for she was holding up and actually making something to windward. The waves in this protected place were enough to make the fat boat canter, and her bows caught the slapping tops and threw white spray that arched upward and whipped across the cockpit to bring a salt taste to Tom's lips. He leaned down once and turned on the ignition key and pressed the starter buttom; then after

146

some moments he bent down again and saw by the tachometer that the engine was running, and he threw the shift lever into forward gear and advanced the throttle.

Now! *Harmony* was under control, and his own mind was as profound and clear as a windless Arizona sky—antithesis of Esmé there and then. He felt a flood of exuberance, and he glanced down at the two girls, who had pulled themselves up from the cockpit deck and were sitting on the seats and gripping the coaming with both hands and often looking up at him. He was keeping balance by holding the coaming himself with his right hand, and he let go for a moment to hold his hand up and form a circle with his thumb and forefinger. Flick was throwing gestures to the wind and still crying out from time to time—or at least opening his mouth like a goldfish into enormous O's that should on another day have produced huge shouts—but his lips were blue; he was beginning to look like a child who had been swimming too long and didn't want to come out yet. Just once more, just one more time.

If they could come about from one tack to the other, head-to-wind, and providing that no vital gear gave way and that they did not run down a floating danger, there was no reason why they could not reach straight back and forth right here in the pond and not lose ground to leeward. The test on tacking would come very soon. The alternative? To turn tail-to-wind might capsize *Harmony* or take her mast out like a matchstick snapped between thumb and two fingers, for a jibe in such a wind as this was surely the most dangerous maneuver in all of seamanship. Tom realized with a sickening dive of his confidence that he had already passed the point of no return, for he could no longer simply bear off and run down the pond

147

and out the channel; if she failed now to come about head-to-wind, he could not avoid the possibly fatal trial of a jibe.

There remained, as he remembered the chart, six or seven hundred feet of good water in a cove in the shoals to the right of that black can. Better try to come about now, leaving some room to maneuver in case she could not make it. He pushed the throttle forward dangerously far, to get as much thrust as possible from the engine, and he put the helm all the way down, and in all the clatter and shivering of the storm he felt his heart leaping in his chest.

The prow moved smartly at first toward the teeth of the wind, but then, as the sail luffed, no longer pulling, and commencing again its racket of gunnery, and as *Harmony*'s generous cheeks presented themselves to the hurricane, the boat stopped with a kind of thud, so abruptly that Tom had a moment's fear that she had run aground on a mud bottom. But then he saw that she was being hurled off again onto the same tack as before.

He decided to try once more, running off this time to get up as much headway as possible. But it was the same story: She hit that wall of wind and simply bounced off. She would not go round.

There was nothing for it but to turn downwind and try to get *Harmony* around with her stern to the blow.

He would need extra arms—one man at the helm, one on the main sheet to try to help the sail to flip over with the least possible damage. He'd better put Flick on the wheel and fight the sheet himself; it would be a matter of sweet timing—a chance on the wrong split second to lose the palms of one's hands on the lay of the rope, to say nothing of toppling the mast.

148

He beckoned urgently to Flick, who was, however, so passionate in his celebrations of something he had obviously never experienced before—the naked, feral claws of man-killing weather—that it took him an eternity, a hundred feet of *Harmony's* scudding across the pond, to react. Then he lumbered to his feet with the happy stupid look of a souse hearing the high-pitched inner squeaks of nerveless ecstasy; he was really in a state.

Tom made a hand-swimming gesture: around, we're going around tail-to-wind. A gripping gesture: take helm. You. You take wheel. Me on sheet. Flip-flip: urgent. O.K., all set? Traffic cop stop gesture: hold it. Wait. Keep us on a broad reach.

The spit was coming close; the whole arm of land appeared to be moving, swinging like a huge club of earth in a nightmare of elements displaced and natural laws scandalously broken.

Then, with a hand to Flick: All right, swing. No! Less helm. Wide curve. Right! That's right!

Tom uncleated the sheet but kept a full turn around the cleat. The moment of danger would come when the boom would go hurtling across the boat; he would try to ease it over by trimming and then letting it slip fast but not too fast, with always a turn on the cleat. There was no way of knowing how much strength he would need beyond all that he had.

How *Harmony* scudded down the edge of the big curve!

Now to the unlikely task of gaining a little on the rope. Now. Marvelous new surprise: He heaved and got some. Now. It was coming in. That tiny sail was a wonder. Once again.

Crouching and squinting upwind Tom saw the crucial instant flying across the water at them like a manifestation of the shortness of life—it was a moment he thought he could actually see winging like the fastest of birds.

Here! Let the rope run!

Harmony dug in on her starboard bow as if she meant to go straight to the bottom and end this mad game men seemed to want to play. But the boom had gone over with a bump, not a splintering crash; the mast stood like the noble tree-bole it once had been. *Harmony* came up with a bounce and heeled hard on the port tack. She had jibed.

Tom saw at once, recovering the helm from Flick, who looked goggle-eyed with his own accomplishment, that *Harmony* had run so far down the pond in this maneuver that she would never be able to climb back upwind sailing across toward the pier again. The main issue was settled: He would have to take her out to sea. His wild joy at having pulled off the jibe, erupting from his chest, was choked down with a dry-mouthed effort to swallow. There was much bitter salt on his lips.

They recrossed the pond, not fetching the marina pier. He set Flick at the wheel once more, jibed again in good order, and eased *Harmony* off toward the channel at the bottom of the pond, and he found that he was filled, now that the wind was at his back, with a fathomless calm. He would not probe that calm. It was not easy for the others to look at him here, for to do so meant exposing their faces to the buckshot of the rain; for a few moments he was in a way alone. But then, almost at the same instant, as though they were all wired to each other by some contrivance of Flick's, those three seemed to realize that he was persisting down the gale, that he had given up so soon the effort to reach back and forth, and that he was going *out,* and they all turned, blinking and sputtering, and it was Audrey who raised an interrogatory hand pointing to the barely visible gap of the channel. Tom nodded. Yes, they were.

At this Flick raised two fists and pounded at the onslaught of wind. To Tom the gesture seemed an ambiguous display of rage-in-joy, of cruelty yet of a sense of sheer fun. A man might beat a drum with the same double energy. It came through that Flick had personified the storm; the storm was a shrew, and he intended to have his will of her. Some women had to be treated like alley cats. Poor Audrey, jilted so soon in favor of new proofs! Yet this sky-beating of Flick's was pathetic, too, because—Tom could not help exulting even now— Flick was condemned here on *Harmony* to a passive role. He was a passenger, really quite ignorant of the power of the sea, and he could not fight but could only watch the fight and hold on for life.

Audrey, on the same side of the cockpit with Flick, did not seem concerned with his tantrum. She was a woman, and she was not interested in abstract ideas, of mastery and participation, or of the durability of the male spirit; she was concerned with practicalities, and she reached out the snaphook of her safety belt beyond the coaming and tripped it onto the lifeline, and she made signals to Dottie, who was in a daze across from her, to do the same. More significantly, she reached forward and picked up the strap dangling from Flick's waist and snapped *his* harness to the lifeline; she seemed to know that he would never have done this for himself but that he would not restrain her from doing it for him. Tom, grateful for her alertness, attached his own.

Dottie seemed to be all of a heap—weakened by incredulity. When *Harmony* ducked and bobbed on a pair of seas

151

outrunning the hull, Dottie's head wagged as if it were afloat quite apart from her body, like a lobster-pot buoy. Yet when she understood Audrey's suggestive hand-flips, she reacted soundly and quickly and fastened herself; to her the passive state was home. Though bewitched, she could respond and do what had to be done.

Fat *Harmony* almost planed like a Dragon or a Sunfish! Tom bent down to see the dial of the Kenyon. Whee! She was spooning along at her maximum hull speed under that tough little kerchief of a sail: nearly ten knots. Tom had flown often in jets—six hundred miles an hour through the thin fluid of the pure blue stratosphere—but *this* speed on the angry green water, with the forefoot plowing out curving sheets of white urgency and the following seas almost pooping the stern and the rain flying and the stays whining, this was surely faster than any other swiftness on earth. Yet the thrill of it, close and real as it was, scarcely penetrated the core of stillness at the center of Tom's being. In a sense this calm was harder to face than the rain-pricked wind: a little sail, he was taking them out for a little sail as his unfaithful wife had said he would do. He was not at all afraid, but he was bathed, soaked, submerged in such profound doubt about his wisdom and indeed his sanity in doing what he was doing that he could only wonder at the calm. It must be the eye of his own personal storm.

And yes, how soon the pond was eaten up by that speed! The Coast Guard station was in sight to the left: the flagpole, the Stars and Stripes surprisingly left flying in the rain, and out to one side the two square hurricane-warning flags, red with black centers, one above the other, frantic at finding themselves out in what they were announcing. Too late to proclaim it! And the launching rails—succor, the shore people caring about mariners in peril on the deep. Tom hooked a knee over a spoke of the wheel and pulled back his wet left sleeve with his wet right hand and saw the time through the wet face of his watch: eight minutes to ten. Was that all? Three hours till Esmé's eye would pass overhead between here and Montauk?

Tom was overcome with a need to enter one piece of intelligence—*Passed CG station, 9:52 a.m., on way out*—in his log book. He was convinced he would never be able to carry that in his mind, and he felt it was an almost historic item. He leaned forward, tapped Audrey on the shoulder, and made hand motions commanding her to take the helm. She looked up at him in astonishment but at once reached out, unsnapped her belt and re-snapped it on the after side of one of the lifeline stanchions, and slid back into position to steer. Tom sliced a hand toward the center of the channel, between the two long white lips of breakers on the inner shores of the pond, and she nodded with a grave, rather childish look— acceptance of a too-heavy responsibility. Tom, feeling sorrow pouring into the calm place, tore himself away, piled down the ladder, sat at the table, got down the book, and opened it. No time for endpapers now.

What were the other data he had wanted to remember to record?

For a moment his mind was totally white, then he saw Audrey's face, a crease of concentration and willingness between her brows; and suddenly the blanked-out details came to him in a rush, and he jotted a series of telegrams to himself. And slammed the book shut and shelved it, recognizing that he was a fool to have come below to do this; and scrambled above.

They were already half way along the heavy jetty. He took the helm; patted Audrey's shoulder. She slid forward, adjusting her safety strap.

Ahead Tom saw an amphitheater of gloom so deep-vaulted, so dark, such a mare's nest of contending energies of air and water, that he suddenly wanted with a frenzy equal to that of the surface of the sea beyond the jetty—knowing that his yearning was hopelessly tardy—to turn back: *not to go out there*. The actuality of the jetty close at hand on the left, its huge jagged dynamite-sculptured stones glowing in the reflected light of myriad whitecaps, and the wet tubular reality of the channel buoys, black cans and red nun, their designating numbers ghostly white in the storm, past which marks *Harmony* now scooped in her headlong dash, and the evidence of the low land to the right, the pigtail of Indian Head, sandy, grassy, barren, anciently windswept and sea-swept yet still brownly there—the vivid clarity of these nearby sights of a stationary world made the distant view all the more appalling because so uniform. It was a huge arch of gloom in which there was no hope of seeing anything but wetness and motion. Nothing relieved the monotony of vague danger that lurked in motion. Clouds, rain, waves, darkness, all rushing into—what? Invisibility. A huge cone of uncertainty. The one element that rode all others, the dominating force of the seascape, the wind, could not be seen; but one could see what it was doing all too well. Tom realized that in erupting from pond to sea he was going to be moving as far as it had been to climb that morning from still cabin to hurricane abovedeck. He held himself tightly to meet this new shock.

At the same time he must think; he had only a hundred

yards in which to make a decision. His original plan had been to trim sails and turn northward at the outer can off the end of the breakwater, and to sail up along the lee shore of Indian Head, clinging near to land, not more than a hundred yards off the long beach. But now that he had found that he could control a jibe in waters that were not too disturbed, should he not instead jibe as close as he could to the end of the jetty and reach southward under the lee of the much higher main body of the island, where Beacon Hill and Monich Hill rose to two hundred feet; and where, besides, there would be six miles of lee shore compared with four of the less good shelter to the north? A kind of whining buzz at the edge of his mind told him that it made no difference; there was absolutely no point in making a choice. He kicked at the loose sheet lying in disorder at his feet, as if trying to boot that sense of futility out of the vicinity.

Audrey saw his kick, and at once she bent forward and began to coil the line. There was only time for one short blurt of inner response: If only she knew how much she helped him!

Fifty feet left. The trouble with going south would be that the wind would be shifting as the eye of the storm moved through, and *Harmony* would be sailing more and more into the teeth of the gale—and toward the center of chaos. But there was the danger, to the north, of the long reef running off the end of Sandy Point, and one would never be able to see the black bell that was three miles above the tip of the point; after his search of the chart in the cabin before the cutting, its forms were engraved so clearly on his mind—light green land, blue shallows, white depths, compass rose off Cow Cove, another off the mouth of the pond—that he could almost read off the hair-raising soundings along the North Reef: four feet, one foot, three feet, four feet, five feet, a long comb of the sea to catch at the keels of fools. Oh, no, he wouldn't let *Harmony* be tipped there.

The decision, as it came to him, was of a kind he did not like to make: almost on an impulse, and in fear of that hidden hazard. He liked to be more deliberate, to weigh and weigh and know he was right; but there was no time left.

He leaned forward and whacked Flick's knee, and he shouted at the top of his lungs, almost screeched, "Prepare to jibe!"

Flick sat there, his face turned back to the storm and to Tom, grinning in his stupor of auto-intoxication. Tom could tell that the wind had torn the shrieked words from his teeth like bits of dandelion fluff and had blown them out to sea, where they would fall barren.

Audrey was pushing at his side; Audrey wanted the helm; Audrey had understood. Had she read his lips—or his mind? That same inner blurt: If you only knew!

Tom jumped to the sheet and hand-flapped to her to put the yawl around. *Harmony* had begun to buck, and it was harder here to keep a purchase. Here went the boom. Bang! That was too rough; but at a glance Tom checked the stays and boom and machinegunning sail, and all the gear seemed to have held. He trimmed in the sail, and *Harmony* began to move.

When he relieved Audrey at the wheel he was horrified at the first glimpse to see how far offshore *Harmony* had blown in taking this turn. Was it half a mile? He wondered if the dread that had come over him of the universal bleakness out there away from land made his mind exaggerate the distance the yawl had fallen away from the beach.

Flick had stood up. He was turning this way and that, and the motions of his face suggested that he was singing loudly and (for Tom remembered other songs at other times) badly off key, though of course nothing could be heard, and he was making hugging motions, opening his arms and grasping at the wildness and embracing it, over and over again. Tom, who was seated now, trying to concentrate on getting *Harmony* driving, nevertheless gave a split second of his mind to wondering what Flick was singing. "O beautiful for spacious skies . . ." "Embraceable You" . . . That nice old one, "Stormy Weather"?

Audrey, bless her, was not in the market for serenades. She was coiling the main sheet again.

Only now, after the flurry of action died down, did the shock of being outside suddenly grip Tom. The irrevocability was what hurt the most, for this lay heavy on the back of the judgment he had made. He had been inside, where he could have beached *Harmony* in shallows, and now he was outside in this infinity of wet motion, and there was no such thing as deciding that he had made a mistake and that he should go back in. He looked down: Someone—could it be he?—was clutching the wheel with white-knuckled hands. He looked quickly away from those bloodless joints.

The modes out here were darkness and confusion. The water was a dull greenish gray, and off the tops of all the waves the wind knocked breakers that were themselves gray and foul. The seas, behaving like those of a furious tidal rip, were not inordinately tall, but they were steep and foam-tipped, and they seemed to come from every hand at once in spite of

157

the concerted drive of the wind in the one direction, and *Harmony* was thrown about without rhythm, with no steadiness of rise and fall. She pounded, shuddered, rolled, pitched, wallowed, and shook, heeling all the while under the wind, and her sail was now full and making her rush down a wet riffled hillock like a train of cars, and now luffed up, as the yawl's headway was killed by a frontal crash of hard water, so that the cloth rattled with one of the few distinguishable noises of the general storm-racket: that machinegunning. Every time the bow hit, a blanket of green rose to windward, and the air shredded it into stinging spray that flew flat across the boat along with the rain. She was moving. He could see the end of the jetty; they had traveled perhaps two hundred yards more or less southward since the jibe. She was moving. Whether she was holding up to the island it would have been hard yet to say. He glanced at the compass several times and found that she was heading on the average almost truly south—in toward the bulge of the land; but doubtless, with the pounding she was taking from both wind and air, she was being set down to leeward as she went.

Something struck Tom a sharp small blow on the shoulder. At first he could not see what it might have been, but it beat him again: a rope end, standing out horizontally from the top of the cabin trunk and flailing back and forth—the free end of the jib sheet which had jumped its coil. Surveying the boat Tom saw that the whole vessel was a battery of such whips—loose ends of all sorts of lines, standing straight out from their fastenings and licking at whatever might be down wind: two from the lashings of the mainsail, the outhaul on the main boom, the topping lift on the other face of the boom, and many others. He was being flogged by an invisible hand on *Harmony!*—the grim seaman's accounting of old tradition on sailing ships. The sight of all those whips stirred up the dregs of puritanism in Tom, and he was suddenly filled with a righteous anger, which was displaced from the storm and from the injustice and indignity of his position, and was now aimed at these reminders of unfair discipline of long ago. He tapped Audrey again—by now he had given up on Flick in his endless act of congratulating the wind—and urged her to the helm; then he began to climb here and there subduing the cruel ropes. He knew it was a mission of folly, but he could not help himself. His father had never punished him except with looks and words; but he thought of his father now as cruel—a tall, thin man in a carpenter's apron; he was a schoolteacher, not a carpenter, but had a hobby of woodworking, and Tom visualized him in a cellar room under a cone of electric light. He thought, as he crept forward, hooking his safety belt as he went, of the boatswain's mates on the square-sail frigates carrying ratline rope-end whips called colts coiled up in the straw crowns of their naval hats, and, conscious of the incongruity and on the edge of laughing at it, he imagined his father as one of those petty officers, with the colt coiled like a cobra on the top of his head.

The yawl was heaving under him, and Tom was aware that he was expending great amounts of energy on what amounted to a fool's labor of political liberalism; nevertheless, he secured every last one of those whips. Then he started carefully aft to take back the helm, his anger assuaged, his fear of the dark, endless world of the storm outside the harbor for some reason diminished.

He crept past Dottie on his way into the cockpit. She turned up her face and gave him all she could give him, which was a trusting smile. It seemed to him that her endurance would be inexhaustible, and in fact that mere endurance was somehow refreshing to Dottie. She was growing sweeter as the wind grew more harsh. Audrey looked cross; she seemed to be in a fury, yet Tom was aware how quietly responsive she had been, all along, to his seamanship. Maybe she was angry at the opera singer. Flick had made his point; his joy was getting boring, and in truth it was beginning to look trumped up.

Seated again at the wheel, Tom checked the bearing of the end of the jetty. *Harmony* was excelling. She was sailing; she was not falling away much from the land, if at all; she was, good ship, not going very fast in the miserable chop, and that meant it would take her a fair amount of time to go down the five or six sheltered miles.

Which caused Tom to remember that the engine was running, and at a high speed at that. They might need the motor badly later; better try her under her handkerchief alone and see how she would manage. Tom leaned down and switched off the ignition key. For the next few minutes he could feel no difference at all in her painful progress. Glorious little trysail!

Tom, settling to close care of his helmsmanship, thought how really odd had been that vivid photographic glimpse, a few moments ago, of his father, in the naval uniform of the middle of the nineteenth century, with the looped scourge in his hat, standing by the gratings near the mast in the place where ship's court was held. In school and college, and actually through medical school, Tom had bridled at his father's schoolteacherish droning about steadfastness, hope of a better world, loyalty, service to others, honor, kindness—as totally sentimental and obsolete; Tom had laid the foundation for this momentary snapshot of the thin man on the frigate deck by having thought for so long of his father as a nineteenth-century soul, one who rationalized self-service with mouthings of altruism and liberalism. Tom's father simply had no under-standing of how Korea and the bomb tests and the Calcutta famines and the white response to the Montgomery bus boy-cott and the exposure of Stalinism and (especially for Tom) the shock of his hero Camus dying in an automobile accident as if encapsulated within the full irony of his own writings—the downhillness of *everything* since the Korean war—how all this had made the generation of sons in this time mistrustful of slogans, sharply sensitive to cant and hypocrisy, suspicious of big and good words . . . Yet . . . Yet how that picture had burned itself in his mind just now, as he had fought those spontaneous whips of loose cordage! Father, Father! I didn't do it! Don't look at me like that! No! No!

Tom turned his eyes to the water to evade that piercing stare of the man who wanted his son to be a good boy. There was a queer phenomenon on the waves: Wherever the wind could get at any flattish surface of water it made a new pattern of tiny ripples of fantastic swiftness of phase, so that with tremendous speed small wavelets were being built on the backs of the bigger chop, and chop on waves, and waves on swells as they backlashed around from the open ocean. The generation and regeneration of roughness was—majestic. That word had a way of renewing itself in his mind.

And gripped by the majesty, looking briefly into the dark bowl of fury to leeward, Tom was suddenly aware of *Harmony's* isolation. They four were alone on the sea. No eye was watching. The Coast Guard would not know to come for them; futile entry in the log! They were alone in the storm with their private troubles. Tom thought of fighting his way onto the Lexington Avenue subway in the afternoon rush hour on a summer day. Numberless humanity, rancid and struggling for breath under the slow, dusty, wood-bladed rotary fans. How often, gripping the overhead handles, he had thought: There are too many people—that's what stirs up the impulse to violence, to riot, to war: mere crowding. Give me air! I'll kill for a lungful of air! . . . And here was air coming at a hundred miles an hour, in plentiful supply; of all humanity there was no one else anywhere. Just three other pairs of lungs besides his on the whole sea.

Those other three were glancing at him from time to time; each in his own style—Audrey irritable yet answering with alacrity his most obliquely suggested commands of abstract skipper to abstract crew, not as his wife but as a nautical hand, reacting even to gestures and motions that he had no idea implied demands or requests for action; Flick more subdued now, his solo tapering off, for he must have realized his inner resources of wildness were never going to rise even to the level of parody of those of Esmé; and Dottie, this Dottie who had worked up a sharp little quarrel earlier on this dangerous morning, seeming now to digest every horror and fright and make her own kind of carbohydrate of it—each looked around at the skipper now and again to read his face, as though it were a barometer of some sort, a dial of the pressure of their fate. Their looks—each with its own accent—were trusting and confident, and he found that he was gaining faith in himself. *Harmony* was plunging along; he had thought of things, and they had come this far. He reveled in his preparedness. What did they think of his prudence now, his cautiousness that showed in every tiny detail of the regime on *Harmony?* What did these three free spirits, who had expressed, whether they had consciously intended it or not, such contempt for his prudence that hot, still afternoon at Quicks Hole, think now of his trait of being careful? Their lives depended on it. They adored it. They looked at his face to scan it for readings of just that very thoroughness of mind. How grateful they were for the spoilsport now!

And just as they checked the dial of his face again and again, he came to realize that he was repeatedly checking the face of his watch, as though he could push the hands forward faster with the rays of his eyes. But those hands were incredibly sluggish. He wanted the worst to be over soon, but, it seemed, the swifter the wind, the slower the minutes. Eight minutes past ten. The eye was promised for one o'clock. He could get through three hours. Then the eye; he wouldn't even think of what lay beyond the eye. Three hours were nothing. Where had most mornings of his life flown to? Three hours?

But now he waited as long as he could, felt the tiredness in his shoulders from fighting the monstrous weather helm set up by that tiny sail, waited, alertly watching the oncoming seas to try to avoid combers hitting broadside and cross-chop slamming the bows, and waited and waited, checking gear all over the boat with a roving eye, and waited, giving his boatmates, with whom he was in such deep personal trouble, encouraging looks as the man who thought of details and would watch out for them, and waited as long more as he could, and waited still longer, and finally looked at his wrist again. Three massive minutes had managed to struggle away. It was eleven past ten.

He could not let himself think any more about space and

163

time; with a tremendous effort of mind he tuned himself in on *Harmony*. Details. Saving details of his yawl. If he could concentrate all his energies on keeping his boat intact—forget human lives, which were in shambles anyway, and think only and always of *Harmony*—perhaps he could get through the immeasurably empty and ominous storm-area and the gaping eternity this side of the eye. Would the main sheet blocks tear their straps out of the boom? Would the splice of the halyard, wire to rope, hold out? Would the rudder gear take the strain? But br-r-r-r. No! This was no way! To catalogue the details that might go wrong, and about which he would be able to do absolutely nothing? No, no. For details to have the capacity to rescue one from fear, they must be manageable. He could steer, that was about all. Be alert, steer. So what could he do but count on *Harmony*? He did, he did! Look at her rise to that attack of water! Listen to that rapid firing of the tough cloth—and feel her tremor under it! *Harmony!* Beautiful old tub!

Sick boat. She was diseased. Remembrance of the flaw hit Tom and intermittently struck him again and again, just as the rope end had kept at him, distracting him as he tried to keep his mind on his helmsmanship. Why had he not hauled *Harmony* out this summer to take up on the big keel bolt? He went back and back to try to trace what had kept him from doing as he had done every year since his discovery of the soft-fibered place in that lazily chosen timber; the answer dodged away from him. He thought he might have been able to trace the source of a decision affirmatively taken, but this was just a not-doing, a putting-off, an accumulation of days when he simply forgot, or omitted, or inwardly refused, to do what should have been done. How could you get at the root of procrastination? He tried to remember whether there had been occasions—in the city, at the office, speculating over a patient's dysfunctional liver; in a taxi, stuck in traffic, enjoying escapist musings about the free play of movement on the sea—when he had suddenly remembered the flaw and said to himself, "I've got to haul her out; I really must; it's overdue; I'll have it done next week." But search as he would, he could find no trace this summer of such determination. At the same time he had kept *Harmony* wonderfully spruce in other ways. He had had refinements and improvements much on his mind. He had rigged new shock cord for quick-furling of the mainsail, he had installed snatch blocks for easier cleating of the sheets, he had varnished and polished and always carried scraps of boat lists in the pockets of his business suits.

Audrey turned her head and looked at him—Audrey, in whom he had not confided about that small fault of spongy wood: after all, it was a trifling matter. *Harmony* was thirty-two feet long, and this place in her guts could not have been more than four inches from edge to edge; perhaps less. Exceedingly small in the whole picture. If he had plagued her about every detail of *Harmony*'s existence, she would have screamed with boredom. Sailing was *his* obsession; she had been willing to indulge it—up to a point. The flaw had somehow always seemed, until yesterday and today, something he should not bother her with.

But now, as she faced around and drank at his expression, he had an overpowering wish to tell her about it at last, before it might be worse than a shame not to have told her, and he actually shouted into the screaming gale, "*Harmony* has a bad place down around the forward keel bolt. It's dry rot! I said DRY ROT! I never told you. I'm sorry, darling. Audrey, darling. I'm sorry. *Keel bolt! Dry rot!*" He knew, in the very act of getting this off his chest at last, that she could not hear a blessed word.

Audrey let go the coaming for a moment and made a gesture, palms of the hands turned up to the sky, shoulders lifted, clearly meaning, "I haven't a clue what you're saying. What do you want of me now?"

Tom beckoned. Helm. Take the helm.

Tom wanted to make an inquiry of *Harmony* by pumping. What was the working of the seams by these vicious seas doing to her? What was this pounding doing to that place?

Dottie was sitting over the pump. Her big eyes were watching everything; she had seen Tom mouthing his confession into the wind, she had seen the beckoning motion, she had seen Audrey relieve Tom. Tom wondered briefly whether Dottie could lip read, whether she was more acute than Audrey in certain areas of intuition. But now when he moved toward her she looked stricken, as if she had inadvertently done something wrong to the depths of wrongness, and she in her turn let go of the coaming and put up her hands in a pathetic gesture of trying to stop his probably punitive approach toward her. He could not stand in the wind on the lurching cockpit deck; he thumped down heavily beside her and began to make motions to her to move—please move aft—want to pump—you move—change places. But it appeared that Dottie was used to that seat; it must have become her safe place. She turned her back on Tom and grasped the coaming again. Tom put his hands on her shoulders, and he felt through the waterproofs the rigidness of Dottie's arms. She would not budge. Then he thought to unsnap her safety belt and refasten it abaft the lifeline stanchion—just as Au-

166

drey did with her own each time she moved back to the wheel. Then he rose and, keeping one hand on the coaming behind her back, placed the other in front of her, also on the coaming, and he leaned over her that way, seeming to keep her safe in his arms, and jerking his head toward the after part of the seat when she looked up wide-eyed at him, and signalling with his eyes that he wanted her to move, and pressing her with his left arm, he felt her give a little, and he smiled to encourage her, though he felt that the wind was constantly molding and reshaping his face into clownish grimaces, but apparently the smile did show, and gradually she slid aft, little by little, moving her tight-clutching hands one by one and inch by inch along the coaming. How shallow her sweet looks and trusting smiles, which had seemed so sincere, must have been! Finally she was settled out of the way.

He went at the lid of the seat and scrabbled for the pump handle like a man dying for a drink and lunging at the pump of a suddenly discovered sweetwater well. Oh, how he thirsted to *know!* He barked a knuckle and saw blood but felt nothing. Pumping was not easy; *Harmony* lurched when he wanted her to buck into a downstroke, and she threw him sidewise when he tried to draw the piston straight up. But soon the pump primed itself and he felt the weight of suction in the pulls. He began to count. A marvelous serenity came over him . . . nineteen, twenty, twenty-one, twenty-two . . . Arithmetic must surely have been man's earliest tranquilizer . . . twenty-eight, twenty-nine—what? air in the cylinder?—thirty, thirty-one . . . Yes! That was all! Nothing but foam! So little water in the bilges!

Tom let the seat cover slam down and he turned and threw his arms around Dottie. Her stiffness slackened at once,

167

and she eased into his embrace. But he was not hugging her! He was hugging *Harmony!* He loved his yawl just then more, he thought, than he had loved anything or anyone in his whole life. How brave and sturdy she was! And how loyal to him! She would cover up his negligence. No one—not Audrey even though he had roared it at her at the height of the storm—would ever know.

But the memory of his confession made him think, in the moment of turning toward the wheel with a heart leaping with relief and joy, and in the act of patting Audrey on the shoulder to say he would take her place—made him think of her unfaithfulness, of his predicament within and beyond the storm; and that same heart of his suddenly felt like a bag of damp sand lodged in his chest. This letdown heralded the return of anger. Flick sat there looking drunk. His lips were bluish now, and for some reason he appeared smaller than usual, as if all his gestures and bellowing had deflated him, and his bigness had merely been gusto. Tom had a moment's thought, which he recognized at once as irrational—but somehow this unceasing shrieking wind made irrationality more accessible and admissible than usual—that this man who refused to wear waterproofs or life preserver was in league with the hurricane. He had been shouting something to Esmé all morning. What had it been?

Dottie was leaning over the coaming to leeward. She was throwing up.

It was getting rougher all the time—there was no doubt of that—perhaps because *Harmony* was moving down the coast and more and more slop was curving round Southwest Point, or perhaps because the first seas of the shifted winds beyond the eye, outrunning the storm as waves could do, were coming in from the south off the open ocean, or perhaps because there was a great rip of tidal currents here, or perhaps all three. *Harmony* was acting like a wild Brahma bull just out of the rodeo chutes. Was she trying to throw Flick off her back? A moment would come when she would rush up a wave front and simply keep going, until half her bare flanks were raised up into the sky. Could the wind pick her up by the belly and flip her over on her back? No! Eight tons? Eight tons of Yankee workmanship, all of it sound as a silver dollar—save for that one lousy piece of pinchpenny lumber? Even this wind couldn't make *Harmony* fly. But when she shot up like that, naked in mid-air to the hips, and hung for a moment on the lip of a wave, it really did seem as if she might become wholly disconnected with the affairs of this earth. But then she came back down—and with what a thump! And out from the cheeks went two curving planes of smooth green shot silk, which disintegrated forthwith into a million driven drops of brine.

The inimical waves were coming at her from every direction. To think of the seas as confused might no longer be accurate; there seemed a plan, a deliberate malice, in the unpatterned turbulence of this water. Esmé the bitch knew what she was doing. The moment *Harmony* leaned to that little trysail's work, a counterwave, driving with macabre ferocity against a ninety-knot wind, would heave up under her leeward chines and tip her right into the teeth of the hurricane, so that the trysail would go dead, rattle, shiver the boat along her whole length, and then, on another rise from another quarter, the sail would pop full of air and begin to draw again, and then still another contrary surge would knock *Harmony* flat to leeward till Dottie's vomit would be flushed clean off the deck outside the coaming.

Poor seasick Dottie! Tom realized that he had not guided her back to her safe place; that had been thoughtless of him. Was she going to be totally helpless from now on?

Tend your wheel. Mind your sailing. Don't think about these people. You're alone in the world, and you had better accommodate yourself to loneliness. No better time than during this endless aeon before the eye comes.

So Tom spun the wheel, trying to guide *Harmony* through a maze. She had, in spite of the methodical obstruction of the waves, a goodly amount of steerageway, and when he turned the wheel something happened. Most of the time, when the sail was full, he felt in the spokes the influence of a powerful windward helm. Was he exhausted? He did not know. He knew that he was working hard, and that his shoulders hurt when he thought about them. The wind was at a new height of frenzy.

He decided to try laying-to in order to rest awhile, the age-old recourse of weary sailors in violent storms in the open sea—lashing the helm slightly to leeward and trimming the sail so that without his steering at all, *Harmony* would settle into a perpetual cycle of heading up into the wind, stopping, going backwards till the lashed rudder, scooping in her rearward motion, made her bow fall off, then, as the trysail would catch the wind again, sailing forward and rounding up into the teeth of it once more; and repeating the whole process without his having to exert a finger-muscle on the wheel. He was just about to raise himself off the lazaret lid to get at a pair of looped lines with which to tie down the wheel, and his mind was so set on this plan of action that all else had gone out of it, when there came an explosion.

There had been machinegun fire before; this was a cannon blast. A violent detonation.

Tom, in the act of rising when the noise came, shot all the way erect and was promptly hurled forward across the wheel—the engine had somehow blown up, and he was being upended by the deck's eruption beneath him as it was driven up in splinters by the blast. His ribs hurt, and as he sprawled there with his face not far from the cockpit deck he could see that its planks were intact, the caulking compound undisturbed. Not the deck. Not the engine. A lurching sea must have dropped him this way. He pushed himself back up and sat down hard behind the wheel. The first thing he saw was that all three of his crew were turned inward in the cockpit toward him. Their faces urgently asked him the question to which he did not know the answer. Their trust this time was ill-founded.

Then he saw. The trysail had blown out. It had disintegrated to shreds. It hung from the track in a thousand ribbons and tabs and flying threads. The heavy synthetic cloth would not tear readily along the weave like cotton duck, and it had simply burst with that dynamite roar. There was a fluttering like that of a congestion of panic-stricken terns around the mast. Now hundreds of tiny scraps of the sail were beginning to fly out away from the mast, still attached, pulling and unknitting the strong threads of the fabric and flying like uncontrollable kites straight out from the mast and away from the hull.

For the benefit of the three faces, still fastened in his direction, Tom gestured. There. Look. That's what it is.

The heads turned on automatic swivels; the eyes looked; the heads turned back again, as if on a single set of cam gears.

Such trust. They wanted to know what he was going to do now.

So did he.

He saw at once what value the trysail had had. *Harmony* had, in instants after the explosion, become a dead thing on the water, and now the wind and waves had her completely at their mercy. One huge forehead of water with blown foam for a head of hair butted her hard and threw her into the dreaded helpless position of small boats in bad weather: she was broached, broadside to the wind, her port flank exposed to the raging air, neither heading into it nor running away from it, the most apt attitude for a capsizing. She heeled over in the wind under bare sticks, and waves began to break on her high port side, and green water roared along the decks, and minute stinging drops of spray flinging themselves over the coaming turned out in aggregate to have been many gallons of salt water, which only slowly drained from the scuppers of the self-bailing cockpit. Within a short time water was sloshing around Tom's ankles.

His first thought, because of *Harmony's* broaching, was to heave to under a sea anchor, a tough canvas cone whose drag would at least hold the yawl's head into the wind and keep her out of this danger of swamping. Oh, yes, he had one, and with a heightened clarity of mind he could place it exactly: It was stored in what he called the canvas locker, at the after end of the cabin on the starboard side, under the breadbox, a deep cavern where he kept the hood for the forward hatch, the bosun's chair, the canvas bucket, the lead line, and many odds and ends not often needed but needed badly when they were. Not once used, the sea anchor lay, as the trysail had, at the foot of its heap.

But then, thinking it through, he knew he would never in this storm-world be able to rig that big cloth cone, which would rip itself out of his clutches and take off in the air like a spinnaker; he'd never get it overboard from that prancing foredeck in such peremptory wind. There simply was no chance of it.

The unclothed boom was thrashing viciously back and forth. It would be too risky to try to lift the rack of the gallows and fight the boom down onto it. He uncleated the main sheet and strapped it down as tight as he could and cleated it again, at a high cost of time in danger.

Then—so tardily!—it hit him: Steerageway. He must get her out of this helpless wallowing before she went over and down.

His big brain wasn't as crystal clear as he had thought, by a long shot, because he knew he should have dived for the ignition key at the very moment of the loud noise. He did now. With a trembling hand he set the throttle and spark and pressed the starter button, and he kept his eye on the tachometer.

Lovely engine! Off it went at the very first contact.

He threw it into forward gear and pushed it to two thousand r.p.m.'s and put the helm down. And yes. Slowly. Nothing like what that absurd ten-foot sail had been able to do. But yes. Up she moved toward the wind and out of that particular kind of unsafeness.

Patches and ribbons and tag ends of the small sail were still fluttering along the bolt rope against the mast, little flags of Dacron to taunt the storm. But now his motor was holding her up. The faces were turned toward him; they followed his moves like radar-tracking aerials. The motor was doing well.

He must reassure them. He chose to nod—curious dignified gesture of his hooded head, signifying a satisfactory state of affairs but promising nothing. He had the engine revved up too fast, he must throttle it down before the whole block overheated. At fifteen hundred—a taxing rate itself—the ticker kept *Harmony* out of the worst gutters of danger.

Now to think ahead. He could turn—not head-to-wind but transom-to-wind, a kind of dry jibe—and keep as close under the lee of the island as possible, going back northward. There the big bulk of it still was—half a mile away?—three quarters of a mile? *Harmony* was probably not holding up quite so firmly as she had been under sail, and it was likely that she would gradually slip to leeward away from the land. But the protected water, though turbulent, was a known condition; if nothing went wrong *Harmony* could survive in it.

What time was it? Tom nonchalantly lifted his arm and let the hurricane push up his sleeve so he could look at his watch. Might as well let the damnable horror work for him. Eleven sixteen! Marvelous adversity! It had ripped all those tough-textured minutes away like scraps of the sail. Two hours, or less, till the eye.

And with that remembrance of the eye of the storm Tom knew he would have to sail out into the open ocean.

The eye. After the eye the wind would come in, probably harder than ever, from a new direction—and since the eye would be passing close by them, the new direction would be almost precisely opposite to its present one, for the eye was the gimlet center of a counter-clockwise vortex of winds; and instead of being under the shelter of Block Island then, *Harmony* would be in close peril of being driven down onto the land; there were rocks all along this shore. He could not turn north again. The motor might not take them clear of Sandy Point at the northern tip and clear of that keel trap of a reef north of that, in two hours. Indeed, he had no way of knowing how far south they had come up to now, and whether there was enough time to get away from those rocks before the eye arrived and, after the eye, the new onshore hurricane winds. There was nothing to do but head for the open ocean.

Having decided, Tom felt, once again, an unsureness that had all the discomfort of a surge of guilt. The lives behind the three pale ovals facing him depended on his judgment. Was what he intended to do really wise and right? Like the sea around him he had been confused in these last minutes—should have started the engine right away after the sail blew out, should not have toyed all that time with the fantasy of setting the sea anchor, should not have grappled all that more time with the slatting boom. If he was confused in small things, what of the fatal ones? Should he not have gone north in the first place? What had their "little sail" become, anyway?

Flick's lips were the green of scuppernong grapes, his skin was white as a table cloth. The man was standing up. Was he going to sing now? There was a look of astonishment on that discolored face. He opened his mouth and, standing straight up, vomited into the wind. The stuff—Flick's interior color was vivid enough—blew back into the cockpit.

Tom put the wheel over in sheer disgust and headed out to sea.

Escape and confrontation. When one said, "getting away from this world" by going sailing, what did one mean? What world was there, what world had there ever been, besides this one, with foam at its lips and a single evil eye that took forever to look at one? The storm was the true world. Camus' shade of existentialism had seemed the only viable set of thoughts for Tom in college and medical school; *The Rebel* had been the bible then. Somehow the man whose eyes had been sharpened by the sand-edged sunlight of Algeria, and who had had the guts to fight Hitler in the French underground, seemed to be able to see after the war precisely the absurdities that one felt most galling in the years of America's catching up with Europe in disenchantment and disgust. But now: Now all *that* was absurd. All that had been a miserable blindness and affectation of pretended existence. What one spoke of as "this world"—the city; the office; people with putrescent livers and distended pocketbooks; himself going down Madison to the Westbury for a lunch of lobster bisque and chef's salad and a nice little Riesling—"this world" was only a shadow behind the reality of a vicious and ceaseless wind blowing on a sickly sea. "This world" was the fugitive memory of a rather bad dream. He thought of what he had said to Flick that first evening in Edgartown about the illusion of fighting nature that you could get on a sailboat, when a line squall hit you. It was over soon; it was only an illusion of dealing with forces. What nonsense all that was! Illusion? *That* had been the imaginary existence—sipping drinks in a fat unyacht on a mooring in Edgartown harbor; this fight, to the death, was the reality of life. Out to sea! Take her out from under the lee of the land! Somewhere—perhaps under the eye of the storm—one might find the dead center of reality, the self. Look at her go! Whee!

He was no longer trying to fight her up into the wind. In order to get clear of the base of the island he was driving

Harmony off in a more southwesterly direction, keeping her head up just enough so as not to broach again and taking the steeper and steeper down-wind waves on the port bow, climbing, perching at the crests, then charging down, moving better now all the time. The wind kept the masts canted and gave the whole boat a semblance of the stability of a close reach under sail. The engine marched; Tom's one lingering fear was that in the midst of these violent motions some sea-water might slosh past the traps of the exhaust and go steaming back up into the works. He must not dwell on that thought. She was going well; he should take each wave as it came and be thankful for surmounting it, if he did.

Up there the land was dim in rain and spray, and at times Tom thought the intermittent glimpses he was having of a shadowy bulk of solid earth were imaginary; that elusive shape was not solid at all, but was just a cloudbank, a thickening of the fluid of gloom that stretched out to the limits of sight in every direction. Had *Harmony* fallen so far away from the shore that it could no longer be seen? Had they moved out from under the lee? Not yet, to judge by the seas. But . . . but had there ever been a Block Island? Had there ever been dirt, rocks, grass, bayberry bushes clinging to the ground under a brilliant sun?

Two of the three faces kept turning towards him. Flick, in his vomit-and-rain-soaked shirt and with his hair spray-plastered to his skull, had sat down after being seasick on the starboard side, over the pump, in what had been Dottie's safe place, and he was looking steadily away from the wind into the darkness off to the west. The girls kept checking in with the skipper. They must have sensed a new direction, for *Harmony* was not laboring now as she had been; but Tom did not want to signal to them that they were headed out for the ocean. Let them deduce. Let them guess.

Starting the descent of one long wave in a rush Tom was aware of a vibration which half way down the slope presented itself as a deep thrumming. He could not be sure whether he heard it or felt it. It seemed to be a sound. It stopped as they climbed the next sea and did not sound again until several rises later when *Harmony* plunged down another particularly long and precipitous swell. It was a beautiful deep humming harmonic sound. Something about the engine—a bearing at play? The wind in the rigging? Was it a song of the shrouds and stays and halyards? Had *Harmony* become a huge Aeolian harp? No, this was no such light music as that. This had a resonance, a deep-chested sound, as if from beneath, as though the hull were the chamber of a monstrous cello. It came only on the swift, planing dives. It was a lovely sound—if it was in fact a sound rather than a feeling. Tom heard it or felt it when it came and enjoyed it as a diversion in this soaked chaos. It made him think of myths and mysteries of the sea—of Odysseus with a god's gift of storm winds trapped in leather bags and tied with a shining silver wire, of Argonauts pulling at fifty oars, of Poseidon's voice, of mermaids and sailors' heartbreak, of Jonah in the cavern of arching ribs, of sirens on ship-killing rocks—and these relieved his mind for a short while of its awe, which was worse than fear. Lovely sound, *basso profundo*. "Down at the bottom of the sea" . . . He thought it weird and magical.

But before long even this music of his boat communing with the deeps passed into the general noise of the storm and became commonplace, and there was nothing left to Tom but the hard work of steering, and monotony, and a sense of being all mixed up in time, as one is after a trans-Atlantic flight on a jet, and a bone-weariness that could not be admitted even to himself, to say nothing of the awareness, which he had brought into the storm, of being alone, all alone. He steered the yawl. He dared not look at his watch for fear it might be going backwards. Was he sailing into the past? Would that make things better?

Now at last, within a short span that would have been hard to measure in minutes or miles, a sea-change took place so vast and radical that Tom knew he was, all over again, for the *n*th time on this one day, suffering the shock of birth from a safe and protected place into an outer world of more profound truth. If there had ever been a Block Island, *Harmony* was now moving out from under its lee. There was nothing essentially new outside; it was simply that having lost a sense of time one now felt that the sense of scale was also going out of whack. *Harmony* was shrinking. Tom could not bear to think of waves as big as these were getting; he preferred to think of his own diminution.

They were outside in the realms of hugeness now, no question about it. He decided to try going down wind. Perhaps that would be easier than fighting his way up these mountains of wet wrath. Running more with the waves would carry *Harmony* away from the island; he would keep edging out to sea. They would be going down where Flick kept staring. Tom signalled with a hand to the two exposed faces: a turn. Audrey smiled. Tom realized it was not the first time she had smiled. She had smiled quite often when she had caught his eyes. But what was the meaning of her smiling now when with a turning fish-swim of a hand motion he announced the coming change of course? Was she encouraging him, or was she smiling because she had realized all along that he was out of his mind? Didn't she even know that he was alone on the sea? What business had she to smile at him any more?

At first Tom eased the wheel and then he spun it fast as he came to see that he must swing *Harmony* as quickly as possible in order to avoid her being broached and swamped in *these* waves. There!

My God! Look at her go now with both wind and sea following, and hear her making that deep thrumming all the way! The girls, turning to him, had suddenly put on roller-coaster faces. They were opening their mouths—squealing, no doubt. Flick? Still staring off to starboard. Did he know he was looking in a new direction?

Except for the great relief of having the wind out of his face, it was harder for Tom this way, not easier. Everything was headlong and too swift. Fleeing down the enormous waves that were themselves in flight, *Harmony* tucked down her fat bow and lifted her duck-bottom stern so high that the rudder kept almost no bite at all, and when she reached the trough she would nose in and heave her whole white torso to one side or the other without regard for the skipper's wishes, and this sudden wallowing skid would make her roll onto her beam ends and ship green water even over her high coaming (Flick sat there impassively as water scooped into his lap; the girls held on with straight arms, ducking their heads, looking at Tom); and then she would make the slower way up the steep slopes, hanging, the wave careening along too fast to be easily mounted, and at last she would reach the crest, where a constantly self-renewing breaker boiled along, and she would veer wildly in that froth as if in the rapids of a river, out of control, then down she would start to schuss again, with that towering overcurve of the breaker threatening to pounce on her from astern, and down she would rush, burrowing her nose, down, down, toward that dizzying lurch at the bottom.

There on a wavetop was Audrey smiling. Tom did not expect any more to live, and Audrey was giving him a big smile. Was this some abstract force of womanhood showing itself, a mother instinct more powerful even than chaos, and having not much really to do with its object; the ultimate feminine self-love in the encouraging curve of those lips? She was not his, but she wanted, even here, to make him hers. To possess him by taking care of him. As though by her smile she was conning him *and* his toy boat through the most precipitous perils . . . And down, down the sailboat plunged.

Tom was sharply conscious of two dangers—not that he feared them, exactly, for out here all that adrenalin could do for a man was being done, and all emotions were being put, like all muscles, to work: the danger of being pooped from astern by one of those rollers breaking along the tops, and the danger of wallowing over so far in one of the troughs as to backfill the exhaust right over its looping water trap and thus to kill the engine.

He thought of trailing a rope from the stern; he had often read about the miraculous effect on following combers of such a tiny thing as a long length of line. But he did not see how he could spare the time or strength—for he was alone now, alone with this storm and that smile—strength both to hold with one hand to the wheel, which despite the evident loss of control by the rudder tugged this way and that with astonishing ferocity, and with the other hand to fetch a line from the lazuret behind him and feed it out astern; too many problems of strength and balance. And in time he observed that in any case each breaker held its place at the top of the wave, and that the great structure of the wave itself never came toppling down.

What had happened to the proportion of things? How insignificant *Harmony* had become, what a gnat—or louse— Tom was now! Did he think that Audrey and Flick had made him feel small the afternoon before, when he had tapped that look of theirs? Now he was literally next-to-nothing; his heart was no bigger than the tiniest grain of sand, and worth no more. How gross the seascape was! The spray from those breakers astern, when she was half way down a wave, seemed to be leaping over the spreaders more than half way up the mainmast, and when *Harmony* fell into the out-of-control squirming of her consternation at the foot of one of those troughs and Tom looked up and around, he found her in a bowl of raging water, an amphitheater with steepest galleries, the topmost of which seemed to tower over the windvane at the head of the mast, which he knew to be thirty-eight feet high, and again when, a few seconds later, she trembled at a crest in the froth of a breaker reaching up her flanks with its willful steel fingers deceitfully camouflaged by millions of soft white bubbles, she seemed to be on a pinnacle, an Alp of water capped with snow white, commanding a peak's panorama if one could overcome his vertigo and look, and yet again, when she started the headlong descent of that mountain and Tom looked ahead and downward, he half expected the sea to part down there at the bottom, to open up all the way down to sand and rocks bearded with glistening kelp and barnacled shells and fishes flapping and gasping on dry land and green lobsters scrambling in terror across the open place seeking the cover of the salt sea. But Tom had begun to distrust his eyes;

the borderline between seeming and being was growing vague. That smile of Audrey's seemed as vast as the gap between two of these hurricane-built seas. Did he exaggerate those waves, that indulgent molding of her lips—or, thinking of himself, of his own heart, did he minimize, cut himself down too far? Time was shot to hell—was space going, too, especially the space filled by the self? His loss of Audrey was beyond belief; was he losing his perception of heights and depths, and of how far it was from wavetop to wavetop, or from fingertip to fingertip, heartbeat to heartbeat? Was he seeing and feeling things all wrong? Had he really lost his wife? Or even his life, in the terms in which he had recognized existence before seeing these seas and that smile? Or his mind? His mind?

Now came an event to test his perceptions. Near the top of one of these gigantic waves a smaller wave climbing the bigger one's back came charging, with sudden fury, at *Harmony*, and it slapped her with the brute strength that water possesses in more abundance than any other element, even fire, and *Harmony* jumped suddenly, bucking so hard in pain and annoyance that the life ring, a canvas-sheathed cork doughnut with the name of the yawl painted on it in blue block letters, burst its marlin lashings and leaped right out of its cloth cradle slung between the mizzen shrouds quite close to where Tom sat, and flipped overboard into the sea. It flashed astern, yanking after it the coiled lifeline that one hoped would be long enough in an emergency—and snaked it clean away. The ring was gone. Tom saw it go. But he was able to tell himself that nothing more than an idea had fallen overboard. A life ring would be meaningless in this water— and that was the very essence of the trouble out here. All the usual meanings of objects, of words, which could no longer be heard anyway, of persons, who could no longer be reached, except perhaps by smiling, of relationships between persons and objects and, alas, between persons and persons—all the usual meanings were distorted here. The apparent distortions of time and of scale had made all that should seem familiar seem, to the contrary, unreal, senseless, broken down, moribund, totally gone to pieces.

At the crest of a wave Tom had a vision of his telling a lie to Audrey. This had happened; or at least he believed it had happened. It had been such a stupid, bizarre, pointless, ridiculous lie. He had come home late. He had in fact been at the hospital; a man named Smallens, who, knowing he should not, had eaten in a restaurant in Jersey some clams that must have had their beds in a boardinghouse of ordure at the gate of a suburban sewer, because the man's liver at once became an inferno, had detained him with endless arguments—on top of everything else the man was a lawyer—about the treatment Tom had prescribed for him. This had put Tom in a crazy mood, and when he got home to a spoiled supper and four tight guests he told Audrey that he had had to have a long consultation with a lawyer because some nutty girl whom he had examined several months before in the presence of Miss Slattery had now slapped a paternity suit on him, alleging that he had, as she put it in her complaint, "molested her" on the examining table. What ever made him tell such a story was beyond him at the time—unless it had to do with some suppressed impulses with respect to female patients which he had never clearly admitted to himself; he had had to go through weeks of subsequent elaborations of the basic lie—settling the mess out of court, keeping the scandal from getting in the papers, steadying the nerves of the lawyer who was overly fearful for Dr. Medlar's reputation. He saw himself now, beckoning Audrey out of the living room and along the hall to the bedroom, whispering the story to her so the guests would not hear it—and now in the hurricane he was suddenly caught by a grotesque gap in the memory. He could not remember whether the Hamdens were guests that evening. Maybe—he recalled Dottie lying in her bikini on the sun-heated cushions, and how close he had come to a reckless theft—the lie had been the truth. It was he who had been unfaithful to Audrey, not the other way around . . . Down *Harmony* plunged on a dizzy descent.

The whole world had become one great eye-fooler, and suddenly a large number of things—opposites that had dissolved into each other, paradoxes, lies that were truths, troughs that were crests, wests that were easts—struck him as funny, and he began to laugh. What was humor but a sense of the incongruous, and what was this storm at play with *Harmony* but a counter-clockwise turmoil of incongruities? He threw back his head and roared at the big joke of Esmé and what it was doing to his beliefs and perceptions; the howler of Dottie and Flick and Audrey and the self, lovers and betrayers, out for a happy cruise in this storm. It was rich! Tom's ribs began to ache with the joy of the joke.

But then he saw Audrey looking at him. It was clear that she could not hear his guffaws, for he could not even hear them himself in the crash of rain on his hood and the rush of the breakers and the moaning of the rigging and that baritone thrumming from down in the caverns of the sea, but she could see all too well the eruptions of the laughter at his mouth; and she looked horrified. Her smile had been quick-frozen, and her eyes were full of suspicion. It was as if she, too, had suddenly

185

come to realize that the paternity-suit lie was an everlasting truth.

Which brought them, on a theme of lack of faith, around to Flick—and for Tom this intensified the joke. Flick was a lump. Flick just sat there and stared off to whatever offered itself as being the view to starboard. Dottie reached up and caressed the hair out of his eyes, and the sight of this gesture thawed the eternal smile on Audrey's lips; yes, the women would take care of him. It had turned out that this man who celebrated communication in all its most sophisticated forms had fallen into a profound silence, where he appeared to be utterly unreachable. All that waving of his arms, all that shouting and singing, which had looked so much like the ecstasy of a man throwing himself at life, taking delight in the tests of manhood—all that had proved to be some kind of ceremony of removal. It had been addressed to no one, not even to the bitch Esmé. Now in this festival of incongruities which Esmé was, it struck Tom that it was precisely Flick's impulse toward human silence that had made him become, in the first place, a technician of mechanical communication. All his devices would lead in the end to a deaf, dumb, and blind earth; a desire for withdrawal, for separateness, for isolation, was at the root of his choice of a career devoted to soldered connections, circuitry, electronic computation, wiring, waves of energy reaching out into space and bearing coded messages. In medical school Tom had used to play a game of predicting students' specialties—this man, with a childlike sweetness and deep nostalgia, bound to be a pediatrician; this one, powerful and subtly cruel, a surgeon; this one, a tiny bit sneaky where girls were concerned, a gynecologist. One could have known that Flick would choose to be a computer man of some sort, for what he really wanted was a vast network of silence. And now he was caught in it. In the height of the hurricane he was serenely moored in port. He was a lump. Let the smiler have him. He was inert; he would be a heavy weight on her hands, if not on her conscience.

She had trained that smile on Flick now. She was going to take care of him. Yes, she really was: She was unsnapping her safety hook, and darting one look at the enormous seas she slipped to her knees on the cockpit deck and eased herself across the way and threw her arms around Flick's legs and pulled herself up on him and sat beside him—between him and Dottie. She snapped herself into that intervening place. With one hand on the coaming she used the other to turn Flick's head around toward her, and she beamed her smile into his face, and then she began a series of hand signals which Flick, with eyes that seemed to have scales over them, did not in the least comprehend, or even watch and follow. What was she trying to tell him? Tom, who was having to keep an eye on the swooping of *Harmony* down into the gaping hollows of water, could not make it out himself. Suddenly Audrey was standing over Flick, and she reached under his armpits, and she was lifting him, or trying to persuade him to rise. He did stand up, looking extremely dull, and Audrey hauled him toward the opposite side of the cockpit. What, Tom wondered, was this ploy—merely taking him away from Dottie?

Ah, delicious! This was in the true spirit of Esmé: She had unsnapped her safety belt but not his! She was tugging; he was anchored. They waltzed in mid-cockpit, hanging there from his harness like some grotesque him-and-her puppet.

Dottie saw the difficulty, but not, for some reason, the

187

humor of it, and she leaned forward and unsnapped her husband.

Audrey and Flick fell in each other's arms into the seat on the port side.

Audrey attached the lump to the lifelines, and, his lips blue, downcast, shivering, holding on tight, he began at once to stare off to port. She left him then, crossed the cockpit on her knees again, raised the seat cover from a kneeling position, and—oh, God, this storm was confusing—began to pump.

Tom felt a flash of triumph; then he felt a spurt of guilt; and then, flooded by a realization that in this storm of opposites and paradoxes both feelings were fatuously inappropriate, he returned, as if homeward, to anger. But fear crept into the anger as he wondered what its object was. What could he be angry at? At last he picked, of all targets, the most foolish: the storm. He was furious at its persistence, he raged at its strength.

Grinding, he zeroed in on his loneliness and began in his anger to wonder what *it* was. His wife was no longer his; his friend was no longer his; goose pimples had prevented him from making Dottie his. Nobody was his. Was it then simply the non-functioning of the third-person masculine possessive pronoun that defined his loneliness? Was it a matter of having lost equity in certain properties which were incidentally human? Was there any difference between Flick's isolation of silence and staring, and his, of having been dispossessed? Audrey had stopped pumping—was *Harmony* dry? He could not tell. She had stopped. She was smiling at him again; it was precisely the same smile as she had lavished on the lump; it was the badge of *her* loneliness. Did she have an intention of coming over and lifting him, her husband, by the armpits and

188

transplanting him in the cockpit so she could do what?—get in the driver's seat? He would knock her down if she tried it; he would belt her. She was no longer his, and he was damned if he would let her even try to make him hers.

Then he knew why he was angry at the storm: Within its confusion all the assumptions of "this world," all its values, all its pretenses, all its civilization—all had turned out to be false here, useless here, ludicrous, dishonorable, hypocritical, "nice," and essentially unreal. Here the thrumming descent to the trough was a descent to the id. He would give Audrey a big poke in the chops if she started that armpit gambit. And yet—and here were the very liver and lights of his rage—he wanted to bring *Harmony* through. To what? Surely not just to the eye of the storm. To what beyond, to what? How could there be an end to *this* loneliness? Toward what was he steering? That was the mystery of mysteries—the enigma of his desire for life.

This desire was, even now, very strong. He felt it in his shoulders, spinning the wheel to try to offset, by anticipating it, that sickening skid at the foot of the trough. He was too late! The rudder was out of the water. He could feel the deck beneath him begin to rise and seem to twist. Seeming! What was the difference between seeming and being? His craft was out of his control and out of her own. She could not decide which way to skid and roll. She was twisting her back. This must surely be the last plunge. This time she would dig her nose into the water ahead and with her enormous impetus she would drive down into it, scooping, burrowing, and she would simply turn turtle. A sea somersault. The masts would point downward, the glistening green keel would reach toward the sky.

189

How powerful, at this moment, in his head and chest and guts and loins, was that unaccountable desire! Life! Buoyancy! A refusal to go under! He stood up at the wheel. He could see that *Harmony*—brave *Harmony!*—had the same desire as he. By God, she did! Green water curled at the cheeks, the bowsprit had plunged like a swordfish's weapon into the flank of the foe, the prow was on the verge of plunging under and wore a mean collar of flying foam. Every influence of the hurricane was driving her in and down, to burial, but she fought on the very edge of it; she trembled and hummed. Her head was still up. Tom felt a slight tug at the rudder. He threw it, not knowing which way to commit his influence, to port. That way, if she answered, the exhaust would be pointing downward (a detail! details added up to the life force!) and the engine would be safe. For a long time she shuddered and thrummed, her bowsprit wholly covered.

The first sign was an end to the thrumming, and he realized: it was the keel. The keel had taken hold, and the scooping rudder. *Harmony* shook her head. Before she turned she began to roll, and now Tom saw that the danger was that she would roll right over on her side. Yes, that was it: sidewise rather than head over heels. She began to sheer away from the solid mass of water ahead. Her masts, driven by both wind and the centrifugal impulse of the great skid into which she was now surely swooping, plunged toward the horizontal. Hoo-o-o-o! What a surge! Over, over. Here came the sea into the cockpit. Poor Dottie was alone on the lower side; Tom, falling, saw her put her head down, and she disappeared. Then Tom was under water, somewhere near the wheel; he had a hand on a spoke. And in that spoke he felt something. A trembling, a trying. Yes, yes! His head came up. He was in a soaked heap on the cockpit deck. The cockpit was full. The masts were drawing big, slow, upward arcs on the sky. Dottie was beside him in the flooded cockpit, shoulder-deep, with eyes like painted saucers. And there were Flick and Audrey, still on the higher seat. She was smiling; he was staring; the world was right side up.

And *Harmony* was going ahead up a riffled hill of grayish green. Slowly the water began to drain from the cockpit. Thank God, the cabin hatches were not stove in. The tachometer came awash; the engine was steady!

Tom knew she could not run before it any more; that had been too close. Indeed he clearly knew now, with salt water nearly up to his knees, that he should have turned long since. Opposites! The desire for life, the persistence in dangerous error. How could he have held a wrong course, running before the wind and waves, so long? Had it really been necessary to keep moving out and out, away from shelter, toward the eye of the storm? Yet here they were, here they still were.

He put the wheel way down to port and began the overdue turn.

He and his yawl were shot full of luck; that was all he could think as, amid powers immeasurably greater than that of the tiny tab of tapered oak hinged to the rudder post, or of his weary hand wrapped around a thin spindle of mahogany, chance rather than judgment on his part chose just the right phase of a huge swell for her to swing on, so she was in the vulnerable position, wind abeam, on the rise of the great hump, and by the time the crest came, with its curling and breaking comber, she was well up into the teeth of the blow.

That was all very well: she had turned. But coming round

to face the wind brought, besides the breath-stealing fact of facing the wind, a new revelation with a new shock on its back. This was not going to be any better than going down wind. Indeed, he saw that he had sustained a new and frightful loss: There was no longer any such thing, out here, as relativity. The concepts "better" and "worse" had lost their meaning; faster and slower, bigger and smaller, more direct and more devious, and better and worse and worse and better—all gone. Here there was only one medium, driven wetness; one temper, rage; one condition of life, danger of a uniform density.

Tom saw what he must do—or what he *thought* he must do, for Esmé was a trickster and had made Tom distrust what he had considered his greatest strength of all, his ability to watch out for "things"; he was tired, muddled, deprived of all the usual measures of decision, and it was hard to tell his beloved details from dreaded wholes. It *seemed* that he must wear off on a close reach, southwesterly in tendency, driving down away from the island; that he must advance the throttle, take the prolonged risk of three thousand r.p.m.'s; that he must try to keep *Harmony*'s bows fairly well up into the wind by holding the helm far to leeward as she ran down a great sea-back and through the valley of skids and most of the way up the next oncoming mass; but that then he must head her sharply up—the only way to do this being to ease the wheel to midships just before the crest and then whirl it back down again to make a kind of flapping fan of the rudder and so nudge her bow up—in order to come into the breakers nearly head on, to keep the boat moving by taking the wavetop fury equally down both flanks. So it seemed, and so he did, or thought he did.

He thought he was doing. This was too hard. He was in a

dream. There had been too much of seeming. One could not live without differentiations, one simply could not get along without being able to see outlines, borderlines, and without being able to feel more or less action in one's arms.

But there was an outline! To windward. A heaviness, a bulk, a darker place. Was that a glimpse of Block Island? If it was, then islands, like boats, could move in the sea, and Block Island, not *Harmony*, was out of place. Perhaps it was just a lowering bank of cloud. Surely she was well away from land by now! There was a reality of something dark there, couching an illusion.

Tom recognized now the final humiliation: not to be sure of anything.

Or was it? Wasn't there something even worse? To be condemned to a monotony of this unsureness? His hand, a glove-shaped bag of weakened sinews and many little bones, curling around a piece of wood ornately shaped on a lathe, repeating an identical action over and over again. Hold down, wait, ease up, whirl; repeat; repeat; repeat. The waves had somewhat different shapes but uniform intent. One had to repeat the action, or else—cease repeating the action, cease being, cease seeming. Camus's rendering of Sisyphus came to him, the aptest picture of modern man—in a hurricane wind. Tom was tempted to stop this repetition, for he felt that if Esmé would take the hint and just stop on her side for five minutes, then he would be able to resume and carry on forever.

But what was that concept that had sneaked into his mind? *Five minutes.* Tom quickly looked at his watch and, without having taken in the message of the metal hands, he sensed a change. Was it in himself? What was it?

Flick was shaking. Monotony for him was to be an endless existence of shivering. Smart bastard who liked to be rained on. (There *was* a change; a tremulous lightening of the weight of monotony.) Tom could only see part of Flick's profile as he maintained his fixated vigil to port: pale, except for the lips, which had a color of no good. The eyes were rapt; they seemed to be reading in a fascinating book a single perfect sentence. But they were, at the same time, sound asleep to anything actual.

After her pumping, Audrey had stayed in that corner of the cockpit, Dottie's former safe place. Now she was steadily watching Flick's trembling shoulders, just as hypnotized, in her way, as Flick in his. But there seemed now—Tom scanned her as he had his watch, without really taking in the message —some kind of imminence in *her* stare; her private monotony was on some kind of verge, and this contributed to Tom's sense of some slight change having set in, or being about to.

And Dottie? Too bad, no visible change there. She sat holding on with the weak hands of one who had regurgitated all energy, sick to emptiness of the sea's anger yet somehow in love with it, watching with huge eyes, passive, helpless except for a tiny dampened spark still in her eye of her quarrel with Flick and of wanting to care for Flick, wanting to hand-brush the hair from his brow, or slap comprehension into his stare.

And what about *Harmony?* (One certain change: a sharpened awareness in Tom, something making him look around again at "things," even if he did not clearly understand them.) *Harmony* was making that deep music all the time now, and even it could be said to have changed. On the edge of the thrumming there was a kind of fluttering, a soft throbbing as of the beating of wings or the trembling of the luff of a genoa jib in gentle airs, coming up from beneath. There was a new edge to the sound; that was a change.

Then Tom realized it had stopped raining. He had no idea how long before. Raising his eyes as *Harmony* made a curvet on the summit of a wave, he saw a sharp horizon far away; then the yawl was in a hollow and the horizon had leaped in heaving and high. He wondered, thinking of the vague illusion of imminent change he had had for some time, whether he had confused it all along with the reality of the stopping of the rain. Shadow and substance: he must have translated a cessation of the stinging of drops of storm-blown rain in his face into a mere sense of becoming, an anticipation. The danger, now, was inward: it was false interpretation. When a man looked at realities and saw chimeras, when he read past events as future promises, he was in a danger more profound than that of the closeness of death; the danger was the horror of being alive and not knowing it.

Tom could still fight the spokes of the wheel; he would with equal effort fight this awful danger. Item the first: look for Block Island. *Harmony* came up on top, and he looked in the direction of the dim shape he had seen, or imagined, a few centuries (moments) ago. There was nothing there. It had been a cloud, a fogbank, a dreamland. He looked back over his left shoulder to where the island actually should have been, and there it was. Anticipation and reality rejoined! How far away? Five miles? What did it matter? He could run to leeward forever in the new wind after the eye, to the Azores, to Portugal, to Casablanca! Hooray for rocks and soil and sand and bayberry bushes, out of the way where they belonged!

But Block Island's obliging location did not mean that the fight against the new danger was won; for now came a new sensory dislocation. Tom saw that the rollers were no longer breaking along the tops of the waves. How long had *this* been true? He was still repeating the robot ritual at the wheel, easing it up and whirling it down near the crests, to head up—into combers no longer there. He could steer a straighter course now.

What else? Look at the water! What else? Why, the vastness was still there, the awesomeness of immensity that made Tom think small, and there were still hard climbs to acrophobic nightmares and then plunges with the lance of the bowsprit aimed down to split the back-scales of slimy dragons of the unconscious crawling on the bottom of the sea—but see: the skin of the waves had changed. That urgent building of ripples on ripples was no longer going on; the furious corrugation had stopped. For how long?

And what did the disappearance of the breakers and the smoothing of the complexion of the seas mean? Translate with care, he told himself. These phenomena may have been there, or rather not there, for a long time, unobserved or misinterpreted. Be careful what you think of them.

Before Tom satisfied himself on this point there was a "thing" to be seen to. *Harmony* was going with more ease than—than in an earlier era—and he wanted to throttle down the engine to avoid overheating. This was a perfectly reasonable and necessary precaution. Bending down and watching the tachometer he pulled back the throttle: twelve hundred, and the thrumming still there but the fluttering gone. Yes, she held her own at twelve hundred. How could she?

That problem of the breakers. The problem of the ruffling-on-ruffling no longer there. The problem, now observed but not yet translated, of no more spume flying off every protuberance and wedge of water.

196

All right, one more practical move: If no more rain, why not take down the waterproof hood? He hooked both knees over opposite spokes of the wheel and after some picking and tugging at the bowknot under his chin he loosened the drawstring of the hood and flipped his head bare.

First things first: the thrumming. It was a sound, sure enough.

Now at last, with a whole face naked and ears out in the open and hair free, Tom understood all those seen changes. The wind had dropped. There was almost no wind. An end had come to the wind.

And as if this were an enlightenment in every sense, as if far more than a mere answer to riddles had dawned on Tom, the day was suddenly brighter. A strange glare, hard on eyes adjusted to the possibility that gloom would last forever, making one squint at its unexpectedness, lay on the decks.

Tom looked up and saw ahead a great curved gulf of blue sky.

The thrumming sound was so much on his mind that it took him some time to feel that blueness as a hope of warmth. He was trying to remember: in that worst of all skids, when turning turtle had seemed a certainty, the first sign had been an end to the thrumming—and what had that meant?

There was blue sky ahead!—as blue as the rim of a summertime high, wafting cool, dry air from pine woods and elk ponds far to the north; only this blue came, less honest, ringed with outrage, from the fetid south. The others should know about this. Tom looked to them, wanting to speak words for the first time in an age. But Flick and Audrey were interlocked, as surely as fornicating animals who get stuck in the act: he staring and shivering, she with that smile and that look

197

of inception. She was really about to do something for him. Let them be. There was always Dottie. "Look up there," Tom said to her, and he pointed at the huge azure curve.

Dottie looked, and then her eyes came back to his in gratitude and uncomprehending sweetness.

And then, two or three score of huge seas later, in a fullness of kindly brilliance, out came the sun. Tom knew the meaning of everything now. Esmé's horrid eye was ogling them. They had made it to the eye.

They had made it. Tom looked at his watch, and this time he understood what the hands had to say: It was exactly one-fifteen. He would remember that for the log. He would buy a new log book, even though this one was only half filled; he could not keep looking at that cut-up endpaper. He'd get a new one.

Then he thought: Sufficient unto the day the winds thereof. Make no commitments for the future; sign no contracts today, buy no log books.

Audrey was unbuckling. The sunlight was dazzling on her bulging orange life jacket over her orange slicker; and a golden light was reflected up on her face, which was illuminated, too, by that look of maternal anticipation aimed at Flick. She undid her hood and shook out her hair, and then she stood unsteadily—*Harmony* was making good time, thrumming along and prancing like a bronco on the queerly unmotivated yet still huge seas, which were now plum-colored and starred with sunglints—and she staggered, looking euphoric and a little foolish like a young girl who had had no idea how strong the drinks were that she had been handed, and she crossed to Flick, whose back was still turned to the cockpit, and she triumphantly put her hands on his shaking shoulders.

It looked as if it would take more than the sun and feminine palms to drive the chill out of him. He did not seem to feel Audrey's touch at all.

The deck lurched, and Audrey, giving Flick a swift knee in the kidneys, jackknifed at the hips and crashed down beside and partly on him, with one arm thrown over his shoulders and the off elbow digging for his groin. Misguided nurse! How she roughed him up!

Then came the first human sounds Tom had heard for a long, long time: a grunt from Flick and an embarrassed giggle from Audrey.

But most of all he heard the inhuman thrumming of *Harmony* in the sea.

Leaving her arm across Flick's shoulders, as if the pair of them were quite alone with the gross monstrosities of the scene, Audrey spoke straight into his ear. Tom could not hear what she said.

Flick's answer was to shiver and chatter his teeth and stare off with undaunted impersonality at the greenish crescent of storm-cloud retiring to the north.

Tom caught a glimpse of a shadow of bewilderment on Audrey's face, but that drained away like a fading blush, and she stood up again, and, leaning on the cabin trunk, she pushed forward the companionway hatch, and she pulled herself upward with the obvious intention of going below to get warm clothes for Flick.

"Watch your step!" Tom ambiguously bellowed at her, but she did not turn her head.

Over and into the rectangular opening went one leg, and then the other—she seemed to be holding on tight—and then she disappeared.

199

What was it he had been trying to remember about the thrumming and the end of thrumming during that almost fatal skid?

Now Dottie was up and unhooded and unbuckled, with her back to Tom, and she was lifting the flap of the seat onto which he had moved her, and she reached down into the locker under it, and up came her hand with the coffee thermos in it. Passive and helpless? Dear Dottie with a quarrel in the bank!

She turned, her big eyes glittering like wave tops, and with a patter of quick little steps she trotted diagonally across the cockpit, holding the cylindrical container in both hands, and plumped down beside Flick. Yes, they *would* take care of him. Making a face expressive of determination and grit in extremity, as if removing the cap of the thermos were in a class with sailing through a hurricane, she twisted once, and made a bigger face, and then again; and then it gave. She drew the cork and poured a capful and held it out to Flick.

Suddenly leaping all the way into a normalcy that was grotesque in its matter-of-factness, Flicker suavely took the thermos cap in his right hand, said distinctly, "Thank you, Dottie-pie," in a tone that made it seem that the coffee was just a bit on the late side but was his due and had to be acknowledged, and holding the cap in both hands blew gently on it to cool it, so he would not burn his tongue. The incredible unconscious nerve of the lump! But then a bout of shivering hit him, and he spilled some of the coffee and scalded his hands and dropped the cap, dexterously palming it out away from his bare, bluish knees, and clearly forgot at once that there had ever been any coffee or wife or boat or storm.

Patiently Dottie put the cork back, placed the thermos in

Flick's lap, and went on her hands and knees on the heaving deck to catch the cap, which was running and rolling like a snide little kitten that knew how to come close and then get away. She retrieved it finally and rose to the seat and poured another round and tried Flick again. But by now he had suffered a total failure of interest.

Dottie sat holding the cap for a long time, looking down at the coffee in it, and then with perfect grace, smiling apologetically, she reached it out to Tom.

He gulped it down, making a hot metal rod of his esophagus, and handed back the cap.

Dottie began to screw it onto the thermos.

"You'd better have some," Tom said very loudly, but at the same time he was thinking of the puzzle of the thrumming and was not humanely interested in whether she drank coffee. What a curious effect, here under the eye of the storm, of a return to reason (was *that* an illusion?) and a wish—but not deep enough to be sincere—to return to the world of amenities, manners, connections one to one. But watch out for Esmé's tricks! That sound under the boat! It was like an obsessive monotone humming of a mad person. Was it Esmé humming to remind one that this eye of hers, though comely and loving, was fickle, fickle?

Dottie, answering Tom's bidding to drink, shook her head and made a comical sign of throwing up, putting her hand over her mouth and puffing out her cheeks.

The seas were indeed sickening, still, and as *Harmony*, no longer obliged to breast the wind, was now making a firm pace, so she pitched more than she had, and drove along with a wild helical motion as if screwing into a vast cork of still air with the intention of backing up and pulling it out of the neck of the windstorm. Sometimes she pounded against a series of short steep seas which were like gaunt ribs on the torso of one of the huge waves. There was a gigantism, a morbidity, about these shapes of water, as of unspeakable mutations from the norm; their leaping and striving under a windless air made them seem all the more freakish.

Tom felt at a loss. He had wanted so desperately to reach the eye that now that he was under it he felt, like any man who has overfed an ambition and then attained it, surprised and a little angry at the taste of ashes in his mouth. There was nothing to savor. Crashes of *Harmony*'s flanks against hard water, as if she were pounding stones? Savor *them?* How should he steer? If south, the storm-day would be shorter but so would this time of calm air. If north, back toward Block Island and a bad lee. He actively did not want to think of the other two quarters of the horizon; a wind had lately come from one of them, and from the other, eventually . . . He would feel too foolish steering in circles, like a man lost in a forest, and with such a struggle to reach a goal so recently won he was incapable of stopping dead. Inertia and indecision carried him along on the same southwesterly bearing with his mind humming in tune with the droning down under the sole of the yawl's stamping foot.

The housekeeper in Dottie obliged her to replace the thermos in the seat locker to starboard. She seemed restless. She tried awhile her original safe seat; she glanced once at Flick and shook her head; then she stood up and on a rising sea was thrown forward and with both lands leaning on the cabin trunk she craned and looked down into the hatchway.

What she saw below made her wheel around and show a newsy face to Tom, for with Dottie every experience seemed

referable to a responsible man. The face she showed wore a
stressful look which Tom could not (with half his thoughts on
the humming) immediately decipher, though he could not
help seeing the elements. Part alarmed, she was; part guiltily
triumphant; part tempted to tattle; part secretive; part pitying; part implacable, with a fierce sense of a rare chance. It
was a direct and transparent look of strong feelings she could
not have understood herself. She opened her mouth, and her
throat tightened; but nothing came out.

She turned in a driven hurry and scrambled recklessly
down the companionway.

Yet Tom sat twiddling the wheel, pinned there, in what
must have looked like serenity, on a recognition: He was
suffering a mental block. Sometimes seeing in the city a well-
known face he lost the name that went with it; he would
struggle, associate, grope, and have a feeling that the name
was being whispered to him just out of earshot. The books
would say that this meant the name was linked in the towers
of his head with hatred, but he would doubt it. A good friend.
He knew the name very well. Too late the answer would
come. So it was now, about the thrumming. Something mem-
orable had come into his mind at the swiftest pitch of the
skid, just before he had committed himself to throw the wheel
to port. It was something so obvious, so significant—so easy!
But as to that, there was a synapse locked wide open; a gap of
loud, humming blankness.

He told himself to think of something else; this swollen
item would come back into his head with a resounding slam,
as of a door blowing shut. Audrey had gone down to get Flick
a sweater; she intended to make him put on the slickers after
all. That must have been her errand. Audrey of those many

nights; that bumpy face which had seemed once to proclaim with its odd planes and surprising curves certain inner grips on life, having to do with loyalty, ability to digest setbacks, a woman's patience and courage, a kind of taking wrapped up in giving. But now? Now? It was all for the lump. She and not the sun would warm Flick's cold blood.

Suddenly Dottie's look from the hatchway came back in memory to startle him. He rose with a gasp from the wheel, astounded once again at the sluggishness of his responses and the unreliability of his scanning apparatus. That look of hers had been a silent scream.

He stopped by Flick, bent down, and sharply commanded, "Take the wheel!"

Flick's eyes swung around as if on a slow compass card from the northeast and came to rest on the attraction of a look of Tom's which Tom felt to be very cross. Flick's eyes were not empty by any means; only insolent. They seemed to say, "Audrey said she'd be right back." Tom imagined a black patch over the left eye: the playful masquerader who never worked.

Tom careened on a violent tipping of the deck and found himself looking down the hatchway.

Dottie was killing Audrey. There were two feet of water in the cabin, and there were waves on the water down there. He had a glimpse of blood lapped by water on Audrey's styrofoam-white face. She was lying on her back floating in the water, her life preserver was keeping her up. Her hair was fanned out like seaweed. Dottie was bending over her, hitting or clawing, partially blocking Tom's view of her. Dottie fell and sloshed and rose again dripping. Gentle Dottie, helpless Dottie—she was taking her dark, dark revenge on Audrey:

204

murdering her. What was the weapon? Somehow Dottie had drawn blood from that ashen face, and now she was going to drown Audrey, fight the buoyancy of the life jacket and hold her face down under. Were Audrey's eyes open? Was Audrey conscious? A striking sleeve blocked his view; a shoulder got in the way. Yes, Audrey was fighting! An arm came up, raking fingers. Dottie fell again, and they rolled on those inner seas in a ball of a death struggle.

Tom quickly raised his head and saw that *Harmony* was still going in more or less the same direction as before, as if, cold to her innermost timbers, she was homing towards the hot sun. Tom looked at Flick—could he possibly believe that gentle Dottie was trying to take Audrey's life on account of *that* lump of lard?—and he shouted, "Steer! Steer the boat!" And he pointed with great authority at the wheel, wagging his forefinger. All he got was the pirate eye.

He floundered into the hole of the hatch, clumsy in his precautionary gear, and crashed down the ladder to restrain the killer. Dottie was up again. She was surely no match in strength for Audrey, yet somehow she had gotten an early advantage—struck her on the face with something heavy; a winch handle?

With his feet on the cabin deck and water up to his knees, Tom took in with a glance in the dim cavern the seriousness of Dottie's assault. Audrey's face was so wan, the blood on it so stark! Dottie had taloned hands on Audrey's shoulders. Audrey's head went under water. After all he had done to save lives—

But while his eyes were reading the murder his whole head seemed to have been grasped by the ears. The thrumming. Down here the waves on the water were miniature; it was sound that had become monstrous, gigantic. It was all around him. It bathed him. As if it were solid water, it would engulf him and drown him. Here he was in the sounding box of the instrument; he would shatter like crystal in these vibrations.

In the very moment of reaching out his hands to pull Dottie away from Audrey, the synapse tripped and closed, and, filled with the thrumming until his whole skeleton shook with it, he remembered what it was he had lost in his head. Of course; so obvious. The keel. When the thrumming had stopped in that great skid, he had thought: *The keel. The keel has taken hold.* It was a vibration of the keel, that sound—a sum of vibrations, building on one another like those ripples on waves on seas on swells, accumulating into the flutter effect that could topple steel bridges when they began to hum in high winds.

His hands touched Dottie briefly, in nothing but a kind of double pat, almost a caress, and then, as she toppled again across Audrey, kneeing the floating orange chest to force the victim under, Tom with great urgency lifted a leg high and splashed past the two of them. His hip hit Dottie, and he was dimly aware that she fell sideways and that for a moment Audrey's head came out of the water. But his back was turned on the act of killing, and he was sloshing forward through the cabin, gasping for breath as if the sound he heard was itself pouring into his lungs like some choking, poisonous miasma. The water, made wild by the wildness of *Harmony*'s plunging, lapped the cabin settees, and in his haste Tom tripped and fell between the folded-down table and the starboard seat, and he went splashing onward pellmell on his hands and knees into the forward cabin. With the rising deck up there the water was somewhat shallower. Now he was at the very pole of the thrumming; it swirled in a vortex around him.

He rose to his knees and flung open the lid of the locker in the vee of the forecastle bunks and with flying hands he dug down past sail-mending kit and light tool bag and balls of twine and marlin, down through heaps of unwanted spare items, until his right hand closed on the great shank of an enormous Stillson wrench. He pulled it up and out. It was nearly three feet long, oiled, sleek, and hideous. If anyone wanted to murder, surely this was the aptest tool.

He pivoted where he kneeled, crawled back into the fore-part of the cabin, turned with his back to whatever was happening in the rest of the cabin, and, plunging a hand into the water, tore up the removable floorboards. There, clearly seen under the sunlight pouring down through the cabin skylight, red, six-sided, magnified by these inner shallows, distorted by the refraction of the waves so it seemed to bulge, swell out, wobble, shrink, and jump, was the cap of *Harmony*'s flaw and his negligence, the nut on the vital keel bolt.

He whirled the worm grip of the wrench to open the jaws wide, wide, and he took a fast hold on the nut with the mouth of the wrench and with both hands under water tightened the vise of the wrench onto the nut. With some part of his mind that had managed to keep itself islanded away from the thrumming he knew that what he was doing was folly, hopelessly impossible while the two tons of the keel hung down, but most of his mind urged him on, and he took purchase and heaved to tighten, as to close a faucet, he thought, and he heaved, till his back hurt, and he heaved. But at the peak of his efforts the vibration seemed to become a growl, a snarl; and a power beyond reckoning took hold of the weird me-

207

chanics of loosening, and the nut turned of its own thrumming accord on its thread counter-clockwise, in the *freeing* direction, pulling wrench, arms, and man in the opposite direction from all his willed strength. With its flutteration the keel was working itself loose before his eyes and against his every sinew. He was filled with a sense of horror and of blind superstitious dread: a malevolent, purposeful, vengeful force was at work against him. Was this what the porpoises had been trying to warn of? The island in his mind whispered: *Illusion! Illusion! It's not really turning, it only seems to turn.* But much louder and dominant over his hands and arms and straining back was the continual fluttering of a lowered keel. How far down had it worked itself? An eighth of an inch? A half inch? He was hit by the appalling idea of the keel's dropping right off and plunging to the bottom of the sea, the towering spars toppling, the hollow chest of the hull lying on its side in the water as Esmé would return in the high fury of the other half of the storm beyond the eye. He knew, he knew, he *knew* this could not happen. After all, there was another huge keel bolt aft lodged in good sound wood. Yet he shook with frustration and wild forebodings.

Then, in a shoulder-stooped attitude, he checked himself. He would not allow the unseen hand below to loosen the nut any further; not a single thread would he let it be unscrewed. He would use cunning in place of strength. He let up the bite of the wrench on the big nut and reset it, taking up the jaws tight and then wedging the huge handle against the nearest floor beam, in such a way that the nut could not turn without tearing out the guts of the hull. He settled back, kneeling in the sea's invading salt water and with his own inner salt water streaming from his pores down his face, feeling clever and, yes, smug. The thrumming continued, but it no longer set up those excruciating harmonic vibrations in his nerves.

His sense of completion and mastery, however, was short-lived. Staring down at his nut-trap, the braced wrench undulating in refractions under the sunlit bilgewater, he succumbed to a horrifying conviction that the keel bolt was not a mere detail, and could not be dealt with as if it were.

The full force of the sunlight pouring down through the plexiglas skylight struck the crown of his head—was the boat turning?—and as if penetrating his skull flooded his mind with a dreadful bright light of understanding: He had got everything all wrong! All that about the loosening nut had been a seeming; there were two human beings in a death lock back there in the cabin. Details! Details! Life was running away!

"Jesu, let her go down! Let her sink!"

At the outer limits of despair, he did not know whether he had shouted that curse-like wish out loud or only heard it rush through his head. He rose and keeping himself upright with stiff arms, which reached out to each side like shoring timbers, he rushed aft, wearing skirts of splashes of his churning knees, and he scarcely paused at the orange-colored confusion of Dottie's intention to do away with Audrey, except to think: Why was she so inept? Why had she half-hauled Audrey up onto the starboard settee, where the victim's back was arched, blood scarfing half that milky face? He recognized a flickering half-thought that Dottie was not really trying to kill Audrey at all. He could not wait for clarity but fled up the ladder. Let her go! Let her go down!

Flick was at the wheel. The big man with plastered hair sat there as nonchalant as ever a steersman could be. Tom saw at once that Flick had turned the yawl around and was going toward Block Island.

The impetus of Tom's charge up from the bowels of the boat was spent; and so was whatever had made him do all that he had done, and not done, below, and he thought: Let the bastard steer north. We have plenty of sea room. The storm will be back right away.

And yes, there, lying low to the south and east was the new scudding circle of torn shreds and solid sickish gray.

Tom lifted the seat lid and began to pump.

He did not even wonder why. He pumped two hundred strokes and rested.

He was well into another hundred when a bloody hand hooked itself over the companionway door-boards. Two heads came up over the edge at once: Audrey's crimsoned, shock-pale face and drooping eyes, a half-dead face, and, behind, Dottie's, twisted, a lip being bitten hard. The bungling murderess was helping her would-be victim climb the ladder!

Tom went right on pumping.

Dottie propped Audrey against the door-boards; pushed from behind until Audrey stood waist-high at the boards. Then on a sea-bounce Audrey fell face forward over the boards and hung limp there. Dottie climbed over her and with a surprising strength hauled Audrey bodily out from the hatchway and lowered her into the cockpit, stacking her up like some awkward flexible object, a narrow mattress perhaps, against the high seat-back on the port side.

Flick left the wheel. He appeared to have become bored with the activity of steering. But no: He had an errand; he sat beside Audrey and retched beyond the coaming.

Audrey weakly turned in the seat and also threw up. The pair of lovers were heartily sick side by side.

Tom had reached four hundred strokes. There would be no end to this work.

Dottie sat beside him. She was smiling. The sunlight picked out on her sensitive face a look of appeal for help. She was saying something.

Tom let go the pump handle and leaned toward her, the better to hear.

She repeated: "It's all over, isn't it?"

"Over? What do you mean?"

"The storm's over. It's finished, isn't it?"

"No, lamb," Tom said. "This was just the eye."

As if to grant him, in the maelstrom of his losses, at least a stint of truthfulness, a cloud just then covered the sun. Tom kept himself from saying that the worst was yet to come. What he did say, kicking his chin toward the convulsive gatherings of Flick's back, was: "You'd better get him his waterproofs."

But she shook her head; her dainty, golden earrings trembled, though her wet hair hung heavy. "I couldn't go down there again."

"O.K., then. Pump."

Tom went below himself and got the brand-new waterproofs, and he climbed up and stuffed Flicker into them, limb by limb. It had grown dark. Dottie was pumping with a will.

Lifting up and cording tight his hood, Tom sat at the wheel, and as he was in the process of turning *Harmony* toward the northwest a seething edge of white froth came across the lumpy waters. The new wind, rain-laced, took his breath right away.

4

The Secret Place

There stood the gate of heaven, gleaming in evening sunlight: the marker bell outside tolling with that true-bronze tone of good cheer that sea bells have when the sky is blue; the long jetty of blasted rocks with veins of quartz and flecks of mica giving off diamond glints; the black cans and the red nuns and the two spindles steadfastly marking the sweet channel; and there, off to the left, on Indian Head—yes, that primitive dream of dry land—rocks and sand and bayberry bushes bathed in the light of the sun. The breeze, fresh but dry, was out of the north; the sea, so soon, was growing calm. They were coming back, all alive and afloat.

Harmony looked like one of those old junkmen's wagons that used to clop around city streets picking up scrap metal and rags and broken furniture and mildewy-dusty magazines and papers, the driver chanting or perhaps pounding with a hammer on a clanging gong of a rusty wheel rim. Everything portable was coming up from below to dry; Dottie was scurrying with a pursed mouth, bringing things up, wringing them out, and spreading them here and there. The matresses were slung over the main boom, clothing and towels flapped along the lifelines, and with Tom's help she had even rigged bed-sheets on the fly from the main and jib halyards, enormous flags of truce.

Audrey was at the wheel, her face like an ancient cliff; the rocks of her endurance had been rounded off not by weather but by pain. The gash over her left cheekbone, no longer bleeding but blood-caked, was putting out all around it a bloom of greenish bruise. Her right shoulder slumped; she steered with her left hand.

Flick rocked on the pump like a satyr at his endless labor of intrusion and withdrawal, up and down, in and out. He had pumped now with a mechanical insatiability for two hours, and he had won: there were only four inches of slop above the cabin floorboards now. Mute and dull, he was gaining on the flaw.

No one spoke. They were automatons, Tom thought, performing what had to be gotten through, not with energies of blood sugar and flash-flaming oxygen and sparking nerves, for those had been spent long since, early in the morning, but rather with some deep, sluggish reserve of aching and yearning tenacity which seemed to be drawn from the very marrow of the bones; or maybe (though he knew better) it somehow came from the gruesome liver. In any case, they moved; the crew did work as they had not in fair sailing. Tom's own exhaustion was so profound that he felt as if he were hip-deep in some viscous quagmire, were being sucked down not by a quicksand but by a slowsand, if there could be such a thing; yet his legs and arms functioned as if some damp gray power akin to the invisible force of storms were pushing at them, some terrible wind of life and motion that he did not want to try just yet to understand.

214

He went forward to rig the Danforth anchor. There it lay in its seating near the mainmast, firmly lashed down and ready—could that be a tiny glimmer of smugness he felt on *this* side of the storm over something he had done?—and when he had untied its stock and shank and flat, angular palms and had lifted it to carry it forward, it seemed as light in his arms as papier-maché. How could it hold a yawl in a wind? With dead-looking fingers, wrinkled by hours of wetness, he unlashed the linen anchor line from its rack on the port side and made fast the shackle and cleated the line and hung the anchor out over the sheave on the bowsprit, all set to be let go once again to that deep mud bottom where its big brother, the fluke anchor, lay derelict, lost forever.

He looked up and saw that they were already inside the Great Salt Pond, and that they were in fact just passing the Coast Guard station, where, he noticed, the flags, both of warning and of patriotism, had been taken in from the huge cross-treed flagstaff; the huge doors at the top of the boat track yawned open. A jerking reflex made him look at his watch; it was running, and it said: six-twenty-three.

A frantic question suddenly beat at his mind. What time had it been—what day had it been—when they had passed that squarish white building on the way out to look for Esmé's eye?

Tom went below in a great hurry to find the answer in his log book. The item would be dated; the item would be timed. He was coming back to "this world"; he needed to know about time in all its proportions; he wanted to put the hours in order.

Order! The chaos in the cabin must have been the product of some cosmic humor, a practical-joking bent of Esmé's.

215

The jack of hearts was on one burner of the stove. All the drawers, latched though they had been, were open, as though a prowler had been looking in nervous haste for jewelry. Knives and forks and spoons glinted in the shallows of the bilge; one walked on cutlery. A pair of dark glasses was lodged, lenses out, to view the world, astride the ship's clock, which had stopped at three minutes past noon, as if in dismay at the effort of pushing into a new twelve hours of *that* sort. Time! Yes, he must find his log book.

The book shelf was empty. The tide tables lay outspread on the ice chest, open at a page giving distances in nautical miles. Tom leaned forward, gripped by the pervasive irrelevances of this setting, and learned from the top of the column that it was two hundred fifty-nine nautical miles from Bar Harbor to Halifax. This struck him as nonsense and annoyed him, and he shut the soaked book and threw it toward the bookshelf; it fluttered to the wooden slats of the settee on the port side.

Dottie, leaning in at the opening of the companionway, called down, "Audrey wants to know where you want to anchor."

"Tell her I want to know where she stowed the books."

Dottie wore a kindly look of astonishment; it was as if she had been slapped and forgave. At last she turned away and seemed to be talking in a friendly way to the woman she had tried, a few hours before, to—to do *what* to? Soon her face came back toward Tom showing a bland look that may simply have reflected the total disinterestedness of total exhaustion, and she said, "She wants me to tell you we're right at the anchorage. She wants to know if you want her to anchor where we were before." Then, her expression modulating just enough toward puzzlement to indicate that what followed was her own contribution: "Would that be bad luck?"

"God damn it, tell her I want to know where she hid my log book."

Dottie turned away again, and just then a blush, so hot as to make Tom perspire, burst on his face, for he remembered that he had come down and made entries in the log book in the channel on the way out, and that had been *after* Audrey had secured things in the cabin. The books had been on the shelf behind their restraining lee-bar; where were they all now?

Dottie's face again. The same vacant expression. "I think you'd better come up here."

Tom took one step up the ladder and saw that Audrey had slumped sidewise to the left away from the wheel. Flick had gone to her and was fumblingly hauling at her and turning the wheel without looking where *Harmony* was headed.

Tom ran up the ladder, jumped into the cockpit, cut the throttle, and pushed Flick aside from the wheel. Let him take care of the women; they'd been nursing him all day.

In the relative quiet of the idling motor Tom heard Audrey murmuring in Flick's arms, "I'm all right. I just . . . I'm O.K. now." But she still lay cradled, and Tom heard her say, "Darling, that black paper for your eye patch, couldn't you have understood what his log book meant to him?"

"Don't talk about me as though I were dead," Tom grimly said.

"We're all tired," Dottie said, as if that extenuation of insults and rages made acceptance of "this world" any easier.

Tom put the engine in neutral, let *Harmony* shoot till she had no more forward life, and went up on the foredeck and let go the anchor, with a clanking plash of metal on pond surface. Then he returned to the cockpit and shut off the engine. Out of the dregs and lees of his former self came the words, "Good old engine."

Silence. The universe drained of rushing sounds. The rigging quiet; tiny ripples on the water.

Harmony was alone in the port of refuge. Silent along the marina pier were the wrecks of the morning; silent on the shore were the torn and splintered and canted remains of yachts and trawlers and work boats and stink pots and cut-away dinghies and all that could float—treacherous sheds, too.

"If the bottles aren't all broken," Tom said to Dottie, "I could use a great big drink."

"Oooh, yummy," Dottie said; the soft childishness came out of her as if on tape, unbacked by feeling of tone or expression. She climbed below. Tom heard the ice chest top thump, and a clinking of sound bottles. He pumped while he waited.

Dottie handed up plastic thermal cups, dead to the touch, brimming with Bourbon and ice. Tom reached the first cup to Audrey, saying, "You look as if you could use this."

She was still leaning against Flick's chest, but she said to Tom, "Thanks, darling. Cheers to the skipper!" She drank without waiting.

When Dottie came up she said in a flat voice, "Only two eggs broken in the ice box."

Tom was feeling the burning liquor going down. "Imagine that," he said.

But eggs didn't matter. The jack of hearts on the stove didn't matter. This was all so normal: quiet evening in harbor, serene landscape, drinks in the stately cockpit with its coam-

218

ing like a starched wing collar from old times of white ties and tails. Normalcy? With Audrey leaning against the big sea-chantey shouter and waver of arms?

After one drink Tom pumped a thousand strokes and got all the rest of the water out of the bilges, and after the second drink they dragged down the damp mattresses and toppled, each in his own way, into the deep zones of greenish midnight at the floor of the troubled sea.

∽∽∽

They all rose early the next morning into an azure day across whose pale arch a dry easterly breeze drifted like a rumor of good news. Tom, who had been up once in the night to pump in a half-awake daze, was stiff in every fiber of every muscle; his skin seemed to sheath an inutterably tangled complication of copper wires, like those myriad bundles of sinews on the backs of telephone switchboards. Yes, to give Flick his due, Tom had a moment's picture, standing by his bunk when he first stood up, of this first layer of himself as an electronic envelope entrapping his inner meat and psyche in a humming, rigid system of aches—and the sum of the aches was drawn around the circumferences of his head. He groped in the medicine cabinet over the toilet washbasin for two aspirin tablets. The cool water that washed them down tasted like Liebfraumilch on his salted tongue.

Audrey could not get up; the bad trouble was in her right shoulder, and her face was ghastly with a half-moon scab blurring into a swollen purple ripeness of a whole cheek in pain. She stared up at the ribbed underside of the cabin trunk as if she had been awake day and night for weeks on end.

Dottie took over with a willful, mothering sweetness, and the object of her brimming love, at first, was Audrey. Dottie had evidently heard the clink of the aspirin in its bottle in Tom's hand, and she went for it and gave Audrey some; with velvet palms and digits she raised Audrey's head and held it up while Audrey swallowed the pills and the following water. Murmuring and clucking, with a tenderness unblemished by a single instant of roughness, Dottie bathed the wound on Audrey's face. At the galley sink she rinsed the salt water out of some soaked gauze she found in a first-aid kit in the head, and she laid out the wet bandage across the gash. Tom, remembering what he thought he had seen in the flooded cabin under the eye of the storm, stood by, paralyzed by puzzlement. He had a thousand "things" on his mind, to list and fix and do, but he stood immobilized and enchanted by Dottie's display of either irony or total lapse; but, whichever, of pure kindness.

And Audrey kept muttering shockingly unexpected words: "Thank you, dear . . . You've been a darling . . . How good you are to me!" And once she said, "Does Flick know how sweet you are?"

"Sure, sure, sure," Flick blustered, whether to tease or in outrage it would have been hard to say, "she's an all-day cherry lollipop." And at that he climbed above and began to pump with vigor, the rank goat back at his chore of humping.

Tom understood, and even felt for, Flick's outburst— after the storm a man did not know where he stood. One would have to review how he, and how others, had behaved, and see where everyone came out; and wait and see, too, what others seemed to think. Already Dottie's and Audrey's mutual warmth had bloomed to disturb Tom's view of the way things had been and ought to be.

Dottie went to the icebox, and as she lifted the lid Tom realized the source of much of his unease and weakness: none of them had had a bite to eat since the breakfast Audrey had fixed early the previous morning. Tom was ravenous. He fought an impulse to shove Dottie roughly aside and snatch a raw egg out of the box and puncture it at each end with the ice pick and suck it out raw.

"We need ice," Dottie said, head down at the lid of the box, as if it were any morning.

And gas, probably, Tom thought—not a prayer of getting it from that marina today. Another lack that made him feel wan and helpless: he could find neither pencil nor paper wet or dry. He wanted to assess, to make a checklist. Hello, Dr. Meticulous, he said to himself, glad to have you back aboard! Sort of glad. The outlines are familiar. But no, no, don't speak of livers yet! Hold back that glimpse of the operating room; the whiteness, gowns and masks and tight cloth hats, Dr. Simon donning such a hat and, as always, reaching out a hand to his nurse and saying, "My phylacteries and shawl, please"—his everlasting joke about the antiseptic yarmulke of a hat making one go off at a tangent and see the cutting of human flesh as a ritual after all. Enough for now to want to make a list. See: the ice pick is not in its little safety-holder; that should be written down.

Dottie's head went into the breadbox and she gave out twice cries of revulsion that sounded like the Latin expletive of woe: "Eheu! Eheu!"

Tom leaned forward to see what the matter was. The matter was this: Someone at some time—no doubt Audrey when she had gone down, after the eye had arrived, to get Flick some covering—had salvaged all the books, which must have knocked out their retaining batten early and jumped from their shelf and floated around in the deep cabin water; and had put them in with the bread. And now the breadbox contained a mealy mass of dissolved bread and bent cardboard and disintegrating printed paper. Tom reached in past Dottie's shoulder and pulled out a dough-smeared shape: his log book.

He was furious, but when he turned to Audrey to say, "Look what you've done," he was deterred by the sight of the gauze bandage just lying there on the wound and of her eyes glittering in steady gaze at the rounded ribs above.

He took the book to the sink and washed off the leatherette cover. The pages were of good rag paper and were firm; he saw that the printed lines had faded and that his entries were still mostly legible. He looked and saw: *Passed CG station, 9:52 a.m., on way out.* It had been six-twenty-three on the way back in; he could remember details!

He was thinking about taking the book above to turn the pages, air them, drip out moisture, so they would not dry all stuck together, when Flick came piling down the ladder, saying, "My wallet. I've lost my wallet."

Flick charged up into the forward cabin and could be heard banging out a hurried search.

"Dottie," he bellowed, "where's my wallet?"

"In a minute, sweetheart," Dottie singingly answered in full knowledge of her value. "I'm fixing breakfast." Then, in a quieter voice: "Tommy, be an angel and light the stove. It scares me to death . . . Oh Gawd, no dry matches."

"Allow me," Tom said, suddenly pleased with himself, for he had quickly stooped down and found unbroken a

222

tight-sealed mayonnaise jar full of wooden kitchen matches in the somehow still-shut locker under the stove, along with the polishes and bug bombs and special lubricants.

As Tom began to pump up the air-pressure tank of the stove Flick came, in his crashing, snorting style, out of the forward cabin, saying loudly, "It's not the cash I mind. It's the credit cards."

∽∾∽

When the steaming breakfast was spread on the table, Audrey sat up, and the bandage fell from her face. Dottie fetched the cloth arm-sling from the first-aid kit and arranged it so as to hold Audrey's right arm still.

"Yow, Dotkin," Flick, not waiting, said with his mouth full, " 'ose eggs a greatest."

Audrey forced out a whimpering laugh at herself when she missed her mouth with a forkful of scrambled egg held in her left hand. Dottie said to Flick, "Move, you big lummox. Get out of the way." And she slid in beside Audrey and began to feed her with a spoon. "Is that coffee too hot, dear? Blow on it, I'll hold it . . . Do you want another pillow? Tom, hand over that pillow. I know it's soggy, can't be helped . . ." At one point, interposing a leaf-like hand between her own mouth and Audrey's eyes, she shaped toward Tom with exaggerated lip movements the silent word, "Doctor," and pointed behind the shelter of that screening hand at Audrey. They should get Audrey to a doctor. But for God's sake, Tom thought but did not say, I *am* a doctor. What if I am a specialist, a hater and cutter of livers? I know what to do for a common sprain . . . Yet he had not even looked at

Audrey's shoulder. What was the matter with him? Was he too exhausted to have any judgment left? No, he stubbornly told himself, that wasn't it. *Harmony* had to come first; for all their safeties, he had to get *Harmony* to a boatyard and haul her out on dry land. Then a doctor. You weren't going to find either a boatyard in commission or a doctor who could take X-rays on Block Island on this day; the best bet would be New London; wonder about the currents . . .

Dottie went on placidly spoon-feeding Audrey. Wasn't Dottie overdoing her usefulness and serenity? He remembered the rigidity of her shoulders when he had tried to move her from the pump at the height of the storm; and what *had* she been doing in that knee-deep water in the cabin? Was the reproach of that lurid cheek driving her to this solicitude?

Yet Audrey was so grateful; she ate like a baby, hungrily, her pain-reddened eyes blinking adoringly at the provident hand as it lifted the spoon.

"That was super bailing you did yesterday afternoon, old pumphead," Dottie said to Flick. The first word of congratulations of the day. To the lump himself.

"Damn good thing I've kept up on those isometric exercises of mine, all I can say. Damn good for all of you." The bounce was coming back; the big jaw was working now on an empty mouth. "Do you realize," he said, "that some of those waves were higher than the *masts?*" He went on to offer up further descriptive material; and Tom reflected that Flick was now going to prove himself to have been the big audio-visual recording apparatus of the good ship *Harmony*. Ah, yes, he'd been right there all day, watching, remembering. Who was to say that he'd seen everything out of focus?

They're going to rearrange the entire experience, Tom

said to himself. I'd better get that log book dried out in a hurry.

But he blurted out to Audrey, as if nothing had happened to her, "Where's my *Eldridge's?*" Then, abashed by his own peremptory tone, he explained that he wanted to figure the currents through the Race and Fisher's Island Sound. For a horrifying moment he saw himself in Flick's shoes, shouting at his wife to find his wallet for him: the male assertion of supremacy-through-helplessness.

Audrey said, speaking thickly through the pain of her cheek, "How should I know?"

"That yellow book?" Dottie said. "I saw it somewhere."

"It was on that bunk of yours," Tom said to Audrey, holding her responsible, "on the bare slats. Before we brought the mattresses down."

"It's on the bookshelf, skipper," Dottie said. "Where it belongs. I just remembered I put it there."

And indeed it was. Lying flat so it could not be seen from the opposite settee. My, God, Tom thought as he reached over the girls' heads for it, Dottie certainly is feeling sure of herself.

While Tom checked the currents, Flick, full of food, perking up sharply, went on reminiscing about the storm and seemed to be working up enthusiasm for the experience he had had. He talked of things that *he* had been able to do; it suddenly began to seem that a Hamden wind had blown down from a Hamden sky onto a Hamden seaway. I, I, I . . .

Reacting to this, Tom felt pouring into himself what had been so notably absent all morning: an access of sympathy for Audrey. "Darling," he said, testing that word on the day after the storm, "the currents don't look too good until the afternoon. I think we ought to be able to get to New London by, say, six o'clock. Then we'll go straight to a hospital and check you over. Best we can do. That O.K.?"

But Audrey may still have been rankling over his pushing her about the *Eldridge*'s, and she answered, again with a clear show of pain, "What can I say?"

Tom felt rueful and cheated. Where were the ennobling and purifying effects of the hardship they had all suffered together? Only Dottie seemed to have been brushed by them; and what if her gentleness and confidence this morning came not from that source but rather from her knowledge that she was capable of doing what she had done to Audrey under the eye of the storm? Why had no one congratulated *him*, the skipper, for anything *he* had done? Was he going to have to descend to Hamden's level and sell himself to the public?

He went above, sore and confused, and pulled at the pump.

In a few minutes Flick came up and he dropped with a sigh into the seat where he had sat so silent on the way out to the eye. "That sun feels good," he said.

"What are the girls doing?"

"They're looking for my wallet."

" 'They' are? Audrey, too?"

"Aud says she feels tops now that she's had some breakfast."

"And she's down on her hands and knees looking for your wallet?"

"I don't know, they had some plan of dividing up the boat, fore and aft. They're picking up some other junk, too, that got tossed around."

"And you came up for a short rest?"

"No, Tom, for Chrissakes don't be such a sourpuss. I
came up to tell you some of what I got to thinking during the
storm. About how to improve this old thing of yours. You
know, I kind of got to love her during the storm, she really was
good to us, she's really some tub; so I began thinking, I should
pay her back some of what I owe her, and I began thinking
how we could fix her up. You know, Tom, we could automate
this old girl from tip to toe. Now, look," he said, and he
moved over and straddled the gear box behind the wheel, "we
put the console right here, a slanting top for easy viewing and
manipulation—and all you need is buttons, switches and dials.
I think after what I had to do yesterday my candidate for
Switch Number One would be a bilge pump. Ye Gods, an
ordinary submersible pump—well, you'd have to brine-proof
it—it'd accomplish in thirty seconds what it takes a thousand
strokes of that idiot back-breaker to do. Steering, you'd just
have port and starboard buttons, get rid of this incredible
antique of a wheel; then you'd have a trim-tab dingus on the
rudder, like the ones on a plane's ailerons, to take out the
windward helm when you were on a beat. There'd be power
winches—pull up the sails, pull up the God damn anchor,
trim the sheets, do any lousy thing it takes muscle to do now.
Of course you'd have all the standard navigational and pilot-
ing stuff they have in planes, like Omnirange and Distance
Measuring and ADF. Of course surface radar. You could tie in
your auto-pilot with the radar: in a fog you clamp the auto-
pilot on some target the radar picks up, and it zeroes you right
in. Then you'd have a fathometer and an *accurate* speed
indicator—boy, that's a horse-and-buggy job you have now.
And oh, one of the best things I thought of is an automatic
helmsman, you'd call it maybe the Apparent-Wind-Angle

Steering Device. The apparent wind is a vector of the real wind and the speed of the boat; you probably know that."

"Yes, I *do* know that," Tom said. He had stopped pumping; he was aghast.

Flick charged ahead. "You have a wind-vane that registers the apparent wind, see, and you simply set the angle away from that direction that you want to sail, and you tie in the steering gear with it, and the device takes over. It responds to every slight wind shift—more alert than a man sailing, especially if you're out all day—or like yesterday, where you know it wasn't easy."

"Yes, I know that, too."

"In other words, the device sails us, we don't need a helmsman . . . You want frills, you can have any you want. Like a hi-fi system, an eight-track music tape thing with those cartridges, and you sail along with 'The Eroica' going or in light airs you'd want Mozart or like yesterday you'd have *Götterdämmerung* or *Night on Bald Mountain*, something ghastly. We could have used eight-track for the dancing in the cockpit when we anchored the other day in Quicks's Hole."

That brought it all back. Tom was beyond rage; he felt the humming of those wires of the aching under the skin. "Listen to me, Flick," he said. "Number One, my boat *Harmony* is the last place in this world you'll invade with all that claptrap of yours. I'm a sailor. I just don't want any part of that shit. A sailor doesn't need it; he needs his wits. Going up those waves yesterday, one had to do a quick swing"—why couldn't he say, "I had to do"?—"up into the combers. It was a very tricky maneuver, each time was different. Only a man—"

"All right, a man is at the console. You could do it. I

228

mean, it would take practice: you can't just sit down at *any* mechanical device—take a piano—and start in cold. Sure, you'd have to have some experience with your buttons, you'd—"

"And Number Two, when are you going to account for yourself?"

Flick's face had that dissolving look that it had had each time Tom had given him an order on the boat. "Account? What do you mean?"

"I mean Audrey."

"Oh, Audrey." At that Flick stood up and stepped to the companionway, and he called down, "Find it?"

Audrey's head appeared in the opening, and she spoke in pain. "We can't seem to find it anywhere." Then she held up with her left hand a T-shirt of Flick's, and she said, "I rinsed the salt out of this. You want to hang it out to dry? Warm today, you'll need it."

ᔕᔕᔕ

They were taking the storm away from him. He felt that they were stealing the experience of Esmé right out from under his nose.

Harmony had reached out of the Great Salt Pond under full sail at a few minutes before noon—as a sort of superstitious rite he had entered in his drying-out log book the time of passing the Coast Guard station once again—and she was now well out on Block Island Sound smoothly plying the meeting-plane of the two conditions of blue, pale and pure firmament above, pure and deep fundament beneath. In all

229

this blue she carried white sails and made a white path. Getting off the rags of the trysail and suiting her up with her three dazzling triangles had been a trial: he had worked and Flick had talked. Flick was feeling more and more magnanimous; he had even begun to give Audrey some credit for the pumping she had done during the storm; it was astonishing to Tom that the lump had even noticed that. As to Tom himself, Flick had not been openly critical but, like Dottie, with that funny pursed mouth of hers, hanging clothes out on the lifelines to dry, he had simply hung out in the sunlight some undecided points, questions of judgment flapping in the gentle morning breeze. Flick's methods were oblique, crafty, and subtle. Before setting out for New London they had all done a smart job of cleaning *Harmony*. Audrey, her arm in the sling, worked intermittently; Flick's praise of her came intermittently, too, and it was so effective in stirring her to new efforts that it soon seemed meant as a goad rather than as a reward. Dottie divided her time between maid-work and nurse-work; she gave Audrey unwavering tenderness. Tom worked muscle-stiff and more and more bewildered.

What Tom simply could not get his mind around was Flick's emerging heroism. It was coming out, little by little by little, that Flicker Hamden had somehow brought *Harmony* and her crew through the storm to the evening haven. The largest element in this emergence, of course, was the pumping Flick had done. How this pumping had happened to start at all was already blurred; the entire second half of the storm was in fact a hideous blur in Tom's mind. Tom's foggy memory was that Dottie had pumped, Audrey had pumped even though hurt, then both had screamed and screamed at the then waterproofed lump, sitting on either side of him and howling into both his ears simultaneously, and finally he had moved in his thorough-going daze to the pump and, once fastened to it, had been gradually transformed into a kind of sex-mimicking reciprocal engine. He had done a lot of work, there was no question about that; there may have been a question whether he knew what he was doing. At the time. Now he more than knew.

But here as they slanted along Flick was eking out a new claim. This seemed to be to the effect—never blurted explicitly but tossed out in deceptive little jigsaw-puzzle pieces—that he had taken the wheel under the eye of the storm and had turned *Harmony* onto a course that made sense and saved them all, back toward Block Island. One got whiffs of a bad smell: *Harmony* had somehow been on a wrong bearing, negligently and possibly criminally wrong. Flick had set her right. Homeward bound.

Tom felt gagged; he wondered if he was going to be seasick. Lumps of protest stuck in his throat. All this structure had been built so airily, so imperceptibly, that he could not begin to strike it down until it was solidly there. He could not begin to say that Flick's idea, if it had been that and not simply an infantile running for the womb-harbor or some such idiot behavior, had indeed had a certain danger in it. No, the structure was built on beams of hinting and girders of innuendo, and so unshakable was it becoming that Tom finally lied to himself—told himself that he couldn't care less.

"The reason I took over," Flick finally said, full-cheeked, like a man eating potatoes *au gratin* hot from the casserole, "was that—Godamighty, this was a shocker, I *tell* you—I suddenly found myself all alone. I thought for a minute there that you'd all gone off your chumps and done the lemming

231

routine. But I guess you were all below." Then, as Tom felt his stiff muscles grow even tighter along his weary bones, Flick asked the most obvious question on earth. "What the hell were you doing down there, all of you, anyway?"

Tom was promptly in a fright such as he could not remember having experienced during the whole of the storm, asking himself with a suddenly running heart: How am I going to say what I was doing below? I don't want anyone ever to know what I was doing down there. I won't tell. That's a secret place down there. I won't tell. I can't.

It was Dottie who took the pressure off—Dottie who answered with innocent eyes like dew-cleaned petals. "We had a time. Didn't we, Audrey dear? We sure had a time."

"Amen," Audrey said. There was pain advertised on her face by the cut and the bruise, but her eyes were brimming with benign feelings. "I haven't had the good grace to thank you properly, dear Dottie."

"Pooh," Dottie said. "Don't thank me." Her manner was sincere and glossed her disclaimer into: Don't thank little me.

Tom thought of what he had seen Dottie doing in that knee-deep water. How grotesque this winsomeness of hers was! Was she acting? Tom wondered: Is that feminine little piece of poontang of a dark avenger just about the shrewdest little actress you've ever seen? Look at her hanging her head in modesty! Was Audrey thanking Dottie because Dottie had not been able, for some reason, for some mysterious and irrecoverable reason, to finish whatever she had been doing? Either there was something inexpressibly creepy in this behavior on both sides, or—what *had* he seen down there in the cabin?

"So what happened?" Flick asked.

232

"There was an accident," Dottie said. "Right, Aud?"

"Hey, don't put me off that way," Flicker said, working into the tones of a prosecuting attorney. "What were you all *doing* down there?"

Tom, torn, had a painful wish to hear what Dottie Hamden would say she had been doing but was himself barren of the first approach to a defense. Waves of curiosity and alarm beat at him from opposite sides as the water had at *Harmony*'s flanks in the confused cross-forces under the lee of the island the previous morning.

"Let me tell my part," Audrey said.

Dottie asked, "Doesn't your cheek hurt when you talk?" How cool she was!

"It's not that bad. Talking about something will help me to forget it."

"I mean, I'd be glad to tell the part I know, what I saw of the whole business."

"I'd rather," Audrey said with some firmness.

"O.K.," Dottie said. "You tell the beginning."

"Let's see—where to start? All right, when we got to the eye out there, you looked so miserable, Flick, you were chattering and shivering so, that I shifted over to your side of the cockpit—do you remember this?—and I asked you if you'd let me get the waterproofs for you; there was going to be more storm, I knew that. But you wouldn't answer. I knew you, you were too proud, the way Tom had made us go ashore to buy you the slickers, you were determined to get triple pneumonia before you'd lift a finger to put them on. But I decided to get them anyhow. You really were going to need them. I hope you'll forgive me. So, anyway, I went below, and do you know, it was the most incredible sight I'd ever seen? In the first

233

place, the water—up to the tops of the bunks. I thought for sure we were going to sink, and yet I realize now that I went right ahead on the assumption that we'd pull through—*someone* would pump us out. I was right; you did."

She was looking at Flick, who was being transformed, right in front of Tom's eyes, it seemed, into the dragon-slayer of all time.

"But the mess and confusion sort of gripped me," Audrey went on, "so I forgot what I'd gone down to do in the first place. I don't know, it was as though I could somehow defeat the storm by tidying up the cabin—triumph of housework over the unruliness of the elements. You know: a woman's broom to clean all the cobwebs out of heaven. That was me. All sorts of gear was floating around in the wash, and when the boat plunged, the water and everything in it would slosh in the spookiest way, and there I was flopping around snatching at playing cards, my fingers and thumbs going *wack wack wack* like a couple of duck's bills snapping at the cards, and latching onto a pair of my best panties that drifted around just below the surface looking like a jellyfish, and I remember there was a pencil that I jammed into the iron stove, and—"

"And the books," Tom heard himself bark out.

"The books, yes. I put them in the breadbox." Then Audrey, obviously sensing accusation in Tom's strange cry, added, "My association, you see, was that the breadbox was supposed to be sort of moisture-proof, at least enough to keep the bread fresh; maybe it would help keep the books from being completely ruined—although I must admit they'd been floating around in that knee-deep bilgewater, so I guess I was pretty kooked up." Then suddenly she stopped and looked piercingly at Tom and said, "What's the matter? Did I gum up your log book or something?"

"No, it's all right," Tom said, embarrassed by Audrey's true aim.

"I must have been down there quite a while; I got a lot done, anyway, most of it pretty crazy. All the time I was stumbling and lurching around, because the boat, you know, was being thrown ear over teakettle by the waves outside, and I'd become really drenched, I'd fallen into the water more than once. Then, it's funny, if I close my eyes I can see the last picture with the most amazing clarity. I was at the end of the table. I'd just fished up that cylindrical bottle of oregano that you like on things, Tommy"—why, at this moment, the double-dealing diminutive?—"and I had the stupid idea of putting it back on the condiment shelf, even though I'd taken it down from there in the first place and had put it in one of the latched drawers that had unlatched itself, and I began to move toward that corner when I could feel *Harmony* beginning to buck and I began to rise and fly, it seemed as if, and on the way up I saw Dottie's face just floating into the hatchway up there, and I arched up over the sink and my face came down on that sharp curved edge of the handle of the sink pump—I can see that chrome bar coming at me, with all sorts of reflections of the interior of the cabin sparkling on it—the sun was out, you remember. And then there was a Fourth of July in my head and I went black. And that's where you come in, dear Dottie—thank God for you!"

"You mean," Tom blurted out, "it was the *pump handle* that put that gash in your face?"

"That's what I assume," Audrey said. "That's what I landed on."

"This happened before Dottie came down?"

"I saw it happen," Dottie said. "From the top of the hatchway."

235

"Let Dottie go ahead," Flick said.

Tom's hands and feet felt frozen, and his guts were heavy. "Wait a minute," he said. "This is important to me. Audrey, you're saying your face landed on the handle and you were knocked out cold before Dottie went down there in the cabin with you?"

"I know I did that swooping act, and I saw Dottie up in the opening, and I saw the chrome and reflections—exactly as I told you—and the flash when I hit, and that's all I remember till—I don't know. Later."

"Come on, Dottie," Flick said. "Your part."

"O.K.," Dottie said in good cheer, "I'd just stood up, up here, and that same wave sort of upchucked me to the hatchway, and I looked down just in time to see Audrey crash into that horrible handle thing. And then she fell backward into the water. I thought she was dead. The blood was simply cascading out of her cheek and she was floating on her back in the water, and the blood was pinkening the water, and if she wasn't already dead she was going to drown in two shakes of a lamb's tail—yeee, that expression—my Daddy used that all the time, I used to *loathe* it—and so I turned around and tried to shout to Tom at the wheel to do something, but I was too terrified, I couldn't get a sound out of my throat. I hadn't been terrified this way by the storm, it's funny, I trusted the men, it just seemed to me that they knew what to do and we'd get home all right, I never did think we were going to sink out there. Anyway, as I say, I couldn't make a sound, so I had to go down myself, though it scares me out of my wits even to go within a city block of the sight of blood. I made myself somehow. But then I had the most dreadful time. That water heaving so, and Audrey was limp. I kept getting some kind of grip on her and then falling right across her—and at some point there you were, Tom, and I thought: Thank God, one of the men is here, I don't have to be responsible for poor Audrey any more, he'll take over. But, criminy, you went bucketing past, and actually I have a bone to pick with you, Tom Medlar. You banged me and threw me down onto Audrey all over again, just when I thought I was getting a good hold. I think she was coming to, and she was trying to help herself and had grabbed at me from underneath, but there I went when you charged through like a fullback, clumsy! So I worked and worked—I could see you doing something on the floor, Tom, up in the front part—and *finally* I got Audrey up on the seat thing. And you went scooting back above without even looking at us, Tom, much less offering to help. And after a bit Audrey came around better and better, and we got up in the fresh air together. That was it."

Flick's big courtroom eyes came swiveling around to Tom.

"And you? What were you doing—on the floor up in the front?"

∽∽∽

Tom's sense of confusion had grown so strong that he had to escape from that question, had to play for time to sift and settle. A horror of being found out had come over him; there was a piece of evidence as to the answer to Flick's question—what had *he* been doing down there?—that he must dispose of: the great Stillson wrench jammed against the floor beam with its jaws on the nut of the keel bolt over the yawl's flaw. He made his voice as steady as he could: "Do you feel up to steering awhile, darling?"

Audrey's eyes came around to his in some surprise; she had clearly been wanting to hear the answer to Flick's question.

"Something I forgot to do below," Tom hurried on to say. "Won't take a minute."

"Hey! I asked you a question," Flicker said.

Audrey moved to the wheel.

"You really O.K.?" Tom asked her, shortcutting away from Flick's insistence.

"Like I said," she indifferently answered, "it's a relief to have something on my mind."

"Steer as we go."

"As we go," Audrey said, checking the compass.

Tom fled below. When he lifted out the floorboards over the head of the keel bolt, he kept his back between the hatch opening and that which he did not want seen. In spite of earlier pumpings the water in the bilge reached nearly to the floorboards again. The wrench, still firmly lodged, seemed already to be covered with a thin film of rust. Tom knelt and looked down—and inward.

His confusion, to begin with, was rooted in anger and vanity. It was he who had brought them all through the storm—his forethought, his comprehension of details that mattered, his helmsmanship, his bodily endurance, his finding a way to cleave the breakers, his thinking out of suitable courses, his being a sailor, his judgment and fortitude and manliness and—yet here in the pit of the bilge was evidence of his having lost his head all the way. He would hide the evidence and salvage his captaincy. He would have to steel himself to hold Flick off. Some people aggrandize on others, using and distorting every experience to their advantage—go in losers and come out winners every time. It is a habit of moral cheating that by subtle turns of phrase in reminiscence, and even by mere archings and hintings of tone, readjusts the shares of honor. Tom wondered, since Flick had carried the process so astoundingly far in this case, whether it was his own nature to submit to such brigandage of good name. Did he, Tom, invite it—this touching up by someone else, this subtle, patient, continual dabbing at the colors and outlines which changed, in the end, not simply the spirit of the picture but its very substance?

Yet who was right and who was wrong? Had Flick really been a lump, or had Tom's own eyes seen an image that had been far from the true one? It now came out that Dottie, far from having tried to kill Audrey, had been trying instead to save her life.

A diametric opposite, and a horrifying one—so monstrous, indeed, that Tom realized he had, just now, been burying his response to it beneath questions of vanity, of credit, of manly competition. Had he really seen murder in rescue's clothing? If he had been so blind, had he any right to accuse Flick of changing the facts of the storm? Who, after all, distorted things? Surely Audrey and Dottie had not colluded in making up this version of the "killing." Could they possibly have agreed, for some weird, neurotic reasons connected with Audrey's entrapment by Flick and Dottie's need for endless repetitions of defeat and recovery, to change their story from one end of the scale of truth to the other? Or had Tom had reasons of his own to see things totally and fundamentally askew? Or—perhaps to grasp at straws—could there be a no-man's land somewhere between what he thought he had seen and others' "truths"? How mistaken had he really been in his image of the powerful, earthy garbage woman— who turned out to have such a mousey, defeated voice? How far from the mark, after all, had been his reading of Dottie's look of appeal as she lay in her bikini on the cushion in the sun? *Had* there perhaps been a strong flavor of killing in her saving of Audrey?

Was one doomed to see all of life in one's own way, only to have to adjust his vision after each livelong day according to the likewise distorted visions of others? Did one see everything with a vivid inaccuracy while it was happening and then bargain out with others an *ex post facto* "accuracy" that compromised the self-serving distortions of all? If one became convinced that this was so, then how could one balance out the profound humility, on the one hand, that this conviction would force on oneself, with, on the other, the need for vigilance against born liars who had not yet realized the nature of these revisions? How could Tom be humble toward Flick?

He reached down for the handle of the wrench and found that it was immovably wedged in place—so tightly, indeed, with its metal handle-tip denting the hard oak, that Tom had a moment's renewed belief that some force had in fact been loosening the nut as the keel had given out those fluttering vibrations. Then how far *had* he lost his head? God, what he would have given at that moment for just one miserable small item of certitude! He began to try to free the worm nut of the wrench, and as he was leaning forward, straining with his fingers at the burred cylinder, he gasped at a thought that had struck him like a hearty clap on the back, of congratulations.

Could there have been, at the core of all his inaccuracies of vision, a misreading of what Audrey felt about Flick? Had he been wrong about that pair? Had he got even that wrong?

He grasped the worm nut and pressed and turned with all his strength, and at the peak of his effort he was flooded by a recollected feeling—that this was going to be a happy cruise. That, he remembered having thought, was all set. And now as a kind of overlay on this memory came another, a visual image: this same wrench seen through the choppy bilgewater under the eye of the storm, wobbling and bent and contorted by refraction and changes of depth and light—an image of wavering untruthfulness seen at a moment when the wrench, the water in the boat, the boat itself, and the calm at the center of the storm were all of the essence of truth.

How he wanted this storm, this cruise, these days aboard *Harmony* to have been a marvelous experience, the joys of which one would never forget!

The worm-set gave with a sudden jolt, the steel jaws surrendered their bite on the nut at the yawl's flaw, and he lifted the tool out and replaced the floorboard and went forward to put the wrench in the locker in the vee of the forecastle where it belonged. No one would ever know what he had done down there.

∽∽∽

When he stepped out into the sunlight in the cockpit he felt himself to be, once again, the master of his vessel. He was determined not to lie outright, especially, if possible, not to himself. He looked around. The day seemed to be larger now, its sky supremely elevated in hazeless clarity, its horizons ringed with distant shoulders of known land: Fisher's Island in view ahead, Watch Hill Point on the starboard bow, Point Judith up to the northeast, Plum Island off to port, Block Island astern; greenish purple promises in all quarters, save the easterly, of sure anchorages. Closer at hand the faces were not hostile. It seemed to him in this bright light that Audrey and Flick, she at the wheel, he close by her side, the two leaning ever so slightly toward each other in that yearning which can never be completely hidden, were, yes, in love, but he felt keenly open to correction on that point. Dottie, arms up, brushing her hair out to the dry breeze, was a giver; she could never have meant to kill. Tom felt that he should rub his eyes and clear away the last of the film of manifold distortions that the storm seemed to have sprayed over his vision. The wound on Audrey's cheek began to hurt him now; he was a medical man and a husband still. "How's your shoulder, darling?" he asked in all sincerity as he took the wheel.

"Not too great," Audrey said, "if you want a frank answer."

"Better have a couple more aspirin by now," he said, and on that roundabout hint Dottie stirred up to go and fetch; but she waited to hear the rest of what Tom might say.

"We're doing pretty well," he went on, looking up at the trembling fullnesses of the sails. "We could make maybe a knot more under both sail and power, but we're kind of low on gas, I'd like to keep a reserve, if you think, Audrey—"

"I'll live," Audrey said.

Now Tom faced Flick. "We're taking in a fair amount of water. You have any pumping left in you, Flick? I'll be glad to do it if you don't feel up to it."

"I'll pump," Flick said. Could it be that his eyes had lost

that dissolving look?—or, Tom wondered, had most of the disconcerting film scaled off his own eyes? "But first," Flick said, "you were going to tell us—"

"What I was doing down below while we were under the eye. Yeah, sorry about the interruptions. Well, it doesn't take much telling. I'd looked down the hatch and I'd seen Dottie struggling over Audrey in the water, and the amount of the water threw me. I was afraid we were going to fill and sink, so I thought I'd better look and see if there was a single bad leak and whether there was anything I could do about it if there was."

"What did you find?"

"Nothing I could do much about."

"Nothing to do but pump?"

"Nothing to do but pump. For ever and ever, amen."

Dottie went below. Flick was more than satisfied; he was justified. He began to sway once again on the pump, and soon he was singing, off key. Tom felt relief spreading like the warmth of a shot of Bourbon in his chest.

A feminine squeak came from below. Then: "I've found it! I've found it!"

A stab of alarm bled ice water into the place where the relief had been. Had he really put the wrench away? Had she found—*evidence?*

But Dottie was standing on the ladder with her shining face exposed, displaying a gift of pleasure for her man; she was holding up his wallet, which was dripping water.

"Where was it?" Flick asked in a rather mournful and reproachful tone, as if Dottie, having found it, must have been the one who had originally mislaid it.

"In the craziest place," she said, and she began to giggle

as Flick darkened with annoyance. "I went in to get the aspirin for Audrey, and there it was, in the—right in the—oooh, it was so *peculiar*—right down in the johnny."

"Wash it off? Did you wash it off? God al*mighty!*"

"Here," Dottie crossly said, reaching it out to Flick and looking suddenly as if she would burst into tears.

And so, although, as to visibility, breeze, and smoothness of the going under *Harmony*'s forefoot, the day itself was almost perfect, there began nevertheless to be moments of distress, and the easing of one sort of anxiety in Tom's heart gave way to another bad feeling: of discontent. He wanted much that he did not have, he wanted to be a decent doctor, he wanted not to hate his noble work, he wanted not to have seen a rescue as a murder, he wanted Audrey back. Perhaps . . . —but in his concerns at the helm of his stubborn vessel which had ridden out the hurricane, everything seemed to trail off into an indefinite series of perhapses. The current turned, and they flew past the hazards of the Sound, and fishermen in dories lying near the reefs looked up sullenly as the old-fashioned craft sailed by, and all the while Tom was oppressed by a heavy sense of the discrepancies between his reading of the experiences of the storm and the versions his crew had brought away. But gradually these differences, too, faded into common issues of busyness, as the future became a matter for agitation. The Hamdens were going to clear out. Questions of transportation arose; Dottie was dispatched below by Flick to pack. Audrey's pain was harsh. Was there a train schedule somewhere?

They rounded the old stone lighthouse and made their way upriver, and at Burr's anchorage Tom had to tie up at the pier for the time being, because he had no dinghy. Not too

244

much damage here; boatyard services were available and functioning; yes, it could be arranged to haul the boat out in the morning. Flick jumped on the dock in a business suit, and Dottie, wearing a dress, exposed a lot of leg as she climbed ashore.

As the Hamdens stood on the pier Tom called out, "Hey, anybody have a dime?" He was going to have to call a taxi to carry Audrey to the hospital.

Flick tossed a dime down. Tom cupped his hands but missed it, and the thin metal wafer tinkled on the deck. The sun flashed on its little circle, and as Tom bent over to pick it up it became the one precise image in all that scene. The storm and all its exigencies, majesties, and contending inaccuracies had already begun to slip away into vagueness, like a dream fading at the dawn of a new day, for ordinariness was showing its lights again, and, indeed, at that very instant, "this world" was claiming them all, Tom, Audrey, Flick, Dottie . . .

In time, in the months and years that followed, Esmé made splendid conversations, and Tom used his memories of the storm to good purpose while dining out many an evening, his vivid tales coming out always as celebrations of how good it was to be alive and how lucky he was to have a wife like Audrey. People were impressed.

A Note About The Author

JOHN HERSEY *was born in Tientsin, China, in 1914, and lived there until 1925, when his family returned to the United States. He was graduated from Yale in 1936 and attended Clare College, Cambridge University, for a year. He was private secretary to Sinclair Lewis during a subsequent summer and then worked as a journalist and war correspondent. His first novel,* A BELL FOR ADANO, *won the Pulitzer Prize in 1945, and the next year he wrote* HIROSHIMA, *an account of the first atomic bombing. Since 1947 he has devoted his time mainly to fiction and has published* THE WALL *(1950),* THE MARMOT DRIVE *(1953),* A SINGLE PEBBLE *(1956),* THE WAR LOVER *(1959),* THE CHILD BUYER *(1960),* WHITE LOTUS *(1965), and* TOO FAR TO WALK *(1966). Mr. Hersey is now Master of Pierson College at Yale.*

January 1967

A NOTE ON THE TYPE: *The text of this book is set in Electra, a type face designed by W(illiam) A(ddison) Dwiggins for the Mergenthaler Linotype Company and first made available in 1935. Electra cannot be classified as either "modern" or "old style." It is not based on any historical model, and hence does not echo any particular period or style of type design. It avoids the extreme contrast between "thick" and "thin" elements that marks most modern faces, and is without eccentricities which catch the eye and interfere with reading. In general, Electra is a simple, readable type face which attempts to give a feeling of fluidity, power, and speed.*

W. A. Dwiggins (1880–1956) was born in Martinsville, Ohio, and studied art in Chicago. In 1904 he moved to Hingham, Massachusetts, where he built a solid reputation as a designer of advertisements and as a calligrapher. He began an association with the Mergenthaler Linotype Company in 1929, and over the next twenty-seven years designed a number of book types, of which Metro, Electra, and Caledonia have been used very widely. In 1930 Dwiggins became interested in marionettes, and through the years made many important contributions to the art of puppetry and the design of marionettes.

The book was composed, printed, and bound by Kingsport Press, Inc., Kingsport, Tennessee. Typography by R. D. Scudellari. Binding design by George Salter.